FALLEN

AN EVERYDAY HEROES WORLD NOVEL

REBECCA BARBER

EH

EVERYDAY
HEROES

Published by KB Worlds LLC.

Cover Design by: KatDeezigns

Editing by: Spellbound

Formatting by: DL Gallie

Published in the United States of America

Dear Reader,

Welcome to the Everyday Heroes World!

I'm so excited you've picked up this book! Fallen is a book based on the world I created in my *USA Today* bestselling Everyday Heroes Series. While I may be finished writing this series (*for now*), various authors have signed on to keep them going. They will be bringing you all-new stories in the world you know while allowing you to revisit the characters you love.

This book is entirely the work of the author who wrote it. While I allowed them to use the world I created and may have assisted in some of the plotting, I took no part in the writing or editing of the story. All praise can be directed their way.

I truly hope you enjoy Fallen. If you're interested in finding more authors who have written in the KB Worlds, you can visit www. kbworlds.com.

Thank you for supporting the writers in this project and me.
　　Happy Reading,
　　K. Bromberg

For my readers.

You wanted a sexy fireman…well here he is.

Enjoy
xoxo

1

ZACH

FLOPPING DOWN ON THE UGLY COUCH IN THE LIVING QUARTERS OF THE firehouse, I was rat shit exhausted. I was coming off the shift from hell. Minutes after starting my shift yesterday afternoon we were called to a house fire caused by someone falling asleep with a cigarette in his mouth. Then a kid got his fingers stuck in the drain in his bathtub and screamed blue murder into my ear as we tried to pry his chubby fingers free. Then a call to a car accident that I wouldn't get over in a hurry. Being first on the scene to a multi-vehicle multi-fatality was never fun.

"Aren't you heading home?" Grady asked as he dropped onto the arm of the couch beside me.

"Yeah, in a minute," I replied running my hand over the stubble on my chin, catching the scent of fuel on my fingers. Even though I'd showered and changed into jeans and a t-shirt, I could still smell it on my skin.

Clamping his hand down on my shoulder, he looked down on me like he was about to impart some kind of wisdom. Not that I was naive enough to believe he actually possessed any. It'd been six months since I'd joined the crew and they'd accepted this Aussie without question.

"Dylan's cooking breakfast. Wanna join?"

"Nah. I'm going to just head home."

"You sure? You know she cooks enough pancakes to feed an army."

"Thanks, but I'm good."

The truth was, I would've loved to go over for breakfast. Dylan was a great cook when it came to breakfast foods, but the last thing I wanted to do was to sit and watch as Grady and Dylan grossed me out with their lovey dovey bullshit. All it did was remind me of Katie. The woman who broke my heart and had me leaving the only home I'd ever known, headed for the other side of the world.

"All right then, I'm out."

"See you in a couple of days then."

"Have fun. And don't do anything I wouldn't do," I replied, already thinking about how to waste my days off. It was funny how much I'd come to appreciate days off. Even something as simple as doing laundry, renovating my house or just sitting out the back on the porch grilling steaks and cracking open a cold beer was about all the excitement I was up for these days.

Standing up, I yawned and stretched my arms above my head ignoring the ache in my shoulders. Finding my phone, I checked my messages expecting to see something from Mom, only to find it blank. Digging in my pocket I pulled out the keys to my truck and headed to the door. The sooner I headed home the sooner I could crash and start trying to put what I'd seen last night behind me.

I'd just clicked the fob unlocking the truck when an alarm I hadn't heard before sounded. Glancing over the hood, I saw that Grady had stopped where he was too. "What's that?" I called out, heading back towards the door.

"I don't know," he answered, throwing his duffle bag on the back seat and starting in my direction.

Two steps from the main door he froze. "Shit!"

"What?"

"The safe haven box."

"Safe haven box?"

"Yeah, I think that's what it is. I never thought it'd get used though. Not in this town."

Instead of going inside, he rounded the corner towards the back of the brick building. Grabbing his shoulder, I stopped him in his tracks. "What the hell is a safe haven box?"

"It was introduced a couple of years ago. It's a place where people can anonymously drop off their unwanted babies knowing they're safe and they can't be prosecuted for it."

"What the fuck? Unwanted babies?"

"Yeah. Bloody sad if you ask me."

"Are you...you okay with this?" I asked, unable to mask the shock. How did I not know about this? Why the fuck was there a place where people could get rid of their unwanted babies? The thought alone disgusted me.

"What? Hell no! But it's better than what was happening."

Scared to know the answer, I asked anyway. "What was happening?"

"People were abandoning them in public toilets, at bus stops or even parking lots. At least this gives them somewhere safe, warm and dry to leave them. It's got an alarm rigged up, so we know straight away, so the kid isn't there for long."

"This is crazy."

"Doesn't Australia have something like this?"

"If it does, I've never heard of it."

"Come on. Let's go see if it's kids playing games, or someone actually needs us."

"Is it wrong that I'm hoping it is kids?"

"Me too. Me too."

Silently we made our way around the corner. There was no one out there. Only a few cars, a couple of old wooden pallets and a stray gray cat prowling. It didn't give me any comfort.

Following Grady over to the wall, he pulled open a hatch I hadn't even seen. My heart shattered. If I thought Katie had destroyed me, the sight before me was the final straw. Lying there, wrapped in an old flannel shirt, was a tiny baby.

"Is that?" I asked dumbly.

"Yeah. Let me get him out."

"I'll do it."

I don't know why I offered to be the one, but I just needed to. Reaching in, as carefully as I could, I picked up the most precious thing I'd ever had in my hands. Once he was in my arms, I looked down at him. He was so small. He barely weighed anything at all. He had huge blue eyes and barely any hair. All it took was a blink of his long black lashes and he captured my heart.

Hugging him close against me, I lifted him to my face and breathed him in. All I could smell was the thick putrid stench of cigarette smoke. "What happens to him now?"

"What makes you think it's a him?"

"He looks like a boy. Don't you think?"

"Looks like a baby to me."

"You're hopeless Grady."

"Come on. Let's take him to the hospital to get checked."

"And then?"

"Then he gets placed with a foster family until a more permanent solution can be found."

"And if one can't be found?"

Grady didn't get a chance to answer before the bundle in my arms started squealing. "What's wrong with him?"

"Let's just get him to the hospital."

After checking the box for a note, or a change of clothes or anything that might let us know who this little guy was, we headed back towards Grady's truck. As we went, the shirt he'd been wrapped in came loose. Juggling the squirming, screaming child in my arms, I dropped it on the ground and kept going.

"Do you need this?" Grady asked from behind me, the shirt dangling from his fingers.

"Nah. It's disgusting."

"We need to wrap him in something. We don't want him to get cold."

Stepping up to the passenger side of Grady's truck, I laid him down on the front seat before pulling my long sleeve shirt over my head and wrapping him snuggly. After checking it wasn't too tight, I cradled him against me.

"Need me to hold him?"

"I got it."

I have no idea why I was so protective of him; I didn't even know his name or where he'd come from, but he completely owned me. Climbing into the truck, I buckled my seatbelt and held him tightly against me as he continued to howl. His cries broke my heart.

As Grady backed out of the lot, he suggested, "Hold him against your chest."

"Against my chest?"

"Yeah. Something about skin-to-skin contact."

Even though I wasn't entirely sold on Grady's suggestion, I was willing to try pretty much anything. Unwrapping him, I settled his head over my rapidly beating heart. A few breaths later, he quietened and settled.

"Zach?"

"Huh?"

"We're here," Grady told me.

Looking up, I saw we were parked out the front of the hospital. I'd been so captivated by my new favorite little man; I'd barely realized we'd arrived. When Grady opened my door, I felt sick. I was going to have to give him up, something I was seriously considering impossible.

Carefully I climbed out, trying not to bump the boy in my arms. "Want me to come in with you?" Grady offered.

Wanting to keep him to myself for as long as I could, I shook my head. "I got this. Go home to your wife."

"If you're sure."

"I am."

"Okay. Call me if you need anything." Clapping me on my back, he draped my shirt over my shoulder before climbing back into his truck and leaving me standing there in the emergency bay of the hospital. When the breeze ruffled my hair and left me covered in goose pimples, I hugged him tighter, trying to ward off the cold.

"Come on, little man, let's get you checked out and warmed up." He answered with a gurgle as I carried him inside.

Stepping inside the waiting room, I headed for the lady seated behind the counter. When she looked up over the top of her black-rimmed glasses, I didn't miss the way her eyes widened, and her cheeks flushed. Not that I could blame her; I could barely believe it myself. I'm sure I looked like shit. I needed a shave, my shirt was tossed over my shoulder, my arms were covered in tattoos, and I had a tiny baby snuggled against me.

"C-c-can I help you?" she stuttered as she pulled her glasses off and set them down on her desk.

"I need someone to take a look at this little guy."

"What seems to be wrong with him?"

Looking around at the waiting room, I wasn't surprised to see people staring back at me. I didn't give two shits what they thought about me. They weren't important. But this little guy, he was. And he deserved more than being gawked at like he was an exhibit at the zoo.

"Have you got somewhere private we can talk?" I asked, looking at the examination room behind her.

Eyeing me warily, she nodded and flipped up the divider in the counter and ushered me through. When the door clicked closed behind us, I sat on the edge of the bed. When I tried to put him down, the screaming started again. Unable to stand it, I held him close.

"Look…" I began as I explained about finding him in the safe haven box and getting him here. As I told her what I knew, I watched as her heart broke and she felt as bad as I did.

"How can someone do that?" As soon as her words came out, she clamped her hand over her mouth. "Sorry, I shouldn't have said that. It was unprofessional and judgmental. I apologize."

"Hey, no need to apologize to me. I'm right there with you. How anyone could give this little guy up, I have no idea."

"Okay. Well, let me check some vitals, and then we'll get the pediatrics team to check him over."

"Then what?"

"Then we call in Children's Services."

"And he'll become just another kid in the system."

"Unfortunately, yes. But it's better than the alternative."

I tasted bile. I hated that she was right. I hated what she was saying, but it didn't make her any less correct. It was bullshit.

Sensing my mood, she stretched her arms out to take him from me.

2

LILY

"Oh. My. God."

"Are you okay, Lily? You've gone very pale. Maybe you should sit down for a minute," my ex-best friend and nurse, Sarah, suggested, reaching for my elbow.

"You didn't tell me about... about... well, about that," I muttered, my eyes unblinking as I stared through the glass at the most beautiful sight I could ever imagine.

"Ah. Zach Higgins. Now I get it." Sarah smirked.

"Zach Higgins? That's all you've got to say? I'm standing over here in physical pain from where my ovaries just exploded from just looking at the guy, and all you have to say is, Zach Higgins? You're fired as a best friend."

"Fired? Why am I fired?"

"You could've warned me I'd be walking into... well... this."

"So what? So you could've freaked out and talked yourself out of it? Nope. No way. It's for your own good."

"Well, a heads up would've been nice."

"Noted. Now, do you want to go and meet her?"

"Tell me again."

Leading me away from the window and the sight that could

incinerate underwear, she took me to a quiet room and went over everything she'd already told me on the phone. A little girl was left in a safe haven box early this morning. The fire fighter who found her brought her in for a check-up. She's about two weeks old, a little underweight and under nourished but all in all in good health.

"Okay. So, I take her home and look after her…"

"Until a permanent solution can be found." Sarah sounded like she was reciting from the unemotional textbook, not talking to someone she'd known since kindergarten. "Lily, are you sure you want to do this? I mean, it's a big responsibility."

"You don't think I can?" As I said the words aloud, I could taste the bitterness there.

"Absolutely you can. I know you can. I just know you well enough to know you're going to get attached."

"You make it sound like a bad thing." I did not like the way this sounded. I was hurt by Sarah's insinuation. She knew me. She knew all I ever wanted was to be a mom. And she knew, she'd stood beside me and held my hand when the doctors confirmed that, for me, it was almost going to be impossible.

"Stow your claws, Lily. All I am saying is I know you, and the moment you hold that gorgeous little girl in your arms you're going to fall in love with her and not want to give her up. And you need to keep in mind, that there's a very good chance you will have to give her up."

She was right. I was already in love with the idea of her and once I had her in my arms there was no way I was going to want to let go. It would hurt and I would cry and it would more than likely break my heart, but I didn't care. I was doing it. I'd deal with everything else later. It was future Lily's problem. First though, first I had to meet her.

"I can do this."

"You can. And I'm going to be right beside you no matter what happens. So, you want to go meet her?"

"Yes," I answered, inside starting to freak out.

Walking back towards the nursery, I saw Zach with the precious little package curled against his muscular chest. His long, tattooed arms wrapped around the tiny pink bundle; his eyes closed. "Why's he still in there with her? Don't they usually just drop them off?"

"Yeah, normally. Poor guy, thought she was a he when he first got her. Got a bit of a shock."

"I'll bet."

"So... he's still here because..."

"Because there's something about him. She doesn't want to leave his arms..."

"Can you blame her?" I spat out, not meaning to. The look of surprise on Sarah's face as she looked at me was quickly replaced with a wide grin.

"I guess not. Anyway, every time he tries to put her down, she screams so loudly she ends up gasping for breath with tears running down her face. None of us, Zach included, could handle seeing her so upset, so he's stayed with her every second."

If looking at him hadn't made me pregnant, hearing how good he was caring for her would've knocked me up instantly.

Pushing open the door, we stepped into the nursery to hear the steady beeping of machines, soft whimpers and snorts of the tiny babies, and the rhythmic snores of the gorgeous, shirtless fire fighter with his finger wrapped in a tiny little fist as she clung to him. As much as I wanted to meet her, I didn't want to wake him or take her from his arms.

Stepping past me, Sarah reached out and touched his shoulder. Immediately, his chocolate eyes popped open and focused on me. Up close he was even more stunning. From the deep dimple on his cheek, the short cropped dirty-blond hair, and the look of pure adoration that consumed him when he glanced down and checked on her.

"Zach," Sarah said, drawing his attention back to her. "This is Lily. Lily's a carer and she will be taking her home for now."

"What do you mean 'taking her home'?"

Oh. My. God. His accent flooded my lacy panties. Sarah was a dead woman the moment I got her alone.

"It's okay. Lily's been cleared by family services. She will look after her until a forever home or a foster home becomes available," Sarah explained patiently.

As carefully as he could, Zach squirmed in the chair, straightening his spine while not waking her. "Why the hell can't I take care of her?" he practically growled. "She likes me. She's happy in my arms." This guy was completely smitten. Not that I could blame him.

"It's not the way it works. You have to have gone through the process to make sure you can offer the child a safe environment. Lily's been on the list for years. I promise you, Zach, I'll vouch for her. I've known her for years. Lily and I went to school together. She'll be safe with Lily."

"You can come visit her any time you want," I blurted out, shocking us all.

Zach looked straight at me, and suddenly I felt breathless. I was a mess. I'd been in the middle of preparing a bouquet when Sarah called, and instead of taking the time to pull myself together, I stuffed the buckets of flowers back in the cool room, grabbed my purse, locked the door and beelined it straight for the hospital. Now with Zach looking me up and down, I was self-conscious.

"Thanks," he replied gruffly, resigned to the fact he was going to have to hand her over.

Finding his feet, he stood up, dwarfing me. I was only five-foot three and I didn't reach his shoulder. As he stepped towards me, I breathed in his scent. I'd never been so glad to be in a hospital as I was in this moment. I may need medical attention soon if he got any more intoxicating. "Here you go." He extended his arms, and I was hypnotized by the way his muscles rippled.

The moment he settled her in my arms, I was a goner. Completely and utterly in love. How someone could walk away and leave something so precious, I'd never understand. I managed a full minute of nursing her and staring down into her beautiful face, jealously admiring her long, dark lashes before I got a demonstration of just how powerful her lungs were.

Rocking back and forth, I tried to soothe her. The harder I tried, the louder she screamed. "Come on, sweetheart. You're okay," I tried placating her.

Five minutes passed and she didn't settle. Her face was bright red and cheeks stained with tears, and my heart was breaking for her. Zach had tugged his shirt over his head, covering the tattoos I wanted to know more about and the abs I wanted to lick. He'd stepped back to give me room, but as her cries echoed, he began pacing back and forth, running his hands through his hair. Anxiousness rolling off him in waves.

"What's wrong with her?" I asked Sarah, hoping there was a simple explanation. Usually, kids loved me. I wasn't being arrogant, normally I was the one parents called for babysitting or at dinner parties I was the one who ended up sitting on the floor reading books and tucking tired toddlers into their beds.

"Nothing. We've checked all her vitals; she's got a clean diaper, she's had a bottle. This is what she's done all day. I can't explain it."

Sarah looked to Zach who looked like he was in serious pain. When she nodded, he moved towards me. "Mind if I try?" he asked.

Reluctantly, I handed her over. Thirteen seconds. Thirteen damn seconds and her cries had fallen silent. From the moment he settled her against his chest to the time she stopped crying, it'd taken thirteen damn seconds.

"What'd you do that I didn't?" I asked, staring at him like he was some kind of magician. If I hadn't seen it with my own eyes, I wouldn't have believed it, but it was undeniable. This guy was the baby whisperer.

"Honestly, I don't know. I've never held a kid before."

It wasn't fair. He had no idea what he was doing and yet he was able to settle her without really even trying. Sarah's phone chirped as her eyes darted back and forth between us. "I'm sorry guys. I have to go. Lily, there's a bag there with some essentials in there.

Diapers, pacifiers, a blanket, a new jumpsuit and a few other bits and pieces. I finish at seven, so I can drop by on my way home if you need."

"That'd be good. Thank you." I couldn't believe it. She was leaving me here with a baby that hated me and a stranger I wanted to lick from head to toe. And I wasn't a girl who did that. I was a good girl. I was the girl who always had fresh flowers on the kitchen table. The girl who dusted twice a week and only ate chocolate once a month. I didn't do hot and sexy firefighters who had me imagining all sorts of decadent things.

"Can I leave you two to sort this out?"

"Sure," Zach answered, his deep voice rumbling through me.

Not trusting myself to speak, I bent down and scooped up the bag Sarah had prepared for me. I was trying to figure out what to do. I couldn't very well take Zach home with me, much to my disappointment, so I was going to have to sort something out.

"We'll be fine," I confirmed, keeping my voice as steady as I could.

"Good luck, guys," Sarah threw out before scurrying out the door.

For a few awkward minutes we stood there, both staring at the beautiful little girl in his arms. Now the tears had stopped, I snuck a look at her. With her wet lashes and damp forehead, she was everything I ever wanted.

"Would it be weird to name her?" I asked Zach, not entirely sure why his opinion mattered to me. But it did.

"I'm not sure," he replied honestly.

"I just feel silly not having a name to call her. Even if it's just something we call her."

"That makes sense. Do you have any suggestions?"

I never thought I'd get to name my daughter. I never thought I'd be given the chance. Even if it was only for me and only for today, I was going to do it. "I always liked the name Ava."

"I like Ava. What do you think, Ava?" he cooed at the baby in his arms. He was so damn adorable. Asking her if she liked her name. Instead of answering, she grabbed his finger—the one he'd been unconsciously rubbing back and forth across her belly—and sucked it into her mouth. "I'd say she agrees."

Pushing the pink blanket away from her face, I looked down at her, blinking back my own tears. "Hi, Ava. I'm Lily," I introduced myself. For a moment, I stood there looking at her before taking a step back. "Well, I guess we should head out. Would you mind carrying her to the car?" I asked, hopeful. The last thing I wanted was to have everyone staring at me, judging me like I was a terrible parent as I carried her through the corridors.

"Sure."

Zach was a man of few words, but he didn't need them. Heading for the door, I held it open and let him pass. As we moved through the deserted halls, me leading the way, I felt the warmth of Zach's huge hand against the center of my back as he steered us through the corridors. If anyone saw us, I could only imagine what they'd think. We looked like a happy little family. Looks could definitely be deceiving.

We reached my car, and I set the bag on the back seat before opening the door to the car seat I already had there. I was lucky I hadn't taken it out after I'd looked after a friend's baby the other night. Even though I went to their house and didn't need to leave, I was the type of girl who preferred to be prepared just in case. Thus, there was already a professionally installed capsule in the back seat of my Prius.

"Did you want to put her in?" Zach asked, looking confused.

Taking a breath, I prepared myself for the squealing to start. Good thing I did. As soon as Zach let go, it started. As quick as I could, I settled her in the seat and buckled her up. Closing the door, I turned to face Zach who had his hands buried in his pockets, his brow furrowed, looking everywhere but at me.

"Well, thank you," I said, not really sure what it was I was supposed to do or say in this situation.

"You're welcome. Well, good luck. I'll leave you to it."

Zach started walking away, and I was hypnotized by the way

his ass filled out his jeans. Chastising myself, I shook my head. Now was not the time to be daydreaming about boys. I had a little girl who needed me. Ava was my number one priority. It didn't stop me calling out to him though. "Zach?"

"Yeah?"

"Did you need a lift home?"

"Nah. It's fine. I'm not going to ask you to go out of your way," he declined politely.

"It's not out of my way."

"How do you know?" he questioned.

Shit! He had me there. The truth was, I wasn't quite ready to say goodbye to him just yet. Besides, I could hear Ava's cries through the closed window. Needing to wrap this up and get moving, I offered, "I live on Main Street above the florist."

"Above the florist?"

"Yeah. I own Daisy's Flora. It was my grandmothers and now, well now it's mine." Good work Lily. Why don't you just go and share your whole life story with the guy? I'm sure he doesn't want to hear it.

"Are you anywhere near there?"

"In that case, would you mind dropping me at the station?"

"Climb in."

3

ZACH

I'D NEVER MET ANYONE LIKE LILY BEFORE IN MY LIFE. THERE WAS JUST something about her. Sitting beside her in her car, Ava screeching and screaming behind me, I couldn't help but notice how she white-knuckled the steering wheel. She was a contradiction. Her almost black hair was pulled back in a tight ponytail with a pale pink ribbon tied in a bow which matched her dress. A dress I didn't think anyone even made these days, let alone wore. It was one of those fifties housewives' dresses with the belt cinched around her narrow waist before flaring out, and when she'd slipped behind the wheel, I could've sworn I saw the hint of a lacy petticoat. But it was the pearls at her neck that had me fascinated. Lily was the perfect image and, given what I'd learnt about her in the first few minutes, sainthood wasn't much of a stretch.

Pulling into the empty spot beside my truck, Lily looked behind me at Ava, sighing heavily. "She hasn't stopped crying."

Not really knowing what to do or say, I went with what I thought she needed to hear. "I'm sure as soon as you get her home and settled, she'll calm down."

"I hope so."

"Look, why don't I give you my number, and if you get really stuck you can give me a call. I mean, I'm not exactly sure what I can do, but I'm willing to try," I found myself offering.

"Are you sure?" Her voice was laced with relief. "I mean, I probably won't call."

"You can call." She handed me her phone, and I added my name and number. Untangling my long legs from her tiny car, I looked in the back seat and saw Ava. Her face was flushed and streaked with tears once again. Even though I probably looked like a complete pussy, I dragged my shirt over my head. "Look, I have no idea if this will help or not but take this."

"You're giving me your shirt?"

"Wrap her in it. It might help. I don't know, it's dumb," I tried to take it back, but Lily wasn't letting go.

"Thank you. It's a great idea. I'll give it a try."

"Okay then. Well, good luck."

Not knowing what else to do, I closed the door and walked away. As I jumped into my truck, I watched Lily back out and head down the street. Dialing Mom's number, I gave her a heads up that I was on my way and started towards her place.

Half an hour later I pulled up to Mom's, feeling completely off balance. After digging a somewhat clean shirt from the bag on the back seat, I bounded up the steps and let myself in.

"Mom, I'm here!" I called out as I toed off my boots.

For as long as I'd been coming here, the place hadn't changed. Everything was still exactly how it should be. The cupboard was lined with photos of my life. Even the awkward prepubescent teen phase was memorialized on the mantel, despite how many times I tried to hide them in the drawer.

"Kitchen," she returned, and I headed in her direction.

Rounding the corner, I found her sitting at the bench trying to finish the crossword puzzle in one of her silly gossip rags. Leaning down, I dropped a kiss at her temple. "Five down. Flightless Bird. Three Letters. Emu."

She jotted it down. "I would've got that."

"I know."

Closing the book, she turned to face me. As much as I loved my mother, it was hard not to see how old she was looking. Time had not been kind to her. The wrinkles on her face were deeply etched lines, and her knuckles clutching the pencil were gnarled. Every single time I looked at her, it just reconfirmed I'd made the right decision to move. Having her live half a world away and fighting arthritis, which was slowly but surely stealing her independence, as well as what I believed was a broken heart. When Dad died, he took a part of Mom with him and she'd never really recovered. Not that I could blame her. Dad was her person and without him, Mom had to find her way without her best-friend and partner.

"So, you hungry?"

"You cooking?"

"For you, my boy, whatever you want."

When I was a kid, I used to cop a lot of shit for being a mommy's boy, but I had the last laugh. Who else could rock into their parents' place and, even at twenty-six, be doted on like they were the spoiled eight-year-old they'd once been?

When I opened the fridge, I tried to hide the wince when I saw how bare it was. There was half a block of cheese, a tub of butter, milk and a loaf of bread that had seen better days. "Mom, where's the rest of your food?" I asked, trying to keep the irritation out of my voice.

Waving my comment off dismissively, she just smiled, cracking my frustration wide open. "It's shopping day tomorrow. Don't worry about it."

Bullshit it was shopping day tomorrow. I hadn't been over to visit for almost two weeks, I'd been too caught up with work and the renovations on my new place to make the drive. Not anymore. That ended now. I had to come over more often. If she couldn't take care of herself, then I'd take care of her.

"Ah, that makes sense," I lied, not wanting to make her cry. I couldn't stand it when she cried. Seeing your mother teary, I don't care how old you are or how tough you think you are, was enough to drop anyone to their knees. "Well, I'm starving. I came off shift this morning and I haven't been home yet. Why don't you go get changed and I'll take you out for a steak?"

"Zach, sweetheart, you don't need to take me out. You go out and have fun, I'm just going to have a sandwich."

"Mom." I came over to where she was still sitting and wrapped my arm around her shoulders, for the first time I realized how skinny she'd become. I could feel the bones in her shoulders poking out, and I didn't like it. Not one little bit. "Don't make me go and sit alone in a restaurant looking like a loser. Would you please join me for dinner?"

With a huff, she pushed me away. "Fine. But I'm getting a glass of wine," she negotiated.

"We'll see, missy," I teased back, loving the way her face came alive. I would've bought her a whole damn winery if I could to keep that look there. "Now, go put your good slippers on and we'll get out of here."

She made it halfway down the hall before she paused and turned back to me. "You know, Zach, you're becoming mighty bossy in your old age."

"Yeah, but you still love me."

"Some days," she mumbled, disappearing into her bedroom.

As soon as she was gone, I slipped straight into reconnaissance mode. Checking the cupboards, I wish I was surprised to find them as empty as the fridge. This was not good. I had no idea when the last time she'd eaten a decent meal was, and it wasn't exactly like I could ask her without pissing her off. Stealing her pen, I found a notepad and started a list. I'd fill this place with food and then make sure I was around enough to make sure she ate it.

Ten minutes later, when she hadn't reappeared, I went looking for her. Stepping into her bedroom, I was overcome by the smell of roses and powder. It was the same scent that used to cling to Grandma when I was a kid. Noticing the anguish on her face, I dropped down on the bed beside her.

"What's wrong, Mom?"

"I can't go out, Zach. What if someone sees me?"

"So what if they do?" I was completely lost. I had no idea where her head was at or why being seen mattered.

"Zach, I'm not what I used to be."

I had to concede there. Didn't mean I was about to let her become a hermit though. "No, Mom, you're not. But you're still my mom, and I would like to take you to dinner. We can even sit in the back corner if you want."

"Zach." Her voice was desperate and needy, and I almost caved.

"I promise I'll protect you." I made the promise so easily, meaning every word. There was no way I was going to let anyone upset her.

"Okay. But if we see Angelica, I'm getting straight back in the car and you're bringing me home. Deal?"

I had absolutely no idea who the fuck Angelica was or why Mom was so damn determined to avoid her, but I wasn't going to let that stop me. "Deal. Let's go before my stomach starts eating me from the inside out."

"Well, we can't have that, can we?" She laughed, standing up and heading towards her closet. "Give me a minute to change."

Leaving her to it, I went back out to the lounge to see if there was anything else lying around that I needed to know about.

We finally made it to a diner that was up to Mom's standards and snuck into a corner booth, carefully avoiding being seen by anyone, especially the evil Angelica who I'd learned in the car was Mom's replacement at the bank. A twenty-something know it all, who refused to listen to anything Mom had been trying to teach her and complained to management that Mom was bullying her. Finally, the truth had come out why Mom's retirement had kicked in six weeks earlier than expected. While she hadn't exactly been fired, it had been suggested that maybe it was for the best if she finished up early. Assholes! Had I known everything at the time, you can bet your ass I would've made sure everyone else knew too.

After placing our orders, with Mom indulging in a steak and

vegetables, we sat back and relaxed. I'd managed two mouthfuls of my drink before Mom turned the interrogation in my direction.

"So, Zach, did you know Evelyn across the hall is getting another granddaughter? Another one! That means she'll have three granddaughters and a grandson."

Mom's favorite topic to bust my balls about was the lack of a wife and children in my life. She was ready for grandkids, and with my sister Maddy too caught up in herself, all her hopes were weighing on me. No pressure.

"Evelyn must be thrilled," I replied, playing along. While I knew exactly what she was getting at, making her work for it wasn't going to kill her. If she wanted to have some fun, then two could play at that game.

"She is. She brought me over photos of the others the other morning. Beautiful kids they are. And Christian, her oldest, starts school this year. Can you believe it? He's so grown up."

"I hear kids do that."

"When am I getting grandkids, Zach?"

"Wow! Straight out with it this time, huh? No pussy footing around today?"

"I don't have time for pussy footing around, Zachary. I'm getting old. I want to be able to enjoy my grandkids. Remember their names. I lost my keys the other day. Do you know where I found them? Do you?"

"Where did you find them?"

"In the freezer next to the peas. I didn't even know I had peas or why my keys were there, but it took me two days to find them."

I couldn't help the snicker that escaped me. I'd been worried about Mom's memory for a while, but hearing this and seeing the annoyance on her face made me laugh.

"It's not funny. You're my only son, Zach. Who knows when your sister is going to be ready to settle down, if ever?" I knew that was something that worried Mom more than she was willing to admit. "I just want to see you happy."

Reaching across the table, I grabbed her hand and held it in mine. I needed her to hear me. Really hear me. "I am happy, Mom. I've got everything I need, right here."

With a heavy sigh, the fight evaporated from her and it turned to guilt, something Mom had mastered over the years. "I know, sweetheart, but don't you want someone to share your life with?"

4

LILY

I COULDN'T DO IT ANYMORE.

It'd been four days since I'd brought Ava home from the hospital. Four days since I'd slept. Four days since I'd showered. Four days since I'd eaten a hot meal. Basically, I stunk, was beyond tired and hangry.

We'd been in my apartment less than fifteen minutes when I realized I wasn't set up to look after a baby. I didn't have a crib or a stroller or, as it turns out, a clue what I was doing. After tossing some of my clothes in an overnight bag, I packed up my chocolate-colored cat, Malteser, and went to my grandma's house. Or *my* house, I guess. Grandma Rose died eighteen months ago leaving me not only her house, but completely alone in the world. She'd been my everything. The woman who raised me. The woman who dried my tears and fed me ice cream after I'd had my fragile teenage heart broken. She was my person. And I missed her every single day.

Opening the front door, I tried to juggle my handbag and a screaming baby only to be greeted with stale, putrid air. While Ava cried herself hoarse, I opened windows and doors. It took me three hours to find everything I'd come looking for. Thank God Grandma was a hoarder. She still had everything from when I was a baby; something I'd teased her about for years.

"Please, Ava. Please stop crying," I begged as I bounced back and forth on the balls of my sore feet.

I was on the verge of conceding defeat and taking her back to the hospital for a check-up. It couldn't be natural or good for her to have screamed for days. The only time she wasn't crying was when she was asleep, which sadly wasn't often enough.

After washing the blankets I'd found in the cupboard, I settled us both on the double bed and prayed for more than a few minutes of shut eye.

Ava didn't agree.

At three in the morning, completely exhausted and cried out, I buckled her in the car and went to the hospital. They checked her over and, once again, confirmed she was okay. A little dehydrated and tired but overall, she was a healthy baby.

At six, as I fought to keep my heavy eyes open, Sarah bounced through the glass doors looking way too happy for me. I wanted to gouge her eyes out.

"Lily! What are you doing here?" Sarah exclaimed as she moved towards me. "Is the baby okay?"

"She's an asshole, but she's okay." As soon as I said it, I felt swamped by guilt.

"Huh?"

Rubbing my eyes, I wished the headache would ease. "She's cried from the moment I got her home."

"Any idea why?"

"Do you think if I knew what was wrong, I wouldn't have fixed it?" I snarked. I was a bitch when I was tired, and even though I knew Sarah didn't deserve it, I needed someone to take it out on. I was quickly realizing why kids usually had two parents. The idea of handing her over and making her someone else's problem, even for half an hour, sounded like bliss.

Dumping her bag on the floor at my feet, Sarah dropped into the uncomfortable chair beside me. The moment her arm wrapped around my shoulder, I fell apart. Having someone to catch me was all it took before I completely lost it.

"Hey! What's this?" Sarah asked, holding me tight as tears streamed down my face.

After a few moments letting it out, I pulled back, wiped my eyes and sniffed. "Sorry."

"Don't be sorry. What happened?"

"She just hasn't slept. She barely eats. All she does is cry and shriek. She hates me."

"She doesn't hate you, Lily. She can't hate you. No one does. It's just not possible."

"Then why won't she settle? What am I doing wrong?" I wiped my snotty nose on my sleeve. It couldn't make it any worse. I was covered in spit up, milk and God knows what else.

"She doesn't hate you. She just doesn't know you. She doesn't know anyone. Just give her time."

Everything Sarah said made sense, but it didn't help. It didn't offer me the answers I desperately needed. A nurse appeared cradling a crying Ava. Standing up, I wiped my hands on my thighs and reached out to take her.

"Look, Lily, I have to get to work. Why don't I stop by after my shift and see how you're doing?"

As much as I didn't want to intrude on Sarah's life and take her away from time with her own family, I was desperate. "That would be great. If you don't mind."

"Of course not. I'll head over around six and bring dinner."

"You don't have to."

"I know I don't. But I'm going to. And you, beautiful girl," she trailed her finger across Ava's cheek, "you need to be a good girl for Lily, precious."

"Ava."

"Excuse me?"

"Her name is Ava. I couldn't keep calling her baby, so we thought Ava suited her."

"We?"

"Zach and I."

"Oh, you and Zach are chummy now, are you?"

Before I had the opportunity to answer, Ava's squealing escalated. "I should get her home. Maybe after a bottle she might nap."

"Fingers crossed."

Sarah disappeared around the corner leaving me standing there, with the eyes of other parents boring into my back. Gathering our stuff, I carried Ava out to the car and headed home.

The doorbell rang at twenty after six and, thinking it was Sarah, I didn't even bother to pull on pants before answering the door. Didn't I give the delivery boy a shock. My pink shirt was wet in patches and clung to me in places it shouldn't from my attempts at giving Ava a bath.

"Ah, I have a delivery for Lily Evans," he spluttered, unable to meet my eyes.

"That's me." I smiled, accepting the plastic bag.

Scurrying away, he left me standing there feeling like a loser. With a loud screech, I slammed the door shut and went back to where Ava was still crying. Picking her up, I noticed she was hot to touch. Forgetting dinner which smelt so good it had my stomach gurgling, I focused on the baby girl who deserved nothing less than everything I had to give.

"What's the matter my sweet girl?" I asked, wishing she could somehow tell me what was wrong.

Swiping the tears from her red cheeks, I felt how warm she was. Not knowing what else to do, I stripped her down to her diaper, hoping that would help. Rocking back and forth on the balls of my feet, I found my phone down between the couch cushions.

Sarah: *Sorry, sweetie. Not going to make it. Chase fell off his skateboard and hit his head. I'm sending dinner though.*

"Shit!" I swore before immediately feeling guilty. I needed Sarah's help, but she was exactly where she needed to be. Looking after her own son was, and should be, her number one priority. I'd taken this on, I'd have to figure it out myself.

I walked into the bedroom we were using and found Ava's pacifier. I was shocked when she took it and her crying faded. Too terrified to move, I just watched as her eyelids fluttered and fell closed as she drifted off. I don't even know how long I stood there. I know my arms were numb and my legs aching. Only when I thought I was about to drop her, I relented and carefully set her down in the crib, holding my breath.

When she didn't move, I backed out of the room on my toes. I'd made it all the way to the lounge room and dropped onto the couch before I risked taking a breath. I had no idea what I'd done differently or what had helped her drop off, but I wasn't about to look a gift horse in the mouth. Whatever it was, I was taking it.

Dropping my head back against the cushion, I laid down and just took a minute. Looking around the room, the one I'd spent countless hours watching movies in and playing with my toys as a kid, I realized I was going to have to make a decision on what I wanted to do with this place sooner rather than later. The paint was looking tired, there was a layer of dust coating everything and the curtains looked like they were out of another era. It was Grandma's home. It was my home. The time was coming when I was going to have to decide whether I kept it or let it go to another family who could make happy memories here.

With a loud yawn, I pushed aside all decisions, making them future Lily's problem and let my eyes drift closed.

I got forty minutes.

Forty blissful minutes.

It wasn't anywhere near enough.

It was better than what I'd been getting, but it was all I was getting. The alarm clock, a.k.a. Ava, was awake again. Rubbing my tired eyes, I trudged towards the bedroom and made my way to where she was crying. Scooping her up, I held her close, breathing in her beautiful baby scent.

"Why don't you like sleep, pretty lady?" I asked as I wrapped her in a soft, pink cotton blanket I'd found in the cupboard.

For the next, I don't even know how many hours, I walked around in circles, sung every lullaby I knew before moving on to Taylor Swift's greatest hits, and somewhere in the early hours of the morning, I buckled her into the back seat and tried to lull her to sleep by the gentle rocking of the car. It didn't work.

After yet another feed, diaper and outfit change, I set her down in the crib, collapsed on my bed and burst into tears. I was beyond tired. I couldn't take much more. I had no idea what I was thinking taking this on on my own. I wasn't cut out to be a mother. Maybe my body knew better than my head did. This was just proof of that.

Sitting up, the room spun around me, and I realized how much trouble I was in. Falling back on the bed, I squeezed my eyes closed, praying for the wave of dizziness to subside. When I cracked my eyes open a moment later, it wasn't any clearer.

Conceding defeat, I did the one thing I promised myself I wouldn't.

5

ZACH

"Last night was insane," Bowie confirmed, collapsing onto the couch in the main room at the station.

He wasn't wrong.

"Yeah. You can say that again," I replied as I poured myself an orange juice.

It was almost seven in the morning, and the closer I got to the end of my shift, the more I looked forward to it. I was ready for some breakfast and sleep. Hell, I wasn't even annoyed at the reality that I was heading home to a full laundry basket and an empty fridge.

Before I had a chance to say anything, my phone started ringing in my pocket.

"G'day," I answered.

As soon as I said it, I cringed. Growing up and living in Australia most of my life, I rarely said g'day. It was one of those words the world thought we said but rarely did. It was right up there along with 'throwing another shrimp on the barbie' and the classic, 'that's not a knife.' Ever since I'd made the move to the US, it'd crept into my everyday language.

"Zach?" a shaky voice asked.

"Ah, hi."

"It's…it's Lily."

"Oh, hi, Lily. How's Ava?" To say I was surprised that Lily actually called was an understatement.

"Ava's… Ava's…"

"Lily. Are you okay?" I wasn't psychic but something was definitely up. Even through the phone I could feel it.

"Ava's okay. Fine. She's fine."

"Okay, Lily. You're worrying me."

"Don't worry, Zach. I'm just… something's not right. I'm so dizzy and Ava won't stop crying, and I haven't slept, and she just screams, and I don't know what I'm doing."

Shit! I knew something was up, but I wasn't expecting her to be falling apart. Glancing at the clock on the wall, I realized I only had fifteen minutes before it was time to call it a day. "Look, Lily. I just finished my shift. Why don't I swing by? Bring some breakfast?" I tried to keep things light while inside I was more than a little concerned.

"You…don't…have…to…do…that." Damn it, now she was crying.

Keeping her talking, I started asking questions while I hurried to grab my duffle bag. With my keys dangling from my finger and my bag swung over my shoulder, I said. "Hey, Lily, can you just hang on two seconds?"

Covering my phone with my hand, I motioned to Bowie who was talking to Grady who'd just breezed through the door looking refreshed and relaxed. "I have to go help someone. Mind if I skip out early?"

Even though I knew they wouldn't have an issue, it was manners to ask. When they both nodded, Bowie asked if everything was okay. I answered him as honestly as I could. "I'm not sure."

"Well get out of here and go make sure it is," he confirmed.

"And, Zach?"

"Yeah?" I called back as I headed out the door.

"Remember to call if you need anything."

"Will do," I agreed with a wave before heading towards my truck. Jumping in, I remembered I still had Lily on the line. "Okay. I'm in the car now. What do you feel like for breakfast?"

Without a chance to answer, an ear-piercing scream boomed down the phone. "Is that Ava?"

"Zach, I've gotta go."

"I'll be there in a few. Sit tight."

Backing out of the parking lot, I took off a bit faster than I probably should've on my way to the florist. Pulling up, I managed to snag a park right out the front. Spying the huge bunches of colorful flowers in the window of Daisy's Flora, I wondered how I'd never seen this place before. I drove up and down this street almost every day but somehow, I hadn't seen it.

Stepping through the front door, the scent of roses and other bright bouquets hit me. I noticed a girl behind the counter with purple hair and a ring in her nose.

"Welcome to Daisy's. Looking for something special?" she asked, setting down her scissors and stepping out from behind the counter.

"Actually, I'm looking for Lily."

"And you are?" she questioned, eyeing me warily.

"I'm a friend of hers. Zach. Look, she just called me she sounded upset. I was just going to check that she and Ava were okay."

"You're the fireman?"

"Huh?"

"The fireman with the tattoos. The one who found Ava."

I was confused, how did she know who I was, but I didn't have time to stand around chatting. Even though I was trying to play it cool, I was anxious to see for myself that they were okay. There was only so many times anyone could hear the word fine before it stopped having any meaning.

"Uh, yeah. That's me I guess."

"So, you gonna show me your tattoos?"

"Who are you?"

"I'm Sage. I help Lily sometimes at the shop. She asked me to cover for her for a couple of days while she gets things settled with Ava."

"Where are they now? Are they upstairs?"

"No. They're at Lily's grandmother's place."

"Where's that?"

After Sage gave me directions and a huge bunch of daises, I headed to the address she'd shared. A moment later, I pulled into the driveway of one of the most beautiful homes I'd ever seen. Sure, the paint was peeling, and the gardens were overgrown but beyond that this house screamed potential. Maybe I was looking at it through paint-stained glasses because I was in the middle of my own renovations, but I could just imagine sitting out on the huge wraparound porch on warm summer nights nursing a beer.

Grabbing the flowers from the front seat, I shut the door and bounded up the walkway. The moment my feet hit the steps, they groaned under my weight.

Knocking on the door, I could hear crying on the other side. "Hello?" I called out as I pushed it open.

"Come on, sweetheart. Please..." There was pleading in her strained voice.

"Lily? It's Zach. Can I come in?"

"Shit! Come in, Zach. I'm in the bedroom."

Stepping inside, I began to get a sense of how much Lily was struggling. Sitting on the table by the door was a plastic bag filled with containers of what looked like last night's untouched dinner. There were blankets and cushions all over the floor. It wasn't dirty, just untidy.

"Lily?"

"In here."

Following the cries, I found them exactly where Lily said they'd be. She was sitting cross-legged in the middle of an unmade bed, with Ava lying in front of her kicking her chubby little legs as she squirmed about in her nappy and singlet. Taking in the sight, a huge hit of guilt sucker punched me in the stomach. Lily, as naturally beautiful as she was, looked terrible. Her hair hung limply down over her shoulders, she was pale and her shirt had a wet patch across her chest. I didn't even want to know what it was.

Not wanting to frighten them, I knocked gently on the bedroom door.

Lily looked up, and the moment her eyes locked with mine, she burst into tears. Not exactly the reaction I was hoping for. Moving towards them on instinct, I sat down on the end of the bed.

"She keeping you up?" I asked dumbly.

"She doesn't sleep. All she does is cry."

"Mind if I…" I pointed to Ava who was looking up at me with the most hypnotic eyes I'd ever seen.

Lily nodded.

Reaching down, I carefully lifted Ava into my arms, cradling her against me. She was so warm and smelt so good. I might have been almost dead on my feet and my stomach was trying to eat itself, but there was no way I was about to focus on anything but the beautiful little girl in my arms.

"She's quiet!" Lily exclaimed in an excited whisper.

I'd been so caught up in her, I hadn't even realized the silence that had fallen over us. When Ava lifted her tiny little fist up and rubbed her eyes before letting out the cutest yawn ever, I was gone. This kid owned me.

"Yeah," I replied dumbly. I had no words.

"Is she… is she asleep?" Lily's voice was thick with disbelief.

Glancing down, I saw her beautiful eyes closed, her long lashes resting on her cheeks. Nodding, I saw a look pass over Lily's tired features, one I wish I understood better. I couldn't tell if it was frustration, shock or relief. Maybe a combination of all.

When Lily flopped back against the pillows and pinched the bridge of her nose, she sighed heavily. Checking Ava, she was completely out of it. Her tiny hands were clenched in fists as soft snores rumbled from her tiny chest. Standing up, I heard a groan and spun around. Lily had rolled over, hugging a pillow tight against her.

As carefully as I could, I set Ava down in her cot and stepped back, holding my breath. I couldn't deal if she woke up screaming. The last thing I wanted to be was the cause of her crying. When she didn't move a muscle, I took a tentative step back and turned to head out. As I went to leave, I looked over at Lily who was now snoring loudly. As I tugged the blanket up over her, she didn't move at all. Poor girl looked like she hadn't slept in a month. Yawning loudly, I resisted the urge to curl up beside her and have a nap. Instead, I backed out of the room quietly.

Standing in the kitchen, I had no idea what I was supposed to do now. Lily and I were practically strangers. There's no way I'd call us friends, and I was in her house while she slept. After sitting at the kitchen bench and flicking through the crumpled magazine on the counter, I knew sitting still wasn't going to keep me awake for long. Instead, I collected the empty coffee mugs and filled the sink. Not afraid to get my hands dirty, I started cleaning up.

An hour later, my cleaning frenzy came to a screeching halt. Dropping the cloth where I stood, I took off towards where I'd left Ava sleeping. Moving as quickly as I could, I found myself half laughing as I hurried along. I didn't have such a severe adrenaline spike running into a burning building as I did trying to get to Ava.

Reaching the cot, I reached down and picked her up. As soon as she was in my arms, she burrowed her face against me and fell quiet. Looking over at the bed to see if Ava's cries had woken Lily, I was shocked to see her spread out but still dead to the world.

"Come on, pretty girl. Let's let Lily get some sleep," I told her. It wasn't until I draped the pink blanket over my shoulder that I realized how stupid I must sound. I was having a conversation with a baby who wasn't even a month old.

6

LILY

I woke up and felt more alive and more human than I had in days. I had no idea how long I'd been asleep, but damn I needed it. Even more surprising, Ava hadn't woken me. Shit. Ava!

Shoving off the blanket, I scrambled from the bed, tripping over my sneakers as I hurried towards her crib only to find it empty. My heart plummeted. With my stomach in my throat, I ran out to the lounge room only to have the wind knocked right out of me.

Sound asleep on my grandmother's ratty old couch was Zach. A shirtless, sleeping Zach with Ava curled on his chest, with her tiny fist wrapped around his finger. Both of them snored softly. Holy shitballs Batman, this was not okay. How was I supposed to hold myself together? How was I supposed to stop myself from falling stupidly and crazily in love with them both when I woke up to find them like this? Shaking my head, I forced myself to walk away. Now was the perfect time to take that long hot shower I was desperate for. With Zach had Ava occupied, I could afford a few minutes to myself to wash my hair and shave my legs. But not before I snapped a photo, you know, for posterity's sake. Not for me to look at later tonight when I was tucked up in my big bed feeling lonely.

Setting my phone on the bathroom counter, I stripped off, turned on the faucet and waited until the water was running hot and the room full of steam.

"Oh my god. Nothing's ever felt that good," I mumbled to myself as I stepped out of the bathroom tightening the towel knotted between my boobs.

"If nothing's felt that good, the guys you've been hanging out with don't know what they're doing."

I froze where I stood. I was naked. Like wearing my birthday suit, wrapped in a towel with another towel tied as a turban on my head. If I'd thought the water had been hot against my skin, then it had nothing on the heat radiating from my core caused by the stare Zach was throwing in my direction.

I couldn't let Zach best me though. He wasn't going away in a hurry, so I couldn't afford to be acting like a schoolgirl with a crush every time we were in the same room.

"Who said I like guys?" I replied, white knuckling the towel, making sure it didn't drop to my feet and show off everything my mother gave me.

He coughed, looking at me like I'd grown an extra head. I watched as he swallowed deeply, his Adam's apple bobbing in his throat. I have no idea why I found that so damn sexy, but I found myself clamping my legs together trying to ease the throb.

"Each to their own," he replied quickly. "Come on, pretty girl. Let's get you changed and leave Lily to take care of herself."

With a cheeky wink, Zach sauntered out of my bedroom, blowing raspberries against Ava's cheek and causing her little chubby legs to kick wildly.

I watched them go before closing the door and sliding down the wooden frame. My palms were sweating, my pulse racing. I felt like I couldn't get enough air in my lungs and my thighs were sticky. This was not good. Not good at all.

On the other side I could hear Zach starting to sing some weird song I didn't know, but his voice, with that damn Aussie accent, was making everything tingle. Forcing myself to my feet, I stomped back into the bathroom, splashed cold water on my face before hurrying to get dressed. In many, many clothes. Layers were my friend. Layers and ugly underwear; not that I really owned any pretty panties, but sticking to my trusty spanx and beige bra was another layer of protection. One I had a feeling I was going to need.

Keeping my makeup minimal, since I had no intention of leaving the house, I stuck to a quick swipe of my mascara wand and a dab of my favorite strawberry lip gloss, I smacked my lips together, straightened the skirt on my dress and headed out to find them. While I knew Zach was more than capable of taking care of Ava, I didn't want to take advantage of his generosity.

Finding them in the kitchen, Ava was in her stroller changed into a light pink onesie with Piglet on her chest, sucking her paci-fier, her eyes drooping sleepily. I don't know how Zach did it, but it seemed like he was a magician when it came to our beautiful Ava. She quietened and calmed when he was near and fell asleep easily. It was a magic I was desperate to learn.

"Don't you own a shirt?"

Wow! I hadn't planned on blurting that out. It was so unlike me to be so rude, but for some reason, Zach brought the worst out of me. Or made me less ladylike, at the very least.

"You look beautiful too, Lily." Zach smiled back at me, his teeth so perfectly white and straight he should be in a toothpaste commercial.

I blushed. I knew I did. My cheeks burned under his stare.

"Thanks."

He bent over and pulled something out of the oven, and my stomach growled embarrassingly loudly. When he sat a casserole dish on the counter, one I recognized from when I was a kid, I couldn't help but smile. Being here, in this house, had that effect on me.

"What's that grin for? Was it the view of my ass when I bent over? Cause I can do it again, I mean, if you want me to." I don't know if it was the mischievous smirk covering his face or the playful tone in his easy-going banter or maybe it was just the fact I felt slightly human, but he made me feel lighter. More like myself.

"You wish."

Zach shrugged. "Maybe. Now, do you want to grab a couple of bowls so we can eat while it's hot?"

My feet were moving before my brain caught up. With my head in the cupboard, I grabbed a couple of bowls and glasses. "You're staying?" I asked, although it wasn't really a question.

"Unless you don't want me to?"

"I'd love you to."

"Then it's settled. I'm staying."

"On one condition…"

"What's that?"

"You need to find a shirt."

"I'm that irresistible, am I?"

Ah, yeah. "Only in your dreams, Captain Kangaroo," I deflected. The last thing I was about to admit was how close to the mark he was. I don't know if it was the abs or the cocky grin or the accent that was making me stupid, but it was undoubtable.

Zach set the serving spoon down and headed for the door. My heart raced. I'd been playing with him. Flirting almost. But if he was making a dash for the nearest exit, it only proved how bad at it I was. "Or maybe it's in your dreams, Lily. I mean, I'm pretty sure I heard some moaning earlier…"

"Don't know how you could've heard anything over your freight-train snoring." Shocked with myself, I clamped my hand over my mouth. Who was this woman saying these things? This wasn't me. I wasn't sassy or a smartass. I was polite, well-mannered, nice even. I wanted to blame Zach. He was bringing the absolute worst out of me, and although it caught me off guard, I didn't exactly hate it.

I glanced down at Ava, who was still asleep. She looked so sweet and adorable, I could barely believe she slept. We were making a racket and she didn't even bat an eyelid. I heard the screen door shut gently and Zach disappeared from view. Guilt crept up my spine, and I found myself creeping towards the door and peering out the glass. I watched as he rifled through the back seat of his truck before finding what he was looking for. As he turned back to the house, I darted back into the kitchen. The last thing I needed to do right now was give him more ammunition to use against me.

I filled the bowls with the creamy pasta and grabbed the jug of water from the fridge, missing the glass and splashing it all over the counter. "Shoot!" I complained as I mopped up the mess with a tea towel.

"Need a hand?"

Looking up, my eyes locked with Zach's, and I almost became the puddle he needed to clean up. The abs may have been covered and those arms, inked with dark tattoos that I was desperate to get a closer look at, had disappeared under his long-sleeve navy fire department t-shirt, but he still looked just as delicious as the dinner I was serving.

"I got it," I choked out.

Dinner was weird, to say the least. The food was delicious, and Ava slept through like a champ, but I had no idea what to say to Zach. We barely knew each other, and if it wasn't for Ava coming into our lives, we probably would never have met.

Even though the conversations had been stilted at best, when he asked about the house, I found that I couldn't shut up. I blurted out way more than he ever wanted to know. I told him about my mother's death when I was only three and Dad's spiral into drugs and depression which resulted in me living with my grandmother. I hadn't heard from my dad since I was seven. Not that I wanted to. Last time I'd seen him, he was all skin and bone, his face was pale, his eyes sunken and his hair wiry. He'd stolen the necklace from my jewelry box, the last thing I had of Mom's, and emptied my piggy bank that sat on my shelf. His own mother, completely appalled and heart broken by his actions, threw him out and told him not to come back until he cleaned himself up. Sadly, I was still waiting.

"She sounds like a remarkable woman. Where is she now?"

Zach's question was innocent enough, but it was a huge kick in the guts. Tears welled in my eyes and I swallowed down the lump in my throat. He didn't know. He couldn't know. It was the reason I hadn't eaten spaghetti in years. One moment Grandma was standing in the kitchen, wearing her pink spotted apron cooking dinner while I sat at the kitchen bench practicing tying the perfect bow, when she dropped the saucepan, boiling water and soggy noodles falling to the floor as she crumpled. I did what I could, but it wasn't enough.

"She passed," I gritted out, overcome with emotions.

"I'm sorry," Zach replied automatically.

I wanted to brush off his sympathies, but the look on his face made me believe he was genuine. "It was a long time ago now."

"Yeah, but still…"

"Yeah."

For a few minutes quiet fell over us, and although I expected it to be awkward, for some reason it wasn't. It was almost peaceful. I was caught up in my own head as memories of Grandma and her crazy antics whirled and then, unexpectedly, I had a light-bulb moment.

"What do you think of this house?"

7

ZACH

I COULDN'T MOVE A MUSCLE. EVERYTHING ACHED. FROM THE HAIR ON my head to the tips of my toes, I was sore. Whoever thought working a double and then using my free time to renovate my house was a good idea was on crack. Thankfully, I'd managed to bribe some of the other guys from the station to come and give me a hand gutting the bathroom and ripping up the old tiles with cold beers and pizza, but I'd still done a hell of a lot of heavy lifting. And I had the cuts and bruises to prove it.

Mom was getting worse, and I knew it wouldn't be long before she was going to need more care, which had me speeding up my timeline. My plan—before Mom tripped down the front steps and took the skin off the side of her face which had the neighbor calling me mid-shift—had been to take my time and work through the place one room at a time. Living in a construction zone was not my idea of fun so I wanted to do it in a somewhat organized way. Besides, I only had so much money to throw around and had to budget wisely. But now, things had changed. That luxury was gone and now I was suddenly in a hurry.

My phone beeped on the coffee table, but it was too far away to reach and too much effort to get up. When it kept going, I heaved my ass off the couch, brushed the chips from my shirt and grabbed it, immediately noticing I'd been added to a group message.

Apparently, beers and burgers were at Hooligans tonight, and my presence was required. As much as the thought of getting dressed and going out sounded like torture, I kinda owed these guys. They'd given up their time off to give me a hand, so being the anti-social shithead I'd been known as back in Australia wasn't really an option.

Zach: *Meet you there.*
Bowie: *Better be, Steve.*
Zach: *Steve?*
Bowie: *Yeah, crikey you're dangerous.*
Mack: *That's better than what Collins called him.*
Collins: *Hey! I thought Skip was good.*
Johnson: *Yeah, you would.*
Bowie: *We gossiping or we meeting for beers?*
Zach: *Beers!*
Bowie: *Good. You're buying first round, Steve.*

These guys thought they were hilarious. They weren't, but they thought they were. At least they amused themselves.

Dragging my tired ass upstairs, I showered and changed into the first clean shirt and jeans I could find. Rubbing some gel in my hands, I pushed my fingers through my hair, shoved my phone and wallet in my pocket and headed out.

"Did you drive?" Bowie asked as I climbed out of the car.

"Yep."

"Not up for a big one then?"

"I'll be lucky to have two beers before I fall asleep on the bar."

"Come on then you pussy. Let's get you some dinner before bedtime." Bowie draped his arm over my shoulder and led me inside.

For a Wednesday night it was busier than I was expecting. Booths were full and there was a crowd gathered around the pool tables. Heading straight for the bar, we managed to catch Dan's attention. I didn't come here often but when I did, Dan always took care of me.

"Out on a school night, boys?" Dan taunted as he wiped the bar with a wet rag in front of us.

"Yep."

"The rest of the troublemakers are over there," Dan pointed in the direction of the back booths where I could see Grady throwing his head back and laughing loudly.

We grabbed our drinks and ordered our burgers before heading over to where everyone was already relaxed and laughing. I slid into the booth next to Grady.

"Cheers," he greeted, lifting his own glass to mine.

The jukebox was playing old-school hits, the burgers were mouthwatering even if they were missing the beetroot, the beer was cold, and the banter was funny as fuck. At least it was when it wasn't aimed in my direction.

Two beers later and I wasn't as sore or tired as I had been and was actually having a pretty decent time.

"That fire the other night was rough. You okay?" Collins asked, stealing Grady's seat who'd run home to his wife the moment she called. Lucky bastard. Dylan was dynamite, and he was damn lucky he'd claimed her before I'd arrived in town.

"Yeah, fine." I shook off his concern not wanting to dwell on it.

It might not be the right way to handle it, but it was my way. For some reason bush fires and scrub fires got to me in a way house or building fires didn't. It was crazy. Where I didn't think twice about running into a burning building, standing in the middle of the paddock with a wall of flames coming at me, scared the shit out of me. Maybe it was because of the devastation back home. Australia had some of the worst bushfires, and for six months of the year, it felt like we held our breath praying for the best but preparing for the worst.

Last week when the call had come, I was first in the truck. I might be shit scared and prefer to face anything else, but there was no way I was letting my boys, my brothers, go in without me. As we got closer and closer, I could see the bright orange flames licking the inky black sky. Smoke filled the air, and you could taste it on your tongue.

We were still waiting on the final outcomes from the investigation but from what we'd seen and found, it looked like kids had been playing in one of the paddocks with some firecrackers when things had gone off track. It'd taken hours to get the blaze under control and by the time we trudged back into the fire house, I was dirty, sweaty, smelly and all I could think about was a tall glass of water, but we'd won. This time.

"Hey!" Johnson nudged Collins before pointing over my shoulder to the bar. "Isn't that Lily Evans?"

"Lily Evans?" Collins replied, having no idea what he was on about.

At her name, my ears perked up, and although I tried to remain casual, I was pretty sure I was doing a shitty job.

"Yeah. She was a couple of years below us at school. Cute girl. Owns the flower shop."

"You know what flowers are, Johnson?" Bowie stepped in.

I reached for my beer and took a sip. I needed to hide the smile that was threatening to break through, and my glass was doing the trick.

"Of course I do. They're those things you buy a chick when you want them to suck your…"

Bowie clamped his hand over Johnson's mouth and just in time. We all knew how that sentence ended. We'd all seen Johnson trudge into the station before a shift wearing last night's clothes and lipstick that didn't match his skin tone.

My eyes narrowed. Shifting slightly in my seat, I turned to spy Lily at the bar looking more than a little uncomfortable. Damn that woman was adorable. Here she was on a Wednesday night wearing a navy-blue dress, cinched at her waist showing off her incredible figure. Her hair was pulled back in a sensible braid, a braid I knew could have many, many beneficial uses. On her feet were silver sandals with a tiny almost pointless heel. But it was what was in her arms that had me vaulting from the seat and making a beeline for her.

"Lily?" I called out as I approached her.

She turned, and I watched with fascination as her face morphed from wary and uncomfortable to a genuine smile that made her hazel eyes light up.

"Zach."

My name fell like a breathless plea from her lips.

"What are you doing here?" I asked.

"Am I not allowed to be? I'm pretty sure I'm over twenty-one and by Californian state law that means I can be here if I want to be."

Wow! I'm not sure who pissed in her Cheerios this morning, but for someone wearing a pearl necklace and clutching at a lace hand-kerchief, her panties were sure in a twist.

"Calm your farm," I held up my hands in surrender and took a step back, not before peering over at the beautiful baby girl in her arms.

"Sorry," Lily apologized quickly, her cheeks blushing.

"Here you go, Lily. Sorry about the wait." Dan handed a plastic bag over the counter and before Lily could juggle Ava, I accepted it for her.

"Can you just sit it on the counter for a second? Actually, would you mind holding Ava too? I just want to run to the bathroom."

She didn't even give me a chance to answer. Not that I was going to turn her down, especially when it came to Ava. A moment later I was standing at the bar nursing the most gorgeous girl in the world knowing that this kid completely owned me. I didn't even give a toss if I looked like a chump about it either.

When a fiery redhead slid in beside me, her hand resting on my bicep, I took a step back. I'd never met her before, and I was certainly not interested. But from the predatory gleam in her eye, the skintight flannel shirt she was almost wearing and could use a few more buttons on, it was obvious she was on the prowl.

Over her head I saw my mates watching the show, amused. I was too far away to know for certain, but I was willing to bet from the way they were throwing money down in the middle of the table there were bets being placed. Bets I didn't even want to know about.

With a wriggle in my arms, Ava gurgled before looking up at me with the biggest, brightest, most captivating blue eyes I'd ever seen. When she cracked a smile, at least I think it was a smile, it could've just been gas, I immediately turned, looking for Lily. She couldn't miss this. This was huge. She needed to see it. I needed her here to see it.

I spotted her in the same moment she spotted the redhead. Her smile dropped and was replaced by a scowl, and I watched as she balled her hands into fists before hiding them in her poofy skirt. I never thought I'd be attracted to a fifties housewife. But there was something about the way Lily wore it that had me imagining turning the good girl bad.

"Lily! You've got to see this! Ava... Ava, she smiled," I gushed, sounding like a proud dad.

"Obviously not because of the company you keep," Lily retorted tightly as she wove the handles of the plastic bag on her arm before reaching for Ava.

I didn't want to let her go.

She was so freaking cute, and she smelt so good, I just wanted to snuggle with her and see if I could convince her to flash me another one of those gummy grins.

"It's getting late. We have to get going."

"Oh. Okay."

I wanted Lily to ask me to come with her. I wished I had the balls to ask her if I could walk her home. Or to her car. Or anything. Instead, I said nothing, letting Lily's eyes bounce between me and the chick whose boobs pressed up against me, pissing me off.

"Have a good night, Zach. And remember if it's not on, it's not on."

And with her final parting retort, Lily and Ava left me standing there, gob smacked. Did she really think I was the kind of guy who'd pick up some chick in a bar and take her home? I wasn't that guy. I might've been, once upon a time in another life, but things had changed. *I'd* changed. I had responsibilities now. Responsibilities I took seriously. And I didn't give a rat's ass how long it took me to prove that to her, I was going to show Lily who the real Zach Higgins was. And she had no idea what she was in for.

8

LILY

"I know. I know. I'm late. Ava wouldn't settle and then she threw up all over me, so I had to get changed or I was going to smell like Ava's breakfast all day. Shit! I'm so sorry, Sage. How busy are we today?" I babbled without taking a breath.

"Firstly, stop. Sit. Breathe," Sage instructed, nudging me onto the stool behind the counter.

Normally I'd be annoyed by her bossy attitude, but today I found myself thankful for it. I needed someone to just make decisions for me for a minute. Until recently, I'd considered myself doing alright in the adulting side of life. I could cook for myself. I knew how to sew on a button. I could do my own laundry without shrinking my sweaters or turning my white clothes pink. I paid my bills, mostly on time. And I'd never had a motor accident. Not even a fender bender or scratched my car in the parking lot. But now, everything felt like it was spiraling so far out of control, I wished I had someone in my life who'd just take control, even if it was only for a minute.

While I'd been caught up in my head, Sage had unclipped Ava from her stroller and was bouncing back and forth on her toes, having a full conversation with the infant in her arms. I hope she wasn't expecting to get any words of wisdom from her. While she was completely adorable, Ava wasn't exactly the best at expressing what she wanted. Or maybe I just couldn't figure it out. She'd scream and I'd be convinced she needed to have her diaper changed only to find her completely clean but hungry. I promised her I'd get the hang of this and sooner rather than later. Most parents had nine months' notice that their life was going to be upended, I'd had nine minutes. Not that I'd change a thing. I was still dreading the moment Child Services called. A call I knew would come before I was ready. A call, I don't think I'd ever be ready for.

"Right. Now, Mom."

My heart stopped. It was the first time someone had referred to me as Mom. Wow! That's what it felt like.

"Are you listening, Lily?"

"What? Yeah. Sorry. What were you saying?"

"Ava, your silly Mom would forget her head if it wasn't screwed on today."

"Isn't that the truth."

"Right. Well, why don't you walk down the street and see about getting us a couple of coffees. You look like you need one, and I wouldn't turn down a coffee and maybe a donut."

Sliding off the stool, I pulled my bag out from under the stroller and swung it over my shoulder. "Donuts aren't a breakfast food."

"No. But they're a haven't-even-been-to-bed-yet morning snack food. So, scoot. I'd like a glaze and a chocolate. Thanks."

I'd made it all the way to the door, pulling it open and hearing the tiny little bells hanging from the handle jingle before I remembered Ava. Damn, I was really bad at this today. "Ava…"

"Is completely fine here with Aunty Sage for ten minutes. So, get. I need my donut!"

Watching them, I realized Sage was right. They were completely fine. Ava was staring up at Sage like she was from another world, not that I could blame her. I'd known her for a while now and some days it took me a while to adapt to her new hairstyle. Sage was one of those funky young women who didn't give a toss what people thought about her or who she offended. She wore what she wanted. Spoke her mind. And wasn't afraid of offending anyone. Today her hair was a deep purple, and I kind of loved it. Part of me wished I had her confidence to do something like that, running my hand down my pleated skirt, but it just wasn't me. I was who I was, and it was going to have to be enough.

It took forever to get our coffees. Everyone was out and about this morning and wanted to chat. Even though it was the last thing I wanted to do, Grandma had raised me better than to be rude, so I stopped, smiled, exchanged hugs and small talk before excusing myself to rush back to the shop.

Crashing through the door, I ran into the back of a tall, broad back, splashing our coffees all over us and dropping the paper bag to the floor.

"Sh—" I started to cuss, before stopping myself.

"I'm so sorry…" I began apologizing, checking out the back I'd walked straight into and a little lower. I just couldn't help myself. That denim-clad butt was mighty fine.

He spun around, snapping my eyes up to his stubbled jaw. Damn, this guy was good looking. "Hey, Lil. Are you okay?" he asked, the deep timbre of his voice doing things to me that it really shouldn't, especially not in public.

"Zach?"

Of course it was him. Why couldn't it have been anyone else? Seriously! Like, why was he even in here? Did he even know the difference between a rose and a daisy? Probably not. Guys like him don't need to buy flowers, not when they looked like that. I'm sure he could just click his fingers and the girls dropped to their knees. They probably didn't even care about being given flowers and having the car doors opened for them or being walked to the front door at the end of the night. All they cared about was what he could do to them between the sheets or on the back seat of his truck. I doubted location was a deal breaker.

"Are you okay? You didn't burn yourself, did you?"

Burn myself? What was he on about? I must've taken too long to figure it out, because he was pointing at the huge wet patch on my chest. At least that's what I'm choosing to believe he was pointing out. Not the fact that in my haste to get dressed, the second time, I'd misaligned the buttons and there was a gape in the middle of my top showing off my boring beige bra underneath. Yeah, if the ground could just open up and swallow me right about now, that'd be great.

Waving away his concerns, I said, "I'm fine. Nothing a few napkins can't fix."

Moving past him, I caught the scent of smoke on his skin and the hairs on the back of my neck stood up. I couldn't imagine doing something so dangerous, but I was glad Zach was here. That meant he'd made it through another shift safely.

"If you're sure?"

"Absolutely. Now, how can I help you? I've never seen you in here before." And trust me, that's not something I'd ever forget.

Ignoring the smirk on Sage's face, she started dancing with Ava in the corner near the buckets of roses waiting for me to start turning into something worthy of delivery. Glancing down at Grandma's gold watch wrapped around my wrist, I realized the time and my heart sped up. At least I was choosing to believe it was the late hour that was making me sweat and not the man standing in front of me, watching my every move.

"So this is where the magic happens. It's nice."

"It's old."

"Old's not necessarily bad."

"It needs a new coat of paint. The sign needs redoing. And the shelves out the back need to be fixed before they come crashing down on my head. But it's all mine and I kinda love it." I was babbling. And I was embarrassing myself but I couldn't stop. For some reason, Zach fried my brain.

Reaching out, he took hold of both my hands, stalling my fidgeting. "It's great, Lily. It really is. You should be proud of yourself."

Straightening my shoulders, I refused to let his cute smile and that adorable dimple in his left cheek knock me over. "Thank you."

"You're welcome."

"Now, did you need something?"

"Actually, I did."

Okay. Wasn't expecting that, but whatever. I could be professional. At least I think I can. "What are you after?"

"I'm not really sure. Flowers?"

Behind him, we both heard Sage snort. Not that it could be ignored. I was pretty sure it was deliberate. "Well, this is a florist, so you've come to the right place. Any idea on color? Type of flowers?"

"Ah..."

"Okay. Let me make this a bit easier. Is it for an occasion?"

"Kind of."

This was going so well. NOT! "Is it for a birthday? In sympathy? For an older woman? For a younger woman? For a guy?"

Zach's cheeks turned red as I threw options at him, and I should've felt guilty that seeing him looking awkward and unbalanced made me feel a bit better. It meant I wasn't the only one. "A woman. Definitely a woman. No occasion."

"Okay. No occasion flowers for a woman."

"Perfect."

"Anything in particular you'd like?"

"Whatever you like. If you could just make me a bunch of whatever flowers you'd like, or someone like you would like, that'd be great." Zach rubbed the back of his neck and looked everywhere but at me. Poor guy. He wasn't the first guy to walk in here and have no idea what it was he wanted, and I doubted he'd be the last, but I had to admit, he was the first I was enjoying watching squirm. For some reason, one guys hadn't quite figured out yet – flowers meant something. They said something. They gave women hope.

No one had ever asked me what my favorite was before. "No worries. When do you need them?"

He let out a huge sigh. "Saturday morning if that's okay?"

"Perfect. Did you want to pay now or when you pick them up?"

After swiping his card, Zach thanked me, but before he left, he walked over to where Sage was eavesdropping and placed a kiss on Ava's head before walking out the door, the jingling of the bells letting me know the coast was clear and I could breathe again.

Plonking my butt down onto the stool, I wondered if it was too early in the morning for wine. I needed one. Or two. Or possibly something stronger.

Just when I thought it was safe to breathe again, Zach's head poked back through the door.

"Forget something?" I asked, squeezing my thighs together.

"Yeah actually. Just wanted to tell you, I love your shoes." With a final wink he was gone.

Sage made a beeline in my direction, as I swung my legs out from behind the counter and looked down at my feet. "Oh. My. God."

Sage's hysterical laughter scared Ava in her arms and she whimpered. "Today's so not your day," Sage teased between fits of giggles.

I wanted to slap her. I couldn't. If it'd happened to someone else, it would've been hysterical. But it wasn't someone else who was wearing one black shoe with a shiny silver buckle and one navy shoe with a red bow. It was me. I was a bloody mess. And Zach had seen it. He'd seen it all.

"This can't be happening," I groaned, fixing the buttons on my soggy, coffee-stained top.

"Oh, it is. Now, sit down and snuggle with little miss here. I'm going to get us more coffee and donuts and then you, Lily Evans, are going to start talking. First topic, that delicious hunk of man meat who was just in here looking all sorts of fine."

I was screwed. So very screwed.

9

ZACH

SWAPPING SHIFTS WAS NOT MY SMARTEST IDEA. GRADY WOULD PAY FOR this. I was going to make him cover one of my Friday nights or something equally as annoying.

This was my second shift in a row, and both were turning out to be torturous. I was used to long hours and the lack of sleep didn't really bother me but dealing with the fallout of idiots grated on my nerves. Last night we'd been first on the scene of a car accident. The guy had wrapped himself around a light pole, and by the time we'd arrived on scene, he'd come to and was sitting behind the wheel, drunk as a skunk singing 'Hotel California'. He smelt like a brewery and there was an open bottle of bourbon wedged between his thighs. After getting him out of the car and helping him stagger over to the ambulance as it pulled in, he proceeded to lecture me about wasting my Friday nights working when I should be out chasing tail, something I'd much rather be doing than dealing with the likes of this idiot, but here I was.

Sadly, that was only the beginning of it. We'd made it back to the station and I was just grabbing a bottle of water from the fridge when the alarm sounded again. Gulping down mouthfuls and trying not to choke as I ran across the common room and climbed back in, we were off again. This time to help an overenthusiastic backyard chef control the fire he'd inadvertently set trying to get the perfect char on his steaks. By the time we managed to get it out, including his back fence, which was now missing sections, his steaks were well and truly cremated.

And so the idiocy continued. All damn night.

By the time Saturday morning arrived, I was so tired and sore, I could barely put one foot in front of the other.

"You got plans for your days off?" Bowie asked as he tossed his bag into the back of his truck.

"Yeah. Sleep. And a lot of it."

"Sounds like a plan. When you back?"

"Tuesday," I replied with a loud yawn.

"Well take it easy. See you then."

"You too." With a two-finger salute, I watched as Bowie slipped behind the wheel of his truck and peeled out of the parking lot.

With a stop to make before I could go home and fall into bed, I got my ass moving.

Stepping inside the small florist shop, the scent of flowers hit me like a wall. It wasn't like I was against flowers, just this many all crammed in such a small space was more than a little over-powering.

"She's not here."

The voice called out and caught me so off guard I almost tripped over a bucket next to my feet.

"Huh?" I replied, wincing at how dumb I sounded.

"Lily. She's not here."

"I wasn't…"

"Yeah okay. Keep telling yourself that."

Deciding that it wasn't worth arguing with the chick with the purple hair and way too much eye makeup on for a Saturday morning, I marched straight up to the counter.

"I'm picking up…"

"The beautiful bouquet Lily came in early this morning to put together for you. I know."

"I'm Zach," I introduced myself, extending my hand over the counter. It took her a moment while she eyed me up and down before dropping her small hand in mine.

"Sage. We've already met"

"We have?" How could I not remember her? Sage didn't look like the kind of girl anyone would or could forget in a hurry.

"Yeah, but you were pretty distracted and in a hurry."

Now I felt like shit. Forgetting someone was an ass thing to do. "I'm sorry Sage. I didn't…"

"Don't even worry about it. I'm not," she shrugged, and I wondered if she really meant it or if she was like every other female I'd ever met and was going to pretend to let it go only to whip it out and make me feel like a dick whenever she needed. "Give me a second and I'll grab your order."

She vanished out the back leaving me standing there, tired as hell, feeling like an idiot. I didn't know if I was glad Lily wasn't there or disappointed. Confused is probably the best description and right then, I was way too exhausted to even consider what that actually meant.

Sage returned a second later cradling a stunning bunch of flowers. I might not know a lot about flowers or flower arranging or even tying a bow, but I knew these were beautiful and absolutely perfect for what I had in mind.

"Wow!"

"She really out did herself, didn't she?"

"Yeah."

"She came in early this morning and put them together for you. Very early."

"Well, I appreciate it. She did a great job."

"You're missing my point. She came in very early. Very, very early to put those together for you. Only you. You were the only order for today and it's her day off, but she came in anyway."

"Why?" I asked dumbly. I wasn't that important, and I certainly hadn't asked for any special treatment.

"Maybe you should ask her."

Sage shrugged her shoulder and when the phone started ringing, I was dismissed. Looking down at the colorful bunch wrapped in purple and orange paper with a giant silver bow, I knew they were exactly what I needed. I just hoped they'd last until this afternoon. I needed a shower and some sleep, then I'd deal with everything else.

———

An incessant and annoying ringing woke me from where I was sleeping, dead to the world. Reaching out, I groped around trying to find my phone, my eyes still blurry.

"Hello," I rasped, rubbing my eyes.

"Zach!" an annoyingly cheery voice exclaimed.

Sitting up, I settled myself against the headboard, knowing this wasn't likely to be a short conversation. "Hey, Maddy."

"Hey Maddy? Hey Maddy? Is that the greeting your favorite sister gets when she calls you?"

Maddy. I loved her, most of the time anyway, but she was always so damn dramatic. No wonder she was an actress.

"Cut me some slack. You woke me up," I grumbled, wishing I was still asleep but eyeing the clock on the other side of the room and realizing it was probably time for me to get up anyway.

"Oh. Sorry, sleeping beauty. How's Mom?"

"Why don't you ring and ask her?"

"You know I can't."

I wished Maddy and Mom would sort out their dramas, but I was not getting involved. Whatever it was that happened between them that had them hiding from each other on opposite sides of the world, I wished they'd just get over themselves and sort it out. And the sooner the better. They were both missing out. But it wasn't my fight.

"She's doing okay, but she's getting old, Mads."

"Don't, Zach."

"How's things back home anyway?" I asked, changing the subject.

"Okay I guess."

"You guess? What's going on?"

"Nothing."

"Nothing?"

"I'm fine."

"Bullshit."

"Huh?"

"Maddy, I love you, but even I know when a girl says she's fine, she's anything but. And thankfully, I'm far enough away that I'm safe, but I'm slightly worried about those who aren't. So, tell me what's going on."

"It's nothing. Bryce just…"

"Just what?"

"He dumped me."

"Dumped you? I didn't even know you two were dating."

"Well…"

"We're talking about my mate Bryce Masters, aren't we?"

"Yeah. I mean, we weren't really dating as such, it was more…"

For the next twenty minutes I tried to talk Maddy down off the ledge. For someone who didn't want to talk about it, once she started, she wouldn't shut up. I don't think she even took a breath as she spilled her guts.

When she was finally done, I reminded her that we loved her no matter what and there was a bed here for her whenever she could make it over for a visit. She'd always wanted to come to America but never made it, and if I was being honest, I really wished she'd come over.

"Call me anytime, Mads."

"Thanks, Zach. I knew you were my favorite brother for a reason."

"I'm your only brother."

"And that's why you're my favorite."

"Love you too."

"Thanks for everything."

"Anytime. And remember, even if they do kill you off, something else will come up. It always does."

"Thanks, Zach. Love you."

We hung up and my stomach rumbled loudly. Jumping in the shower, I got cleaned up quickly, before dressing in a t-shirt and jeans before slapping my baseball cap on my head and heading down to the kitchen. After eating a full plate of bacon, scrambled eggs and a couple of slices of toast, I gathered my stuff and headed out the door.

Sliding behind the wheel of my truck, I wiped my sweaty hands on my thighs. I was nervous. As much as I kept telling myself not to be, I was. At some point I'd decided this was a good idea but now I wasn't so sure.

Giving myself a pep talk, I put the truck into reverse and backed out of the driveway. Navigating my way through the streets, I drove past the station where the doors were wide open, but the rig was missing, probably out on another call. Driving down main street, it was strangely quiet for late on a Saturday afternoon. The florist shop was dark and all locked up for the night, and I glanced over at the bouquet sitting on the passenger seat, taunting me.

I'd taken the long way around, but as I turned into the street, with my heart beating out of my chest, I drove up the driveway and killed the engine.

"I can do this," I told myself as I pushed open the door.

"Can do what?" a sweet voice asked from beside my open window, scaring the crap out of me.

10

LILY

IT WAS A BEAUTIFUL AFTERNOON AND AFTER SPENDING ALL MORNING cooped up inside starting the mammoth job of cleaning, I'd taken Ava out for a walk to enjoy the afternoon sun. Walking back up the driveway, I wasn't expecting to find Zach's truck parked there. I thought he'd be out on a date. The thought churned my stomach.

Stepping up beside his door, I almost laughed listening to him give himself a pep talk.

"Can do what?" I asked, catching Zach off guard.

"Geez, Lily! You almost gave me a heart attack."

"Sorry." Even though it'd been kind of funny to scare him, I did feel a little guilty. But only a little. I stepped back and let him open the door and slide out.

"And how's my favorite girl today?"

I almost answered. The words were on the tip of my tongue when he knelt down and reached into the stroller, letting Ava wrap her tiny little fist around his finger. He wasn't talking to me. Of course he wasn't. Why would he be?

"I need to get her inside. Did you want to come in?" I offered.

"Sure."

Pushing the stroller across the yard, I managed the stairs like a master, thank God, because I could feel Zach's eyes cataloging my every move. After unlocking the door, I unbuckled Ava from her stroller, carrying her inside while Zach did something in his car. Who knows what he was up to?

"Lily?"

"Just a second," I replied, peeling off Ava's wet diaper and dropping it in the trash before getting her cleaned up and dressed again. Nursing her in my arms, I couldn't help but lean in and smell her clean baby scent as I walked back into the lounge room to find Zach looking uncomfortable and kind of awkward.

"Shouldn't you be out on your date?" I blurted out rather rudely.

"Date? What date?"

"The one you ordered the flowers for?"

A sneaky smirk crossed Zach's face, and now I was the one feeling awkward. I didn't know him well, actually I barely knew anything about him, but the mischief dancing in his eyes had me sitting down on the arm of the couch.

"You mean these flowers?"

As he pulled his hand out from behind his back, I recognized the bouquet instantly. It was the same one I'd gotten out of bed early this morning to put together. Three times. Not that I'd tell him that. The need to have it absolutely perfect was driving me. Painstakingly, and much to Sage's amusement, she watched as I added and removed flowers, tossing any with flaws on the floor with a dramatic sigh.

"What…"

"Lily Evans, these are for you."

Zach smiled.

I melted.

Ava cooed.

He placed the bouquet in my arms and reached for Ava. Not knowing what to do or where to look, I let him take her from my arms and tuck her against his chest.

"Y-Y-You bought me flowers?"

"Yeah."

"No one's ever bought me flowers before," I admitted, the words catching in my throat.

"No. Surely that can't be right."

"It is. Sadly."

"How does that happen?" Rocking back and forth on the balls of his feet, Ava's hand clamped around the chain hanging from Zach's neck and instead of batting her hand away, he just crooked his neck to let her hold it.

"Guess it goes with the job. I'm surrounded by them all day, so why buy them for me. I don't know." I shrugged. I'd never really thought about it before but now I was, I felt like shit.

"Well, the men you know are idiots. If buying you a bunch of flowers puts that sort of smile on your face, then they're the ones missing out, Lily. Not you."

How was this man not already tied down? He knew all the right words to make your knees weak, your panties wet and your heart swoon.

"You're sweet, Zach, you know that, right?"

"Yeah, but don't tell anyone. You'll ruin my reputation," he deflected with a wink.

"My lips are sealed," I promised solemnly, making the universal motion of buttoning my mouth.

"One thing I don't get though, every time I've been here, you always had a bunch of fresh flowers on the bench or the table..."

"Ah, you've seen them but have you really been looking?"

"Huh?"

"They're the flowers that I can't sell or give away. They're wilting or missing petals or the stems are bent. I donate what I can to the hospice or the nursing home, but I bring home the rejects. I might as well get some enjoyment out of them, even if they only last for a day or two."

Zach looked at me, and his gaze was intense and made the butterflies in my stomach take flight. "You're incredible. You know that, right?"

"Yep. And now you do too," I sassed back, trying to lighten the heavy.

I was saying all the right things, but inside I was a jumbled mess. Needing to put some space between us, I took advantage of having someone else around. It wasn't something I was used to and definitely something I couldn't get used to, but taking advantage for a few minutes couldn't be that bad... could it?

"Are you right with her for a couple of minutes?"

"Where are you going?"

Squinting, I felt a teeny tiny bit bad. "I was just going to jump in and have a quick shower, I mean, if that's okay."

"Go. Go. No rush. We're all good here," Zach assured me, waving me off. "This pretty girl and I are just going to hang out and debate the benefits of a good night's sleep."

"That's something Ava could learn a lot about."

Zach moved towards the door, adjusting Ava in his arms. I needed to get out of here as soon as possible before I said or did something stupid like asking him to marry me. Hurriedly, I murmured, "Take your time," before scampering out of the room like someone had lit my ass on fire.

After enjoying my shower, I'd washed my hair and shaved places I shouldn't have let get so far out of hand. Knowing Zach was out there had me taking a little longer to apply my favorite raspberry lotion before changing into a pair of cute boyfriend jeans and a sweater, rather than my pajamas which I'd been planning on.

Pulling my hair up in a ponytail, I swiped a coat of gloss across my lips before checking my reflection in the mirror. I didn't want to look like I was trying too hard, but I couldn't go out there looking like I'd just crawled out of the gutter either. Satisfied it was as good as it was going to get, I stepped out of my bedroom and followed the noise, pausing just inside the door to listen to Zach talking to Ava.

"What are we going to do about this, hey, pretty girl?" Zach murmured, his thick Australian accent making everything he said sound sexy.

"Do about what?" I asked as I pushed open the door and stepped out onto the porch, finding Ava curled in Zach's arms, a pink blanket draped around her. Damn he was good with her.

"Oh, hey there. You feel better?"

"Absolutely. It's amazing how good a hot shower can make a girl feel."

"I'm glad." Zach smiled, his dimple popped, and I sucked my breath in.

"Anyway, what are you two talking about?"

"Your porch needs some work. Some of the wooden boards have rotted through and they need to be replaced."

"Yeah. It's on the list. This place is old and needs a bit of work. Hopefully, I'll get to it soon," I lied. There were so many things that needed to be done in front of replacing whole sections of the porch, I doubted it'd be anytime in the next year, let alone soon, but Zach didn't need to know that.

"Ah, okay."

"So, did you want to stay for dinner? It's nothing special. I was just going to make pasta."

"Thanks, but I actually can't," Zach declined, moving towards me and handing over Ava only for her to whine and squirm as he settled her in my arms. His hand grazed my boob as he let go, and our eyes snapped up, meeting as my cheeks burned.

"Sorry about..."

"Don't even worry about it," I dismissed quickly, not wanting this moment to get any stranger.

"Okay then. Well, I should go. I've gotta go pick up Mom..."

"Your Mom lives here?"

"She's over in Kellyville."

"That's nice," I replied automatically, swallowing down my jealousy. What I'd do to have family close by.

Ava started to fuss, and I adjusted her in my arms, but she wasn't having it. As her complaining escalated, I knew it wouldn't be long before she was in full-on meltdown mode, something I'd prefer to avoid.

"I better get her inside."

"I'll leave you to it. Have a good night, Lily."

"See you later, Zach. And thanks for the flowers."

Flashing one final smile, Zach bounced down the steps and headed towards his truck. When he pulled open the door, I turned and headed inside. I needed wine. Wine and chocolate.

"Hey, Lily?"

"Yeah?" I replied, spinning around to find Zach leaning on the hood, his cheeks red.

"Can I take you out tomorrow?"

"Take me out?"

"Yeah." He rubbed the back of his neck, and instead of making him look nervous and awkward, it just made him look even more desirable. "You and Ava?"

"Okay," I agreed. I didn't know him, not well anyway, but there was something about him that had me agreeing to go out with him, no matter where he was taking me. Zach was the kind of guy you'd agree to go anywhere with.

"Great. I'll pick you up at ten."

"See you then."

Standing there smiling like a loon, I watched as he backed out of the driveway. If it hadn't been for Ava's cries, I'm not sure how long I would've stood there, staring like a moron with hearts in my eyes.

"Come on, little girl. Let's go get you some dinner," I cooed, leaning down and kissing Ava's forehead, not missing the scent of Zach's cologne lingering. Was there anything about that man I didn't find attractive?

It wasn't until I was slumped in the lounge, Ava sucking happily on her bottle as I nursed my wine, that it hit me. I had a date tomorrow. A date with the sexy, tattooed firefighter Zach Higgins. Shit! Was it a date? Or did he just want to spend time with Ava? Ugh! I didn't date. I didn't know how to do this. What was I supposed to wear? Where were we going? What did he expect? Maybe dating in Australia was different to dating here?

Grabbing my phone, I shot a text to the only people who could talk me down off the ledge. The devil and angel that sat on my shoulder. Sage and Sarah could help me figure this one out. They had to. God knows I couldn't do it on my own. I'd go crazy trying. Not even bothering with pasta, I reached straight for more wine.

11

ZACH

This was a bad idea. A very bad idea.

I was supposed to be picking Lily up in twenty minutes, and instead of being filled with that nervous energy that usually kicked in when I knew I was going to see her; I was shitting bricks.

"This is a bad idea," I grumbled again, taking another sip of my fourth coffee for the morning.

"It's not. And you're going," an authoritative voice from behind me told me straight.

"Mom..."

Her head came to rest against my arm. Glancing down at her, I hated how old she looked. Yesterday when I'd shown up at her place, I hated what I found. She was vague and not really with it. After a half-hearted argument, I convinced her to pack a bag and come and stay at my place for a bit. My plan hadn't been to move Mom in so quickly, not while the house was still a construction zone, but I couldn't leave her there. Not like this.

"Zachary James Higgins. You are not standing that lovely young woman up because you're scared..."

"I'm not scared," I argued, the blatant lie falling effortlessly from my lips. "Besides, you haven't even met Lily. How do you know she's lovely? She could have a pink mohawk and ride a Harley for all you know."

"Nice try, son. I might not know Lily, but I know you. Even if you'd prefer to pretend that I don't. You wouldn't give someone like that the time of day. Besides, it takes someone special to bring a precious baby into their home and care for it."

"You're not wrong," I agreed, the image of Lily nursing Ava springing to mind, making me smile.

"You know, I think I'd like to meet her."

"Mom," I groaned.

The last thing I was ready to do was introduce Lily to my mother. We hadn't even shared so much as a kiss yet. Bringing her home to meet Mom was a bit of a leap, and one I wasn't ready to make. Not any time soon anyway.

"No, not Lily. I know you won't want me to meet her…"

"It's not that…"

Stepping back, she waved off the argument. "Ava. I'd love to meet the little girl who's captured your heart."

"She hasn't…"

"Keep lying to yourself, Zach. You love that little girl."

"I can't. She's not mine to keep."

"Doesn't matter. It's written all over your face. Every time you mention her, your whole face lights up. But I'm disappointed in you, Zach."

"Disappointed in me? What the hell did I do?" Damn it. That hurt. Mom was the last person on the face of the earth I'd ever want to disappoint.

"You should know that blood isn't the thing that makes someone family. It's love. And whether you're ready to admit it or not, that little girl has captured your heart and you love her."

Bloody hell. I hated it when Mom was right. Especially when I really didn't want to hear it.

"Now, stop trying to convince yourself you're not going. Get your butt inside. Clean your teeth, change your shirt and get a move on. You're not going to be late. Us women, we hate it when our dates are late."

"It's not a date."

"Yeah, yeah. Keep telling yourself that, my boy."

Mom pressed up on her toes, kissed my cheek and ruffled my hair like she did when I was a kid. Turns out, I might've celebrated more than a dozen birthdays since she towered over me, but she was still my Mom and my conscience. Tossing the dregs of my coffee over the railing onto the garden, I headed inside to get myself organized.

By the time I turned into Lily's street, I was nervous. The thought repeating over and over in my head was, 'did Lily think this was a date?' and possibly even more worrying, 'was it?'. The more I thought about it, the more I tried to rationalize it, the more tangled and confused I got.

Pulling up in front of her house, I saw her standing on the porch, pushing the stroller back and forth. She looked absolutely beautiful. With her knee-length white dress, with bright yellow flowers and her hair tied back in a ponytail with a matching yellow ribbon, I realized I wanted it to be. If Lily thought this was a date, then that's what it was. I wasn't going to force the issue, but just seeing her standing there, looking so effortlessly beautiful, I realized it didn't matter. If this was a date, then I was more than okay with it.

Jumping out of the truck, I headed up the path to Lily. The closer I got the more beautiful she appeared. Her lips were stained with a deep red and her cheeks rosy.

"Morning," I greeted, wiping my sweaty palms against my thighs.

"Hi, Zach. You look good today," Lily offered, catching me off guard.

"You too. And how's my favorite little girl this morning?"

"Oh, I'm fine."

"I meant..." I pointed at Ava who was covered in a pink blanket with tiny white rabbits on it, sucking on her fist happily.

"I know who you meant, Zach."

"Oh."

"So... should we go?"

I was acting like an idiot. I couldn't string a sentence together and I was tripping over myself. I needed to get my shit together or this was going to be a disaster.

"Do you mind if we take your car? It's got the seat for Ava..."

"Absolutely."

Lily bent down and pulled her bag out from the shelf underneath the stroller, and my eyes followed her legs. From her creamy thighs, right down to her painted pink toenails, she was gorgeous. Even her strappy silver sandals were cute. I'd never met someone so girly in my life, but despite appearances, Lily wasn't at all precious. She absolutely was delicate and should be treasured, but she didn't complain and wait for someone to do things for her. I hadn't known her for long, and there was so much more I wanted to know, *needed* to know, but I knew she wasn't afraid to take on the world and demand what she wanted.

While she locked the door, I lifted the stroller down the steps and started towards Lily's car. A moment later she was beside me, her scent surrounding me and making my mouth water. The smell of berries and vanilla reminded me of muffins, and suddenly I was starving.

Without a word, we worked like a team. Neither of us felt the need to give instructions or ask questions. While Lily settled Ava in her seat, I folded the stroller and put it in the back of the car, pulling the blanket out and handing it to Lily.

"You drive," Lily advised, dropping her keys into my hand.

Turning them over in my palm, I noticed the daisy key chain which made me smile. "You sure?"

"Yep," she replied, popping the 'p'.

Knowing I needed to treat her like the lady she was, I opened the passenger door for her, waiting until she tucked the skirt of her dress in around her legs before closing it and rounding the car.

Trying to fold my long legs into her car had us both grinning.

"Sorry, I'm short." Lily giggled with a shrug.

Grabbing the leaver, I pushed the seat back, letting out a breath of relief when my knees stopped knocking against the steering wheel.

"All good. You ready?"

"Yep. Where are we going?"

"You'll see," I told her, hoping I'd made the right decision and she wasn't going to hate this.

After a twenty-minute drive where we chatted mainly about Ava, I turned into the busy parking lot and came to a stop. "Is this okay?" I asked nervously.

"The farmers' market?"

"Yeah."

"I haven't been here forever."

"We can go somewhere else..." I offered, mentally kicking myself. I should've trusted my gut and gone with brunch somewhere fancy with silverware and napkins. Not walking around an unused field, browsing stalls of fresh produce and homemade jams.

"No way! I love the farmers' market. I just never think to come out here. Sunday's usually my only day off and by the time I sleep in and then run my errands, I've completely forgotten it's even on. I hope they still have those funnel cakes covered in the powdered sugar. They're so good."

"Funnel cakes?" I asked, having never heard of them. It was definitely not something we had in Australia.

"Oh my god. Have you never had a funnel cake?" Shaking my head, I couldn't help but be sucked in by Lily's excitement. It was infectious and she looked absolutely gorgeous. The more animated she became, the more I wanted to grab her hand and drag her through the crowd to find her funnel cake. Whatever the hell they were.

"They're the best. They're like a donut but so much better. They're delicious and so very bad for me. But they're my weakness. And I don't remember the last time I had one. I mean, I know I shouldn't, I don't need the extra calories… and I'm shutting up now."

"Why?"

"Because you'll think I'm a crazy lady. I'm sitting here practically drooling over the thought of all sugary deliciousness."

"Well then, crazy lady, let's go find you a funnel cake, and maybe you can convince me they're as good as you're making out," I challenged.

"Zach Higgins, you've got no idea what's coming your way."

"Well then, challenge accepted. Let's do it."

After getting Ava out of the car and settled in her stroller, we walked through the markets, Lily waving to stall holders as we passed. After she bought some apples and stopped to talk to an old lady I didn't recognize who was selling lavender in every form imaginable, Lily spotted the food truck selling her precious funnel cakes.

"Stay with Ava," she instructed, not giving me a chance to answer as she scampered away, joining the line.

Ava started to fuss, and I tried to settle her, but she wasn't having it. Unclipping her, I picked her up, rocking back and forth on the balls of my feet.

"What's the matter, pretty girl?" I asked Ava, only to have her blow a bubble in answer.

"Someone looks very comfortable playing daddy there, Higgins."

Spinning around, I came face to face with Grady and Dylan. "Hey, guys. Didn't expect to see you here," I replied, feeling a little embarrassed being caught out.

"Good lord. She's adorable, Zach."

"Yeah, she really is," I replied, not at all bothered by the fact I sounded like a proud father.

"May I?" Dylan stretched her hands out in front of her, making grabby hands in front of me. As much as I didn't want to hand her over, I didn't want to be rude either. Placing Ava carefully in

Dylan's awaiting arms, I tucked her blanket around her, trying to keep her protected from the breeze that was whipping around.

"How's she doing?" Grady asked, nodding towards Ava.

"She's doing really well."

"Have you heard anything?"

"Not yet."

"Hopefully you will soon."

"Yeah. I'm just not sure what Lily wants the answer to be," I answered honestly, but it wasn't just Lily who was getting anxious not knowing what was going to happen. We didn't know if we'd have Ava for another day, another week or another month. As much as the not knowing sucked, it was also a blessing in many ways. Pretending there was no end date was in a way, easier.

Lily appeared beside me, powdered sugar on her face and waving about a napkin in each hand.

"Grady just asked if we'd heard anything about Ava's forever home."

Lily's face scrunched up at my comment. I didn't have to ask to know she felt the same as I did about the situation. It was incredible how quickly the adorable bundle of bubbles had wormed her way into our hearts. Handing her over wasn't going to be easy, and I dreaded the day we had to. But for now, she was here with us and she was beautiful. I wasn't about to ruin it by thinking about what comes next. Or when.

"Nothing yet," she replied, reaching for Ava.

"Well, she's absolutely beautiful."

"Thanks."

"Come on, Dylan. Let's leave them to get on with their day."

"Are you going to buy me a funnel cake? They look soooo good."

"If that's what you want, that's what you'll get." Grady wrapped his arm around her shoulders and led her towards the food trucks lined up along the end of the field.

"See you around." I waved them off.

With one departing barb, Grady tossed out in my direction, "You guys look like a very happy family. Enjoy your day."

Shaking off his comments, I focused on the sugary goodness Lily was handing me. Taking a bite, I did my best not to moan loudly.

"So good, isn't it?" Lily asked excitedly.

"Not bad. Not bad at all."

"It's okay. You can say you like it. I promise I won't tell anyone."

We wandered amongst the stalls, Lily buying more than I think she was planning on, to the point the stroller was overflowing with her purchases and I was carrying Ava, who'd fallen asleep against my chest. A few times we'd been stopped by people I didn't recognize as Lily was asked why she didn't have a stall. In true Lily style, she was polite and thanked them for their support. Damn, this woman was someone to admire.

When Ava woke and started to fuss, it was time to call it a day. I didn't think Lily could've fit another thing in. Heading back to the car, we loaded up her purchases and buckled Ava into her seat, ignoring her rumblings. Once she was settled, I pulled open the passenger door and waited for Lily to get in.

"Hang on a second," I stopped her, grabbing her arm and swiping my thumb across her bottom lip.

"What?"

"You had powdered sugar." Licking the sugar from my thumb, Lily's pink tongue snuck out and wet her lips.

"Th-th-thank you."

"You're welcome."

I went to take a step back to give her room, but she flipped the hold, taking hold of my hand. Not giving me a chance to ask any questions, she pushed up on her toes, grabbed a fist full of my shirt and pressed her lips against mine.

12

LILY

Thankfully this week had been super busy, so I hadn't had time to sit and stress about how stupid I'd been. Kissing Zach. What was I thinking? I'd like to pretend I was drunk, and I could've blamed it on the booze, but the only thing I was drunk on was him.

Sage had been off sick for the last couple of days, so I was trying to do it all myself and it wasn't working. Not when I had four funerals, a school dance, and on Saturday a wedding to prepare for. On top of that, I was still trying to take care of Ava. Thankfully she was asleep at the moment, allowing me to use both hands as I tried to put together Mrs. Straughton's casket arrangement.

As quickly as I could, I stepped over Malteser who was sunning himself on the floor and grabbed the buckets of white roses and calla lilies and got to work. I was just finishing up when the bells on the door jingled. Pasting on a smile, I forced cheeriness into my voice ready to greet a customer. As exhausted as I was, I couldn't afford to offend potential customers.

"Good morning."

"Good morning. Are you Lily?"

Caught a little off guard, I stepped behind the counter and wiped my hands on my apron. "Yes."

"I'm Linda, Zach's Mom."

I don't know if that was supposed to put me at ease or make me even more anxious. "Oh. Hello."

"Please, don't let me get in your way. I was just hoping to steal a sneak peek at the girl who has my son wrapped around her little finger."

Ah. That made sense. She was here to see Ava, not me. I didn't like the wave of disappointment that flowed through me, but I forced it aside.

"Ava's asleep at the moment. But she's just in the office…"

"Oh, she's here. Is her sitter ill? I thought she'd be at home. I was just going to see if there was a time I could stop by and meet her."

"Nope. She's here. With me. Usually, I'm not here as long or as hands on, but unfortunately Sage, my offsider, is sick. So, I'm it."

I hated feeling like I had to explain myself, but I couldn't stand the thought of her thinking less of me.

"Oh, sweetheart. I know Zach's on shift at the moment, but can I help at all?" she offered, looking at me sympathetically.

I was torn. I didn't know this lady from a bar of soap, but I was desperate for some help, even if it was only long enough for me to take a bathroom break and grab something to eat.

"I don't…"

"Why don't you call Zach and check? He'll vouch for me. I raised him after all…"

"And you raised him right," I confirmed, watching as she smiled proudly. "You don't mind?"

"Not at all. I'd do exactly the same if some weird lady walked in off the street and offered to help."

Making the snap decision, I took her up on her offer. I didn't have much choice. I was desperate and she was offering me the help I desperately needed. Grabbing my phone from beside the register, I moved towards the corner of the shop, trying to locate the orange roses I was sure I'd seen stashed over here.

"Thanks. I won't be a second."

I hadn't heard from Zach since I'd kissed him and then put as much distance as possible between us. Knowing I needed to do this, I found his contact and waited for him to answer.

"Lily?"

"Hey, Zach. I didn't catch you at a bad time, did I?"

"Not really. I'm on shift, but all good. What's up?"

"Well, there's a lady here, Linda. She said she's your mom and she's offered to give me a hand."

"What?"

"Your mom is here. Says she wants to help."

"Shit! Do you need help?"

"Well... actually. Yeah. I could use a hand," I admitted, trying not to feel ashamed. Asking for help wasn't easy and it was definitely something I wasn't good at.

"I can't come and help you now. Maybe I can see if I can swap—"

"Zach!" He kept babbling. "Zach!" I tried again to get his attention.

"Yeah?"

"I don't need you to swap your shift or run down here and save me. I was just checking to see if you had any issues with your mother helping me out."

"Issues? Like what?"

"Well, considering I've never met your mother, I was hoping you could tell me she was who she says she is for starters?"

Zach described the woman perfectly down to the color of her shoes and the handbag that dangled from her arm. There was no doubt the woman standing, gazing lovingly into the office where Ava slept was Zach's mom.

"Okay. Well, if you're looking for her, she's going to be down here at the shop with me for a while."

"No worries."

In the background an alarm went off. "Shit, sorry, Lily. Gotta run. I'll check in when I can."

"Stay safe."

Zach ended the call and I pulled my phone away from my ear and stared at it for a few seconds, imagining him jumping into the engine and racing towards a burning building with very little regard for his own safety. Crossing my fingers, I hoped he'd be home safe.

"Everything okay?" Linda called out, snapping me back into the here and now.

"Yep. Zach's just had a call out."

"Ah. That explains the face."

"What face?"

"The one you're wearing right now, sweetheart. The face that's worried for him and wishing he had a safer job."

"My face says all that?" I asked, reaching up and touching my cheeks.

"Yes, but don't worry. I only recognize it because I've felt like that since he announced all those years ago that being a firefighter was what he wanted to do with his life. Trust me, I tried to talk him out of it, but Zach's as stubborn as his father was, God rest his soul. But he's good at what he does. He's got a good head on his shoulders. All you can do is pray he comes home in one piece."

"Wow. I don't know how you do it."

"It's easy. I do it because I love him. And Zach wouldn't be the man he is today if he did something else. So, I just hold my breath, hope for the best and love him no matter what."

"He's a good man."

"The best. But enough about my son. Now tell me, how can I help?"

Fifteen minutes later and I found myself wondering how I'd ever done this without her. Linda had run down the street and picked us up a couple of sandwiches and coffees, before taking over answering the phone, organizing the invoices and keeping her eye on Ava, leaving me free to scurry about and put together orders.

By the time three o'clock hit, somehow, we'd caught up and everything was ready to go. Kids filtered in collecting their corsages for the school dance, and Linda and I worked seamlessly handing them out and taking their payments.

The afternoon flew by and soon enough, I was tallying up the register while Linda swept the floors. Surveying the damage, I was glad a delivery was coming tomorrow morning. I'd been completely cleaned out, which was a very good problem to have.

"Well, that's it. Time to head out."

"Goodnight, pretty girl. You behave for Lily tonight," Linda told Ava, booping her nose and earning her a gurgle.

"What are your plans for tonight?"

"Ah, I'll head back to Zach's. Have a glass of wine and organize some dinner. Nothing exciting."

"Well, how about you come back to my place and we share a bottle of wine instead?"

"You don't have to do that."

"I know I don't, but you really helped me out today. Consider it my way of saying thank you."

"If you're sure, that'd be lovely. Thank you."

While I collected my stuff and locked up, Linda got Ava organized and we were out the door and heading home.

I left Linda and Ava rocking back and forth on the porch swing while I went inside and poured the wine.

Heading back out, I paused inside the door and eavesdropped on their conversation.

"I can see why Zach loves you so much, Ava. You're such a beautiful little girl. And you deserve the world. I hope you get an amazing forever home, sweetheart."

There was a lump in my throat. Even though I agreed with everything she was saying, even the idea of having to say goodbye to Ava was something I wasn't ready to do, and I seriously doubted I ever would.

"Here we go!" I announced, pushing open the door and stepping out onto the porch.

I handed Linda a glass of wine and sat down on the swing

beside her. "Want me to take her?" I asked, suddenly needing her close.

Linda transferred Ava into my arms and instantly a calm settled over me.

"Do you mind if I ask you something?"

"Sure."

"So, you don't have an accent but Zach does…"

"Ah. Yes. I'm American born and bred. I met Zach's dad when he was travelling. I was young and in love and Australia sounded like an adventure. So, I moved to the land down under, got married and then had Zach and his sister Madeline."

"But you came back?"

"Yeah. When my husband died. Zach and Maddy were all grown up and living their own lives, and I wanted to come home. It was time."

"And Zach followed you?"

"I don't know why, but he did. And I'm glad he did. Having him nearby has been amazing. Even if he's a bit bossy and demanding."

"I can see that."

"But he means well. Zach's a good boy."

"I can see that too," I admitted. I mean, there was no point denying it. Zach was a good guy.

Ava started to squirm, and I knew it was time to get her bathed, fed and ready for bed. But my feet were aching, and I just wanted to sit for a few more minutes and enjoy watching the sun sink below the horizon and drink my wine. But Ava didn't seem to agree with that plan.

"Okay. Okay. I'll get up."

"What's wrong?" Linda asked, that motherly worried tone seeping into her voice effortlessly.

"Oh, someone's just had a big day and is ready for her dinner and then bedtime."

"Well, I should get out of your hair," Linda announced, chugging down the last of her wine and standing up.

"You don't have to go," I replied quickly. Actually, the last thing I wanted her to do was leave. I was enjoying having her company. With Sarah working shift work and her own family to chase after, Sage being a million years younger with completely different priorities, mainly men, I spent a lot of time alone. Too much time alone. And since that kiss the other day, even the memory had me wincing, I needed the distraction before I continued to analyze it to death. "I mean, I'd love it if you'd stay. I just need to get Ava bathed and off to bed."

"Can I help?" Linda piped up.

"Absolutely."

And when Linda said help, she meant completely take over, shoo me out of the bathroom sending me to refill my wine and go sit on the porch. When she emerged half an hour later, she appeared carrying the blanket from the back of the couch and what was left of the bottle of wine.

"Dinner will be here in twenty."

"Dinner? Dinner? You organized dinner?"

Shit! I was the worst host in the world. I'd been too busy wiggling my toes to even think about food or feeding my guest.

"Yeah. I hope you like pizza."

"Does anyone not like pizza?"

"I was hoping you'd say that."

"Is Ava…"

"Washed, fed and sound asleep."

"How'd you do that? It usually takes me over an hour to get her down."

"Practice. Oh look. Pizza's early."

Sitting up, I spun around to find the sexiest pizza delivery guy striding up the front path. Damn him!

13

ZACH

It'd been a long couple of days.

I'd done back-to-back shifts with two-day shifts followed by three nights, and all I could think about was a hot shower and some sleep. Lots and lots of sleep. Pulling my truck into the drive, I saw Mom's little buzz box already parked there. I thought she said she was going home, but obviously I'd got my days mixed up. Wouldn't surprise me.

Grabbing my bag off the back seat, I checked the mailbox and trudged up the driveway and through the back door only to be greeted with the smell of bacon. Oh yeah. I could get used to coming home to this.

"Morning," Mom greeted cheerfully as she flitted about my kitchen.

"Ah, hi. Smells good in here."

"Thought you might be hungry."

I hadn't even thought about food but now it was here, my stomach was rumbling loudly. "Starving actually."

"Great! I have bacon, eggs, waffles…"

"Wow! What's the big occasion?" I asked. I couldn't remember the last time Mom had cooked for me like this.

I watched as her cheeks blushed before she lifted her mug to her lips and took a sip. Dodging my question, she sent me for a shower, telling me I had ten minutes before breakfast would be ready. Making a mental note to circle back to this conversation, I headed down the hall, dumping my bag on my bedroom floor and headed for the bathroom.

After getting cleaned up, I changed into a pair of sweats and a t-shirt and stumbled back out to the kitchen. I was halfway down the hallway when I did an about face and turned back to my bedroom. Something was different. Looking around, there was nothing obvious though. Nothing was missing. Everything seemed to be in its place. The blinds were open, but I couldn't remember if I'd just forgotten to close them or not. With a shake of my head, I gave up trying to work it out and followed my nose hoping there was still orange juice in the fridge.

Mom was already plating up as I dropped into the chair. "Looks good."

"I had some time and thought you could use some food before you pass out."

"Yeah. I have big plans for a long day of sleeping," I told her, taking the first bite of the fluffy scrambled eggs she'd heaped onto my plate. I didn't know what her secret was, and for as long as I lived, I was positive I'd never be able to make eggs like she did. It was her superpower.

"I thought you might. I changed your sheets and vacuumed your room, so you can just rest." She smiled as she sat down opposite me and smothered her waffle with syrup.

"You didn't have to do that," I mumbled through a mouthful of food.

"I know. But I'm your mother. It's what we do. We take care of our kids."

"I'm not really a kid anymore, Mom."

"You'll always be my kid, Zachary. No matter how big and how buff you get, you'll always be my baby boy."

"So, you think I'm buff?" I teased.

Rolling her eyes, Mom sighed. "Eat your breakfast."

It was nice sitting here talking about nothing, or not talking at all while we shared breakfast. When I worried about Mom being lonely over in Kellyville, I hadn't stopped to think that maybe she wasn't the only one. Having someone to come home to, even if it was my mom and not the woman of my dreams, was kinda nice.

Rocking back in my chair, I drained the glass of juice that had appeared in front of me. "So, what are your plans today?"

"I was actually going to go give Lily a hand," Mom replied, her voice wavering.

"Lily? Does she need help?"

"Calm down there, Superman. She needs help at the shop, not with Ava. She's doing an amazing job with her. It's just juggling the two."

"What about Sage?"

"Sage is still there."

Yawning loudly, I knew my time was running out. I was going to crash and crash hard.

"Are you enjoying working there?"

"I really am. And Lily's such a sweetheart. Can't say no to anyone, even if it's her biggest flaw."

"What do you mean?" I asked, Mom's comment piquing my interest. If someone was taking advantage of Lily's generosity, then I was going to put an end to that. Tired or not.

"Nothing terrible, so you can wipe that scowl off your face. No, it's more that she makes sure everyone else has everything they need before she goes after what she wants. What she deserves."

Yeah. I could see that.

"How can I help?"

"You don't need to do anything, Zach. I know it's your instinct, to find a problem, run in and fix it. You're so much like your dad in that way, but this isn't a problem that can be fixed."

"Bet it is," I grumbled under my breath.

"Oh geez. Look at the time. I'm going to be late. I told Lily I'd open…"

Mom started clearing the table like a mad woman. Reaching out, I grabbed her wrist, halting her. "Mom, go. I'll clean up."

"You sure?" She didn't look convinced. "I know how tired you are."

"I'm fine. I'm pretty sure I can clear the table and wash up a couple of plates."

Bending down, Mom pressed a quick kiss to my cheek before scooping her bag from the counter. "Thanks, sweetheart. You're the best. Love you."

"Love you too, Mom," I called out as she disappeared out the back door, bouncing down the steps and was gone.

For five minutes I just sat there, my mind slowly whirling, before I stood up, tidied the kitchen, stacking the dishes in the sink and going to bed. Stripping off, I slid between the sheets completely naked and closed my eyes. I didn't know if it was the clean, crisp, fresh linen scented sheets or all the conflicting thoughts bumbling around in my brain but within minutes, I was down for the count.

It was after two when I woke up, feeling slightly more human and a lot less like a zombie, and after tossing a load of washing in the machine, I was craving a burger like no one's business. After a quick call to Bowie, one that was met with a string of curses after waking his grumpy ass up, I was getting dressed and heading to Hooligans. It might've been three o'clock on a Wednesday, but who gave a shit? When you worked shifts like we did, days and times seemed to blend together.

Pulling into the parking lot, I wasn't surprised to see his over-sized red truck missing. Bowie was notoriously late, and we often joked that the man would be late for his own funeral. Spying the bakery across the road, I strode across the street before ducking inside.

Ignoring the fluttering lashes of Phoebe from behind the counter, I grabbed a box full of mixed sugary indulgence and got the hell out of there. Phoebe was a nice enough girl, but she hit on everyone in a uniform in a hundred-mile radius.

With still no Bowie in sight, I walked down the street and entered the florist, those annoying little bells announcing my arrival.

"Back again so soon?" Sage asked sickeningly sweetly.

"Ah, sweetheart. You're awake. Feeling better?" Mom asked, coming towards me.

"Ah yeah. I stopped and grabbed these for you. Thought the three o'clock sugar rush might need supplies," I explained, handing over the box.

"Yay treats!" Sage snatched it away before opening it on the counter and snagging herself one of the pastries, biting into it noisily.

I was trying to be sneaky and catch a glimpse of Lily, but obviously I was doing a pretty shitty job.

"She's not here, Zach," Mom offered, patting my hand.

"I wasn't…"

"Sure, you weren't. She's taken Ava to the doctors."

"What?" My voice was barely recognizable. It sounded like a pre-pubescent teen's, cracking and crumbling. "Ava's sick?"

"No, no. Ava's fine," Mom clarified quickly. "Just a check-up. She wanted to make sure there was nothing…"

Mom didn't have to finish that sentence. I knew exactly what she was getting at. Since Ava had been abandoned, or the correct word so I'd been informed was 'surrendered', we didn't know her medical history. We didn't know if her mother had smoked and drank, or worse, through the pregnancy and if there were any lasting effects. Even though Lily assured me that everything was okay, I guess deep down, she was as nervous as I was.

"Okay then. Well, I gotta run. I'm meeting Bowie."

"Are you home for dinner?" Mom asked.

"Yep. I'll be there. And we can talk."

It felt weird being the one to give my own mother the 'we need to talk' speech, but it was the truth. I needed to know what was going on in that head of hers. What her plans were. Barely two weeks ago she was protesting about coming to my place for a night and now she was keeping my house and cooking me breakfast. Not that I was complaining, it was just odd. Not to mention she seemed better somehow. Maybe it was the loneliness making her symptoms worse? Maybe having her move in permanently was the answer I'd been looking for.

My stomach growled and that was my cue.

"Alright, ladies. I'm out. Enjoy your afternoon," I announced loudly before kissing Mom's cheek and heading for the door.

A chorus of 'byes' followed me out.

Twenty minutes later my burger arrived but still no Bowie. I wasn't even pissed anymore. I'd given up waiting and ordered without him and now I was digging in greedily. Sitting in a booth in the back corner, the last thing I wanted was random company. If I could just sit, eat in peace and get out of here, I'd be a very happy man.

"You Zach? That hotshot firefighter?"

Fuck! There went my quiet meal.

Wiping my hands and face on my napkin, I turned to face the interruption. He was overweight, already drunk, slurring and looked like he had a dribble of barbeque sauce down the center of his boobs. Yep, dude had man boobs. Big ones.

"I'm Zach Higgins. I work at the station," I clarified, ignoring the hotshot comment.

"You're the one shacking up with Lily Evans?"

Putting my hands beneath the table, I balled my hands into fists, quietly reminding myself punching this guy wouldn't do me any favors.

"Lily and I are friends."

"Friends? Wish I was Lily's friend. Went to school with her. She gives head like…"

Thank God Dan, the bartender, cut off his comment. I didn't know Lily's past, but I didn't need to. No woman should be talked about like this dipshit was talking about Lily. If Dan hadn't interceded when he did, I wasn't sure I'd be able to hold back.

"You're out of here, Jack. Come back when you're sober and not looking to get your head knocked in," Dan cautioned him as he nudged him towards the door.

When Jack stumbled and turned back to us, I thought he was going to have another go. Instead, he just shook his head and murmured something about Lily being a lousy lay and not worth it, before falling back out the door.

"Want me to wrap that up for you?" Dan offered.

Looking down at my barely eaten burger, I nodded automatically. Dan disappeared with my plate and reappeared a minute later with a to-go box. "Forget Jack. He's drunk and he's just been laid off. He's spouting shit to anyone whose path he crosses. Lily's a great girl, and I don't know anyone in town who'd say a bad word about her."

"Thanks."

Taking the box, I headed home, not liking the off-balance feeling settling over me. By the time I made it through the door I was mad. I didn't know if I was mad at Jack for being a douche, mad at Bowie for bailing on me or mad at Lily for not being in the shop when I stopped by. I was just generally pissed off. Stuffing my food in the fridge, I changed into a pair of shorts, a tank, stuffed my feet into my runners and took off out the front door. A long hard run along the hiking trails should help sweat my frustrations out. At least I hoped it would.

14

LILY

I can't believe I let Linda talk me into this. I mean, I know I'm an adult and I'm completely capable of saying the word no, but despite my protests, I kind of wanted to come.

After taking Ava for her check-up, something she passed with flying colors thankfully, I went back to work to find an empty bakery box sitting on the counter and everything finished. The floors were swept, the trash taken out. Even the ribbon and paper for wrapping had been restocked for tomorrow. Sage and Linda had done an incredible job. So much so that I couldn't really be annoyed at them for not leaving me a cinnamon roll. And since I'd skipped lunch, again, something that was becoming a really bad habit, I would've killed for a muffin or even a cookie. Especially one of those peanut butter cookies they make at the bakery. Those things were my damn weakness. Probably why I didn't buy them too often. If I did, I'd probably eat the whole thing in one mouthful and end up with a butt the size of a bus.

Having everything done and ready, as soon as four o'clock hit, I was locking the door and we were all getting out of there for an early afternoon. That's when Linda got me. Right when I was at my weakest.

"What are you doing tonight, Lily?" she asked as I was buckling in Ava.

"Ah, probably the same as every other night. Dinner, bath, bed. Repeat."

"Well, why don't you come over to Zach's for dinner? I'm cooking."

My heart sped up. I hadn't seen Zach since he'd been conned into playing pizza delivery boy the other night. Linda was definitely a master matchmaker. As soon as Zach had been bounding up the steps, pizza in hand, she remembered she had somewhere else she had to be. Somewhere my ass. I'd never seen someone hightail it out of my house so quickly. But not before stealing the keys to Zach's truck and telling him to make sure he helped me finish the pizza.

Turned out to not be the worst thing in the world. We sat out on the porch, eating and talking. Mainly Zach was talking, while I peppered him with a million and one questions about what it was like growing up in Australia. He'd almost wet himself laughing when I asked him about the wildlife. How was I supposed to know that not every house was surrounded by things that wanted to kill you? Everything I saw, everything I read, told me as amazing as the Australian beaches were and as sexy as those accents sounded, it was filled with snakes and spiders and drop bears. No thank you. I was staying put. Right where I was. Safe and sound.

"I don't know…" I deflected.

I hadn't heard from Zach since, and I was beginning to think he was avoiding me. Well, I was until the baked goodies mysteriously showed up this afternoon.

"Come on. I'd love to hang out with Ava, and you could use someone looking after you for a change," Linda offered, and tears unexpectedly filled my eyes.

"That sounds so good." I caved, wiping away the tears as quickly as they'd appeared.

"Great. I'm not sure if Zach will be home or not, but it doesn't matter. If he isn't; girls' night. If he is; girls' night."

"Isn't it his house?"

"He won't mind," Linda promised.

And that's what led me to here.

Since it was such a lovely afternoon, I'd loaded Ava into the stroller and we'd started walking. It was so nice to be out in the fresh air enjoying the dying afternoon sun.

Turning into Zach's street, I could hear music pumping. It was old-school Guns and Roses, one of my favorites, not that anyone would ever guess. As we got closer, my grip on the handles tightened. This couldn't be right. Surely. It was too good to be true.

Being super sneaky, I grabbed my phone from my purse and snapped a couple of pictures. Sage would never believe me if I didn't have proof. Hell, I didn't believe my eyes right now and he was right there in front of me.

With the hose in one hand and a sponge in the other, he looked quite the sight. His shorts were hanging low on his hips, hips he was shaking like he was Beyoncé as he washed his truck. Talk about man candy. He had muscles on muscles and those tattoos drew me in like beacons as my feet propelled me in his direction. The only saving grace was his singing. It was terrible. Off key. Out of time and completely out of tune. Thankfully, it made him human rather than the god with the six pack I was practically drooling over.

Knowing he hadn't seen me yet, I kept staring. I mean, who wouldn't. I had eyes and he was there. Movement across the road caught my attention and I noticed the curtain ruffle. Guess I wasn't the only one enjoying the show.

As I got closer, before I had a chance to make my presence known, something I was putting off as long as I could so I could appreciate his assets – arms, butt, back and chest – Ava let out an ear-piercing screech which sounded like she was being attacked. Damn kid almost gave me a heart attack. A few minutes ago, she was sleeping quietly, her fist stuffed in her mouth and now she was screaming bloody murder.

"What the?"

Zach spun around quickly.

Too quickly.

Forgetting he had the hose in his hand, the arc of the spray waved out in front of him, splashing me straight across the chest, soaking me right through.

"Shit, Lily!"

While Zach scrambled to shut the hose off, spraying himself in the process, I checked on Ava who was now lying there silently, her big eyes blinking.

Once the hose was gone, Zach bounded down the driveway, ignoring the fact he had droplets of water running down his chest – definitely not something I could ignore. "Are you okay? I didn't mean to..." He pointed at my chest where the white fabric of my dress was clinging to me like a second skin.

"I'm fine. Just a little wet," I confirmed, which was the understatement of the century. And it wasn't just my dress that was soaked.

"What's going on?" Linda appeared stomping down the driveway looking absolutely ridiculous in a pink frilly apron. When her eyes spotted Zach and I standing there both dripping wet, with only the stroller between us, she burst into an explosion of hysterical laughter. "You know what, I don't even want to know. I'll leave you two to... whatever this is." Pointing her finger between us, she turned and headed back inside.

It wasn't until she was completely out of view, did we crack up. We must've looked incredibly ridiculous right now.

Ava grumbled and Zach pushed back the hood and looked down at her. I couldn't help but watch him. Watching a six foot four, fully built, tattooed guy melt at seeing a beautiful baby girl was enough to make your ovaries hurt. And he did it to me every time. Every. Single. Time.

"You didn't?" he asked, looking up at me and straight in my eyes.

"I...I..."

"You taped a bow to her head?"

"Yes. I know." I dropped my head shamefully.

"I thought we agreed we weren't going to do that?" Zach unbuckled her and lifted her up into his arms letting her nuzzle against his bare chest. Damn she was a lucky kid.

"I had to!" I defended myself, trying to keep my damn hormones in check.

"You had to?"

"Yeah. I had to. Everyone at the doctors today kept calling her a him!"

A smirk crossed Zach's face, making his dimple pop as Ava grabbed for his nose. Talk about wrapped around her tiny finger. That man would take on the world if he thought anyone was going to hurt her. A quality that made him even more attractive than those abs, if that was even possible.

A gust of wind tossed up, and I shivered as Zach held Ava even closer, adjusting the blanket around her.

"Lily?" Linda's voice called out from a window above our heads. I had a really bad feeling our whole exchange had been watched and analyzed from Zach's living room.

"Yes?"

"Come on inside. We need to get you dried off before you catch a chill."

"Oh, I'm fine…" I replied, not wanting to intrude.

"Don't be silly. Now both of you, inside."

"Yes, Mom," Zach replied automatically as he turned and headed back towards his truck, bending over and effortlessly picking up the bucket and sponge he'd been using while juggling Ava like a pro. How did he make everything he did look so easy?

"We don't have to… I can just go home and change," I offered, turning the empty stroller around.

"Nonsense. Now come on in before we both get in trouble."

With Zach carrying Ava and heading away from me, I had no choice but to follow. Or stare at his ass. I mean, it was right there. Wasn't like I could avoid it.

Taking a deep breath, I followed Zach and Ava up the back steps and inside.

15

ZACH

Wet shorts did not hide the boner I was sporting.

Stepping inside, I quickly unloaded Ava into Mom's waiting arms, ignoring the all-knowing grin she was flashing in my direction, and made a beeline for my bedroom.

"I'll grab Lily something dry to wear," I called out over my shoulder as I stepped into my bedroom, closed the door, leaning against it.

For as long as I lived, I didn't think I'd ever forget the way she looked in another one of those crazy fifties' housewives' dresses with the full skirt I wanted to flip up and the belt cinched at her tiny waist. And today's offering came complete with tiny red cherries dotted all over her white dress. Her white dress that went completely see through when it got wet. The see-through dress that gave me a glimpse of the woman she was beneath the prim and proper pearls. Her white lacy bra was visible through the material, and the way her nipples poked the damp fabric told me I wasn't the only one affected.

Taking a breath, I ran my hand through my hair before reaching down and adjusting myself. It took a minute or two reminding myself that my mother was standing on the other side of the door nursing a baby before I could convince the little guy in my shorts he wasn't needed. He wasn't as disappointed as I was, trust me.

Changing into a pair of dry gray sweats and a t-shirt, I snagged another pair and my station t-shirt from the clean pile on my bed; guess Mom was doing my laundry too these days.

Lily had kicked off her shoes and was standing in the lounge room with a towel wrapped around her shoulders while she watched on like a hawk as Mom talked to Ava.

"Here you go. They'll be too big on you, but at least they're clean and dry."

"Thanks." Lily accepted the clothes, and when her fingers touched mine, she stepped back, bumping into the door.

"Bathroom's down the hall. Last door on the right," I directed, trying to play the good host. After all, I was being watched and I didn't need to give Mom any more ammunition she could, and most certainly would, fire back in my direction.

Once Lily was gone and I heard the lock click on the bathroom door, Mom stood up and placed Ava back in my arms. "She's a special girl, Zach."

"I know," I replied automatically as Mom went back to the kitchen.

Slumping down into the couch, I adjusted Ava in my arms. She gurgled and smiled.

"How do you get her to do that?"

"Do what?"

I looked up and saw Lily looking completely different but somehow even more gorgeous than ever. Gone were all traces of the girly girl I'd come to recognize, only to be replaced by someone who looked completely at ease and relaxed. It suited her. Or at least my department t-shirt looked good on her. It hung down almost to her knees, and I shook off the idea of her wearing nothing else.

"Make her smile."

"She smiles all the time."

"Only for you."

"That can't be right. Surely she's smiled when you're talking to her?" I couldn't believe Ava wouldn't. Hell, it took all the restraint I had to stop myself grinning like a fool whenever Lily came close.

"Well maybe once. But I'm pretty sure it was just wind." Lily shrugged it off, moving towards the bookshelf in the corner, making me wish I'd dusted.

She shuffled books around, picked up photo frames, while I watched as she took in my life. One that I'd lived a million miles from here.

"Who's this in the photos with you?" Lily asked, flipping around a frame where I was standing on the beach in my board shorts with my arm draped over a blonde's shoulders.

"Ah, that's my sister."

"Your sister? She's stunning."

"Yeah, Maddy. She's an actress."

"Your sister's an actress?"

"Yeah."

"In anything I would've seen? Movies? TV shows? Was she in the latest Marvel movie?"

"She wishes. Nah. She's in a soapie back home."

"Was it the one Chris Hemsworth was in? *Home and Away* I think it's called."

"What?"

"Or the one Liam was in? *Neighbors* or something?"

"Oh my god, Lily. You're kidding me, right? You know about Aussie soaps?" I couldn't believe it.

Setting the photo back on the shelf, Lily turned back to me with a shrug. "I know about the Hemsworths."

"What is it with you women and the bloody Hemsworths? They're just normal guys. They surf. They drink beer. They watch the footy. They're just like the rest of us."

I don't know what it is about the Hemsworth brothers. Women everywhere thought they were the best thing since sliced bread. I didn't understand it. I don't think I ever would.

"They're not like the rest of you. No way. Hell, I'd even do the other brother."

"Other brother?"

"Yeah, the third one. I'd do him just so I could score an invite to the family Christmas dinner."

Bloody women. I'd never understand them as long as I lived.

Mom outdid herself with dinner. If I was thinking about keeping her around after breakfast, then there was no way I was letting her go now. I can't remember the last time Mom cooked my favorite; a roast lamb leg with all the vegetables piled high on my plate. When I was a kid, I could barely remember a Sunday where we didn't have the hot roast dinner. It was a tradition. One I'd seemingly forgotten until now. But sitting there, with the drawstring on my pants tugging at me under the pressure of too much food, I decided it was a tradition I was going to reinstate. Immediately.

When I'd tried to clear away the plates, Mom handed me a beer and shooed me out of my own kitchen. While I was more than happy to not have to do the dishes, being nudged out the door was Mom's not so subtle way of matchmaking.

Sitting on the bottom step, I picked at the label on my bottle. "Sorry about this."

"Don't be. She's your mom, she loves you."

"Yeah. In her own way, I guess you're right."

"Of course I'm right. At the shop, she doesn't stop talking about how amazing you are and how proud of you she is."

Feeling a little embarrassed, I drained the rest of my beer and stood to get another. "Want one?"

"I shouldn't."

"Why not? It's just a beer."

"Ava…"

"One beer's not going to do any harm. Besides, it's not like you're driving."

"You're right. A beer would be awesome, actually."

Heading back inside, I flicked the outdoor lights on that I'd strung up last weekend, stuck my head through the doorway to find Mom sitting in the chair, her eyes closed and a magazine in her lap while Ava slept soundly in the center of my bed, cocooned by pillows. With the house quiet and everything as it should be, I grabbed a couple of beers and went back out to Lily.

Popping the cap, I handed her the bottle. "Thanks. It's so beautiful out here."

"It's a work in progress."

"Who's doing your work?"

"Mainly me. I mean, I get some help from the guys at the station, but it depends on schedules. Which is why it's so slow."

"Wait until I get started. Yours will look like it's supercharged. It's going to take me forever to get done what I want to do."

"What do you want to do?"

"Everything. Grandma's house is so old and needs so much work, I don't even know where to start."

"Does that mean you're staying there then?"

"I think so. I mean, I love my apartment, but being at Grandma's, it just feels… feels right. It feels like home. Even though I never intended to live there, now that I am, I can't imagine living anywhere else."

"What are you going to do with the apartment?"

"Honestly. No idea. Thankfully I don't have to worry right away."

"Well, that's good. You can take your time. Do what you need to do."

"Yep. And first step, get the rest of my stuff out of the apartment and start making Grandma's house feel like mine. She's not coming back, so I guess it's time to move on."

"Well, let me know if you need a hand," I offered.

"Thanks. Wow! Is that the time? I should get home. I didn't mean to stay this long."

Glancing at my watch, I saw that it was almost nine. No wonder I was starting to get tired. With a huge belly full of food and a couple of beers under my belt, I was fading fast. After collecting the empty bottles, I met Lily standing on the steps, still wearing my clothes. Damn the woman looked good.

"Let me grab my shoes and I'll walk you home."

"You don't have to do that."

"Yes, I do. I'd drive you home, but I don't have a seat for Ava in the truck, so I'm walking you."

With a resigned sigh, Lily smiled. "Okay. If it's not too much trouble. That would be great."

16

LILY

I couldn't believe I'd let Sage talk me into this. Actually, that wasn't quite accurate. I couldn't believe I was allowing Sage to take over my life and drag me out tonight, especially looking like the town tramp. Part of me knew it was my own fault, but I was still blaming Sage. It was much easier to blame her than to own it myself.

It'd been a few days since Zach had shown up before the shop even opened, a group of his firefighter friends in tow, and began loading my life into the back of their oversize trucks. A couple of hours later and the apartment was empty, and I'd been left standing in the middle of the room, staring at the space I'd once called home wondering how I ever fit everything in here. It looked so much smaller.

I must've been up there longer than I thought when Sage came looking for me. I was on the verge of sitting down on the carpet and having a good old cry, something that was long overdue, when she stomped her heavy boots in front of me, leaving a muddy mark.

"What's wrong? Have all the hot firemen gone for the day and you've got no one left to ogle?"

"No!" I defended quickly, swiping away the tears that were threatening to overflow down my face. "Besides, I wasn't ogling."

"Okay. Fine. Drooling then."

"Wasn't drooling."

I probably was, but there was no way under the sun I was going to admit that. Besides, it wasn't like you could blame me. Watching Zach's tight ass run up and down those stairs then reappear carrying something heavy that made his bicep's bulge while he bit his lip in a way that should've been outlawed... The things I'd do to be the one biting that lip had me shaking my head and taking a much-needed time out in the cool room.

"You were, but so was I. Don't be embarrassed, Lily. Own that shit. Hell, if that man looked at me the way he looked at you, you can bet your pretty pearls I wouldn't be drooling through the windows. I'd be smacking that ass and riding him into the sunset."

"Don't you mean riding off into the sunset?"

"Sweetie. You might pretend to be all innocent and naive with your petticoats and pearls, but we both know you'd like to be riding Zach Higgins into the sunset."

My cheeks burned at her words. I couldn't reply. There was no reply. Those were the ideas I had at home, alone, tucked in my bed late at night. Sage did not need to know the things I wondered about Zach and what he could do with his hands.

And that was the problem.

And it was how I ended up sitting in the front seat of Sage's bright yellow buzz box, one that should've been deemed unroadworthy years ago but she adored anyway, out the front of Hooligans on a Friday night instead of being curled up on the lounge in my favorite pajamas with my new book.

"Come on," Sage encouraged as she jumped out and rounded the car.

This was a bad idea. A very bad idea.

It'd been just after lunch when she'd cornered me and told me she was taking me speed dating to help me find someone to, in her words, 'scratch the itch'. I'd begged off, saying I couldn't just go out on the spur of the moment, that I had Ava relying on me, when the truth came out.

Sage had planned this for over a week. And what's more, Linda, someone who I was coming to rely on and adore, was an accomplice in her scheming. So here I was, dressed in Sage's indecently tight jeans that showed off every single one of my flaws, flaws my wide-skirted dresses usually hid. She had me in a pair of her knee-high, black leather boots with a heel that was dangerously tall—and by dangerously tall, I meant with every step I took I wobbled like I'd gotten stuck into Grandma's sherry. But the boots weren't the worst part of my scandalous outfit. No. That particular achievement went to the top that Linda and Sage convinced me was perfect for a night out on the town. The sheer black wrap top fit perfectly if I wanted to show off my tits or my ass, both of which I absolutely did not want to flaunt. If I adjusted it at the front to cover up the massive amount of boob I was showing, then the bottom rode up, flashing my butt. If I pulled it down to hide my massive ass, then my boobs almost spilled out the top. I couldn't win. Sage promised after the second cocktail I wouldn't care, and at this point, there was nothing more I could do than hope to god she was right.

Wriggling out of the car, I was careful not to fall on my ass on the uneven ground. Straightening up, I stuffed my phone in my clutch before turning back to Sage who was wearing a ruby-red tube dress that hugged her like a second skin and her heavy black ass-kicking boots, as she called them. On anyone else it would've looked completely ridiculous, but somehow on Sage, she made it look effortlessly chic.

"You're buying the first round," I grumbled, slamming the car door.

Linking her arm through mine, Sage smiled. "Absolutely. And, Lily, remember this is for charity. It's supposed to be fun and a laugh. So maybe you could wipe that sour puss look off your face and at least pretend you're here to have a good time and not like this is your last night before you're shipped off to the nunnery."

I felt a bit bad. Sage had gone to all this trouble to organize tonight. From making sure Linda was happy to watch Ava, getting the tickets, then spending all afternoon at my place trying to turn me from a Stepford wife wannabe as she'd described me, to a Friday night fun girl. Brushing off the feeling of guilt that was lingering, I pasted on a smile as she pushed open the heavy doors and the sound of the bass pumped through me. Maybe this wouldn't be such a disaster after all.

Or maybe I'd spoken too soon.

17

ZACH

"I'm gonna need a beer," I grumbled, leaning on the bar watching people file through the door.

"Here," Dan replied, sliding the frosty glass in my direction. "And stop looking so damn miserable. What's the worst that can happen? You meet a nice girl?"

Flashing Dan a scowl, I picked up my drink and took a sip. I couldn't believe I was doing this. And where the hell were the others? I was seriously going to kick someone's ass if they all managed to bail and I was the only chump who'd shown up.

Three days ago, Chief had bailed us up after a shift. I was sweaty and tired and looking forward to the steak I'd been craving all day. There were four victims. Those of us who weren't on shift and were single had been signed up to speed dating. At first the protests had been loud and definitive. But soon enough we were caving in and collecting our tickets.

When I'd joined Station 13, I hadn't really understood what it meant to be a firefighter in a community like this. We weren't just firefighters, called out when someone needed us and otherwise forgotten. No. We were part of the community. An important part. We spent time at the schools, not only letting the kids climb all over the rig and try on our helmets, but also teaching them about safety. We visited the nursing home, helped rescue stray cats from trees, and yep, that really did happen. We were always signed up to whatever fundraising event that was taking place, from manning the dunk tank at the local carnival to raise money for the high school marching band, to stripping off and posing for a calendar.

Which is exactly why I was here tonight. Tonight's speed dating was a fundraiser for the children's wing of the hospital. And there was just no way it was possible to turn down raising money for sick kids.

"Hi all," A shaky voice rang out over the microphone. Standing up, I glanced around spotting Courtney, one of the pediatric nurses I'd come to know nervously waving a microphone about. "We're about ten minutes from starting tonight. So, gentlemen, if you could please take a seat at one of the numbered tables, we'll be almost ready to go."

Taking my beer, I headed towards the corner. If I was going to do this, there was no way I was going to be making a spectacle of myself while I did. I was just pulling my phone out of my pocket, ready to start blowing up the other guys' message banks telling them to get their asses moving when they stumbled through the door. Collins, Johnson and the new guy Samuels.

"About bloody time," I mumbled under my breath as Samuels clamped one of his massive paw-like hands down on my shoulder.

Jake Samuels was a good guy, at least so far he was. A Texas native who was a hell raiser and high on adrenaline. He spent most of his time in the workout room or eating. I mean, I loved my food, but I'd never seen anyone put it away like Jake did. The guy didn't stop. If he wasn't eating his serving-bowl-sized salads, he was running down the road to grab donuts.

"Oh, come on, Skip. Keep your pants on. We're here. Didn't want to leave the ladies hanging. You know they love some good ole Texas beef."

"Did you seriously just call yourself Texas beef?"

"Hell yeah! Top quality T-bone right here."

"Geez! Sit your ass down before you hurt yourself, would you?"

Samuels dropped into the seat beside me, pulling a wad of cards from his pocket.

Collins sat a beer down on my table before taking his own seat. "What the hell are these?" He picked up one of the cards, flicking it at me.

"No," I denied, staring at the card. "Tell me this isn't what I think it is?"

"What the hell?" Johnson chuckled, spinning the card between his fingers.

"What? It's my card. Makes it easier to give the ladies my number."

My eyes rolled so hard I was pretty sure I saw my brain.

The confidence, and the cheap cologne were oozing off him, and I was suddenly feeling a little better about the night. Watching him crash and burn could prove to be bloody entertaining.

"Okay let's get this show on the road," Courtney began, gaining a rousing round of applause. "I'm Courtney Harris and luckily for you, I'm the emcee for tonight's festivities. First of all, on behalf of all the kids, families and the staff in the pediatric unit of the hospital, a huge thank you. Just from ticket sales from tonight's event, we've already raised over a thousand dollars. But there's plenty more ways to spend your hard-earned money with a silent auction, raffles, as well as some other surprises. But let's face it, you didn't give up your Friday night to listen to me waffle on. No. You're here to meet the man or woman of your dreams."

Somehow, I wasn't sure how, I managed to hold back the groan that was bubbling in my throat. If I'd have known better, I could've just thrown money at the problem and spent the night in front of the TV.

"Now, ladies. If you'd like to help yourself to a cocktail from the bar, a little liquid courage, if you will, then find a seat. No fighting over the gentlemen. You'll only be there for ten minutes before you move on."

The whispers started as women shuffled around, most of them

clutching their girlfriend's arms tightly. There were a few women I recognized; some nurses from the ER I'd met a few times and a couple of teachers from the primary school. Unfortunately, with the room split in half, with potted plants creating a wall between the sections, there was no stealth way I could see who was on the other side. Not that it mattered, I reminded myself. The last thing I was looking for was a girlfriend.

"Guess this is my seat then," a seductively sweet voice cooed, catching my attention.

"Phoebe," I greeted, trying to sound pleased to see her.

Beside me, Samuels' eyes were bugging out of his head as he checked Phoebe out shamelessly. Something her outfit was begging to have done. Her top, if you could even call it that was basically a bow wrapped around her chest, barely covering her tits. The leather skirt she'd somehow managed to get on, was so tight it left absolutely nothing to the imagination, and I was pretty confident there was not a whole lot on beneath it.

"You ready for our date?"

Fuck me, it was going to be a long night.

18

LILY

I WAS SURROUNDED BY DOCTORS AND POLICE OFFICERS. I'D MET A postal service worker and caught up with a few other local business owners. Eight dates, three cocktails, and I was ready to call it a night. Ava hadn't been sleeping and these dates weren't exactly earth shattering.

Beside me, Sage was having a great time. There was no doubt we were the complete opposite. Where she was a chatty-Kathy, I struggled to find topics to talk about. Especially topics a guy would actually care about. Flowers and babies weren't exactly classified as scintillating conversation starters.

The bell dinged and Luke, one of the local police officers, smiled and slid me his card. "It was great chatting with you, Lily. I'd love to take you out sometime."

While I wasn't interested in Luke, he was a nice enough guy and easy on the eyes, but there was nothing there. No spark. No butterflies. Maybe I'd read one too many romance novels. Maybe I was expecting too much. But for now, I was happy with my life and I wasn't going to settle for anything less than fireworks.

"It was great talking with you too, Luke," I replied, collecting his card and tucking it in my purse. I knew I'd never use it, but that didn't mean I had to be rude and throw it out in front of him.

"We're going to take a fifteen-minute break. So, if you want to use the bathrooms or take a breather, now's your chance. There're four more dates for each of you, so please don't run out the door. If you haven't already met Mr. or Mrs. Right, there's still plenty of opportunity," Courtney encouraged, sounding upbeat and hopeful.

I'd met Courtney a few times with Sarah and I knew how much tonight was terrifying her. If you thought I was an introvert, Courtney took it to another level. She was pretty much a crazy cat lady with a husband. But the moment it came to raising money for the hospital, especially the children's ward, she stepped up and out of her comfort zone determined to take on the world.

"Hey. I'm just going to duck to the bathroom..." Sage started.

"Wait up. I'll join you."

There was no way she was leaving me out here alone.

Following her through the dimly lit bar, I spied Dan at the bar mixing cocktails. It was a busy night for him. The pool tables were crowded. The booths were full and there were a few girls who couldn't possibly be a day older than twenty-one shaking their asses on the dancefloor.

As we got closer to the bathrooms, we noticed the line snaking down the hall. Seems like everyone had the same idea. Joining the end of the queue, I dug my phone out of my purse and shot Linda a text, checking on Ava. If she even hinted that I was needed, I was willing to walk out the door right now and all the way home in these damn boots if need be.

"Well now I'm confused..." one of the women waiting in the line started while I eavesdropped.

"With what?" her friend asked.

"I always thought I liked cops. You know. They have the uniforms. They carry handcuffs."

"Ah, yeah they do. What's to be confused about?"

"Now I'm starting to see the appeal of a firefighter."

"Firefighters? Ew, gross. They're always covered in soot and ash and stink like smoke."

"Yeah. But they carry a big hose."

My ears perked up. There were firefighters here. Why hadn't I met any of them yet?

"I saw that," Sage whispered into my ear.

"Saw what?" I begged off, hoping my face didn't display every single emotion running through my body.

"Fine. Play dumb. I'm a patient woman. I'll just wait and see what happens."

Thankfully the line shuffled forward, and I could ignore Sage's comments, but my mind was buzzing. Was Zach here? Was he the fireman with the big hose they were referring to? Ah shit. I didn't need to see him tonight. Not like this. What would he think of me? Shit! Shit! Double shit!

After ducking into the stall and taking care of business, I adjusted my top in the mirror before stepping back out. There was no sign of Sage but that didn't really surprise me. Knowing her, she'd probably run into someone she knew and was already doing shots at the bar.

Rounding the corner, I looked down to check if I'd got a reply from Linda when I ran straight into a hard chest.

"Whoa!" His arms shot out, grabbing my shoulders and steadying me.

"Sorry," I apologized quickly, forgetting my phone and looking up into the chocolate eyes of a beautiful boy. He was stunning. The type of guy authors wrote books about. Tall. Broad shoulders. Square, stubbled jaw. His nose slightly crooked. And the longest lashes I'd ever seen on a human. Like I had serious lash envy. Even my long lash mascara didn't produce those sort of results.

"You right there, darlin'?"

Wow! His voice was like the smoothest whiskey.

If only he was ten years older. Kid was going to be a heart-breaker when he grew up.

"I'm fine. Sorry about crashing into you..."

"Honey. You can crash into me anytime you like."

Talk about saved by the bell. The jingling brought me out of my hormone-induced stupor, and I scurried back towards my table hoping Sage had at least managed to snag me another drink. I was going to need it.

"Who the hell was that you were hitting on?" Sage interrogated.

"No idea," I replied truthfully as the piercing shrill of the microphone silenced us and had me covering my ears.

The sound of the feedback was stinging my ears. It was worse than fingernails on a chalk board. Even the thought of it had shivers racing down my spine.

"Sorry about that. Now, gentlemen, if you could once again move around one seat, we can get back underway."

The guy I'd just smacked into slid confidently into the chair opposite Sage, and I could see her instant interest.

"Hey there, darlin'," he crooned, and I almost laughed as Sage melted in her seat.

"Nice accent, cowboy."

I couldn't look away. I was dying to see who was the first to whip out the cheesy, inappropriate pickup lines. All I needed was a huge bucket of buttery popcorn and I was entertained for the night. Well, I would've been except for the guy settling in the chair opposite me.

"Hi. I'm Cole Johnson."

"Lily Evans."

He reached out his hand and shook mine. A firm, confident handshake. His face was vaguely familiar, but I couldn't quite place him.

"Pleasure to meet you, Lily. I've heard a lot about you."

"You have?"

That wasn't what he was supposed to say. He wasn't supposed to know anything about me. Who the hell had he been talking to?

"Yeah. I'm a firefighter down at Station 13. I'm one of Zach's—"

Ah crap!

"Right. Zach. Yep. I know him."

"Anyway. We only have," Cole pushed back the sleeve on his navy sweater and checked his watch, "Eight minutes left. How's the flower business treating you?"

"It's been busy actually. Which is good."

Filling eight minutes with small talk when we both knew this was going no further was as painful as having a tooth pulled. When the bells finally chimed, I let out a relieved sigh. Cole stood up and took both my hands before leaning over and planting a kiss on my cheek. He's the only one who'd done that, thankfully. If greasy Grahame, the owner of the hardware store had tried, I might very well have punched him in the nose.

"Lovely talking to you, Cole," I thanked him.

He moved away and the young guy who'd just spent the last ten minutes making googly eyes at Sage, took the seat opposite me. He was as gorgeous as I'd at first believed.

"Darlin'."

"Hi."

"Jake Samuels."

"Lily Evans. Nice to meet you, Jake."

"You too, Lily. What do you do for fun?"

Cole, who was currently sitting opposite Elaine, the town's librarian, leant over and interrupted. "Not you, Samuels. Not if you like your teeth in your mouth."

"What'd I do?"

"Lily's Zach's girl," Cole offered.

"Hey! Wait a minute. I'm no one's girl," I protested.

"Yeah. Keep telling yourself that, sweetheart. Jake, hands to yourself."

I sat there stunned. Is that what everyone thought? What they assumed? That Zach and I were more than friends? Because we weren't. We were friends, and he helped me with Ava but that was it.

For a few minutes Jake and I talked complete rubbish. Mainly he probed for more details on Sage, and I had a feeling I'd be seeing a lot more of Jake around.

"Okay, I've gotta ask. If you and Zach are together, why the hell are you speed dating?"

"Well firstly, Zach and I aren't together. And secondly, I'm here tonight because my ex-friend Sage dragged me out."

"It hasn't been that bad, has it?"

"No. Not really. The cocktails are delicious. Most of the people I've spoken with have been nice guys. Overall, it's been good to have a night out."

"Well then, I'm glad. Now, I have something for you," Jake explained with a wink.

I wasn't sure why I was suddenly nervous.

"Put out your hand."

The bells jingled again, and Jake rose from his seat. With him standing and me still in my seat, he towered over me. He should've been intimidating, but he looked more like a gentle giant.

"Okay, gentlemen. If you could please move onto another table. You all have two more dates to go before we call it a night."

"Was lovely to meet you, Jake."

"You too, Lily. And here… this is for you."

He dropped a card in my hand before wrapping me up in a bear hug. He was warm and strong and instantly cocooned me in the safety of his arms. The only negative about the guy was I was pretty sure he'd bathed in his cheap cologne.

Over my shoulder, I heard a guttural growl. "What the hell is going on here?"

19

ZACH

I hoped Samuels enjoyed his last moment with arms. Why the fuck they were wrapped around Lily right now I had no idea but they wouldn't be for much longer. I was going to rip him limb from limb until he learned to keep his hands to himself.

"What the hell is going on here?" I asked, my voice tight.

Lily shivered. I saw the moment it passed down her spine as she moved out of Jake's grasp and turned to face me.

"Oh, hey, Zach. How's your night going?" Lily questioned innocently.

A crackle over the microphone, scolding us to take our seat had me dropping into my seat opposite Sage. It was awkward as hell. Technically, for the next ten minutes I was on a date with Sage, Lily's friend and employee, while she sat beside us.

"What are you doing here, Lily?"

"Excuse me?"

"Why are you here?"

"Why shouldn't I be here?"

Someone had her sassy pants on tonight. Although I'm not sure where. Those damn jeans she was wearing the fuck out of, were skin-tight and showing off her ass, making my dick twitch. I'd almost lost my shit when I saw Samuels' hands on her waist. Way too close for my liking.

"Where's Ava?"

"Ah. Of course, now it makes sense. Think I'm neglecting your little princess? Well don't worry, hero. She's safely tucked into bed at home and, not that it's any of your business, but I've been checking on her each hour. She's fine."

"Who's with her?" I grunted out, sounding like a damn caveman. The truth was I was jealous as hell. Why did she want to date other guys? If she met someone, I could lose two of the most important women in my life. Something that was not an option.

You'd think this was the worst date I'd had tonight. I mean, all we'd done so far was argue. But somehow it wasn't even close. So far tonight I'd been asked, more than once, about the size of my hose, had multiple offers for women who wanted to slide down my pole, and even one, although I wasn't really surprised it was Phoebe, who'd told me I was the perfect firefighter; I found her hot and left her wet. Their comments would've been funny if they were joking, but I wasn't even mildly convinced they were, and I hadn't had anywhere near enough to drink to see the comical side.

"Someone I trust," Lily spat out angrily at me. "I'm going to get another drink, since it seems I've suddenly got a ten-minute break before my next date."

Next date my ass. There was no way she was having any more dates tonight. Hell! Had I known she was even here, Lily wouldn't have had *one*. Snatching her purse from the table, she stood up, wobbled on her heels and tugged down the bottom of her top. I wasn't sure if she realized what she'd just done, but her creamy tits were spilling out the top of her shirt, and before I knew what I was doing, I was on my feet, following Lily across the bar like a pathetic little puppy, much to the amusement of the guys.

"I'll take another margarita please, Dan," she ordered.

"And another beer please, mate."

"No worries."

We waited for our drinks in silence. It was awkward and

uncomfortable and annoying. This wasn't us. We weren't these people. And I didn't like it. Not one damn bit.

Swallowing my pride, I broke the deadlock. "How's your night been?"

"Really? You actually care?"

The surprise in her voice stung. I deserved it, I know I did, but damn did it hurt. "Course I do."

"Oh. It's been eye-opening, that's for sure."

"Eye-opening?"

"Do guys really think the cheesy pickup lines work?"

"Guys used pickup lines on you?"

"Ah yeah. I'm not sure which was my favorite. It's between, 'they say Disneyland is the happiest place on earth. Well apparently, no one has ever been sitting opposite you' or 'I'm not a photographer, but I can picture you and me together.'"

"They did not say that... did they?"

I was actually almost kind of nervous. That was the sort of shit I could actually hear coming out of Samuels' mouth.

Lily nodded and smirked over the salted rim of her glass.

"That's terrible."

"Yep. How's your night going? Got a pocket full of phone numbers?"

How was I supposed to answer that without looking like a chump? Yeah, I had a few numbers scribbled on the back of coasters but none that I'd be using. Not even Phoebe's who made it very clear it was an open-ended offer.

"It's been okay."

"Just okay? Must be losing your charm."

"Does that mean you think I have charm?"

Lily's cheeks turned pink at my question. Or maybe it was the cocktail. Either way, I was taking the credit.

"We should go and sit down. It must be almost time to move to the final date." Tucking her purse under her arm, Lily wove her way through the tables and back to our abandoned seats.

"You two finished making out in dark hallways?" Sage teased, causing Lily's drink that she'd just taken a gulp of to come out her nose.

Those damn bells tinkled again, and it was time to move. Only I wasn't moving. There was no way in hell I was sliding along and letting Collins near Lily. He was a player of the worst sort. Over my dead body was Lily going to fall victim to his life motto of 'hit it and quit it'.

"Well, Zach. This was…"

"Was what?" I challenged, putting her on the spot as I leaned back in my chair and folded my arms across my chest.

"I'm not going to give you my number…"

"Why the hell not?" My voice boomed through the room, causing everyone to fall silent and turn in our direction.

"Ah, you already have it," Lily hissed.

"Oh."

"Yeah. Oh. Now, move to the next table so I can see if I like the next guy. Maybe he'll get my number."

"Not bloody likely."

"Excuse me?"

Turning towards my mate, I addressed him directly. "Collins. Skip this table. Just go around me and meet Sage. She's a great girl."

He looked confused, not that I could blame him. I was breaking every rule of the night, but I didn't give a shit. I was over this. I was over playing games. I was ending it and I was ending it now.

"Excuse me, Zach. You're not the boss of me. You can't just make decisions like that for me." Lily stood up, drawing herself to her full height, putting her hands on her hips. If looks could kill, then I'd be nothing more than a pile of ash.

Skirting around us, Collins slipped into the seat opposite Sage while they both watched us. I guess we were making a pretty dumb spectacle of ourselves.

Rising to the challenge, I stood and stepped towards Lily. I don't know if she stepped backwards to give me room or to get out of my way, but I didn't care. Without a word, I bent at the waist and threw her over my shoulder in a fireman's carry.

"Zach!" she squealed, clutching my shoulders.

Spinning back to Sage, I grabbed Lily's purse with my free hand before swatting her on the ass with it. "I'll make sure Lily gets home."

"No worries. Have fun, kids."

"Oh, we will!" I promised with a wink before striding through the bar, ignoring the whistles and catcalls.

Outside it was as cold as a witch's tit. The wind was howling, and it was raining. It was that fine spitty rain that seemed to come in sideways, coating everything in a light sheen of freezing cold water. Lily had stopped struggling and her hands were holding my hips, her fingers digging into me.

Reaching my truck, I slid her down my body, caging her between the cold metal of the car door and my heated body. When her feet touched the ground, she looked up at me through overly made-up eyes. She looked like a damn sex kitten. Every day I'd seen her wearing those ridiculous dresses with the wide, flowing skirts and her pearls and she looked like a wet dream. But standing here now, with the rain dotting her cheeks and her breath coming out in white puffs, she'd never looked more fuckable. And it wasn't the clothes or the makeup either. It was her. It was all Lily. Maybe it was the liquid courage pumping through her veins or maybe it was seeing her out of her natural environment. Either way, it didn't matter.

"Zach." My name fell like a breathless plea from her glistening lips.

It was all the encouragement I needed. Cupping her face with my hands, I slammed my lips down on hers, licking my tongue across her bottom lip, silently begging her to open for me. The moment her lips parted, I didn't waste any time, plunging inside.

Lily was as delicious as I'd been dreaming about. Her tongue dueled with mine and I could feel the bite from her nails digging into my biceps. When she wriggled even closer to me, pressing her tits against my chest, my dick hardened in my pants. There was no way she could miss it. Lily shivered in my arms.

Reluctantly, I pulled back, refusing to take my eyes off her. I wanted to know what she was thinking. Rubbing my hands up and down her arms, I tried to keep her warm. At least that was the excuse I was using to keep my hands on her.

"We need to get out of here," Lily murmured, burrowing her head against my chest.

"Okay," I agreed, but I didn't want to let her go. One kiss, no matter how good, wasn't enough. I doubted it would ever be enough with this woman.

Pressing up on her toes, Lily used me for balance before initiating the hottest kiss of my life. Breathlessly, Lily purred against my lips. "Zach, take me home."

"Yes, ma'am."

20

LILY

ZACH DROVE TOWARDS HIS HOUSE, ONE HAND ON THE WHEEL THE other high on my thigh. The heat in the cab was starting to fog up the windows, and I squeezed my knees together. I could barely believe I was doing this, but I couldn't imagine stopping. The last thing on my mind was bringing this to a grinding halt.

"Oh shit!"

"What's wrong?"

Zach hit the brakes so hard I was thrown forward and would've knocked my head on the dashboard if it hadn't been for the seatbelt Zach had buckled me into.

"Ava."

"What's wrong with her?"

The panic in his voice was tangible.

"Nothing. But I have to get home and relieve your mom."

"My mom?"

"She's at my place looking after Ava."

"Is that all?"

"What do you mean, is that all? What more is there?"

Reality was like having a bucket of cold water dumped over my head.

Zach didn't answer. Instead, he punched a few buttons on the steering wheel and the sound of a ringing phone filled the truck.

"Zach?"

"Hey, Mom."

"What's wrong, sweetheart? It's late."

"Yeah, I know. I'm sorry. I was just ringing to see if you are right with Ava?"

"You checking on me too now? Lily's been doing that all night."

"Lily's here with me now. And you're on speaker."

"Oh, hi, sweetheart. How was your night? Meet anyone interesting?"

"Mom! Focus."

"Sorry."

"Look, Mom. If you're okay with Ava, Lily's going to be a bit late."

"A bit late?"

"A lot late. Like tomorrow morning late."

"Zach!" Embarrassed he was telling his mother I was with him and staying for a while, by the sounds of it, I covered my face with my hands.

"Oooo! In that case, I'll crash in the spare room, if that's okay, and see you both in the morning."

"Thanks, Mom."

"Thanks, Linda."

"Have fun. And don't do anything I wouldn't do."

"Mom!" Zach groaned, Linda laughed and the line went dead. "Happy now?"

"Happy with what?"

Zach put the truck back into gear and we were off again. A moment later we were turning into his driveway and my heart was racing again. The nerves were back and my palms were sweating.

He must've sensed my anxiety. Popping the buckle on my seatbelt, he grabbed my arm and dragged me into his lap. "We don't have to do a thing you don't want to do. We can go inside, have a beer and then I can crash on the couch."

Oh. My. Freaking. God.

Like seriously.

Could this guy get any more perfect?

Placing wet kisses up the column of his neck, I could taste his musky and masculine scent. It was an intoxicating mix of sex and sin. The guttural groan was torn from the back of his throat as his hands found my ass.

"These jeans are…"

"Not mine."

"Not what I was going to say."

"Well, what were you going to say?"

Zach's lips found my earlobe and he nibbled, flooding my panties.

"I was going to say…" He reached down, opened the truck door, and swung his legs out before turning back to me and picking me up like I weighed nothing at all. Zach didn't treat me like I was fragile, but he treated me like I was precious. It was odd and exhilarating all in the same breath. Winding my legs around his waist, I cupped his face with my hands and slanted my lips over his.

"Say what?"

"Those sexy-as-fuck jeans, as good as they look on, they're going to look even better on my bedroom floor."

A moment later Zach was kicking closed the back door, carrying me through his darkened house and tossing me on his bed with a bounce. With a giggle, I wriggled up the bed, settling on the pile of pillows.

Zach reached down and grabbed my ankles, dragging me back down. "Where do you think you're going, missy? Get your sexy ass down here."

His gravelly voice gave me goosebumps. Goosebumps of the best kind.

"As hot as the boots are," he slid down the zipper, "they have to go."

"Well then, take them off. Your shirt too while you're at it." I winked.

"You think you're in charge now, do you, Lily?"

I didn't know what'd come over me. I'd like to blame the cocktails but honestly, it was all Zach. He made me want to break free of the shell I'd created for myself. The one I'd spent years hiding in. When I was with Zach, I forgot about who I was supposed to be and was just me. He made me feel everything all at once. I felt sexy and wanted and like I could do anything. Be anything. It was intoxicating.

Propping myself up on my elbows, I looked down at Zach as he peeled my rainbow-striped socks from my feet before toeing off his own boots. I don't know how he did it. He was standing there before me, his hair a mess from my tugging at it, his shirt damp and sticking to his skin. Wearing his jeans, the way a pair of jeans should be worn – tight in all the right places and barefoot, and I'd never wanted him more. Never wanted anyone more. Just looking at him had my whole body tingling and wanting.

Not wanting to waste another second, I reached down and popped the button on my own jeans. As much fun as this party was, I needed to get it moving along before I spontaneously combusted. As I started to drag the zipper down, Zach's hand shot out, taking hold of mine, stopping me.

"What?" I asked, looking up at him towering over me.

"That's my job."

"Well, you're taking too long. I'm going to have to start without you."

The look on his face was priceless. He looked like I'd just told him I was going to take his fire engine away and he couldn't play with the siren anymore. "You wouldn't dare."

"Try me."

Zach didn't answer. Instead, he grabbed me by the hips and flipped me over, maneuvering me until I was on my hands and knees in the center of his bed. Exactly where he wanted me. I hadn't seen his hand coming, so when it slapped down on my wet, denim-clad ass, the sound ricocheted across the room. Not giving me a chance to complain, he peeled my jeans down over my ass, baring my lacy purple thong to him. I heard the intake of breath hiss out between his lips and could only imagine what he was looking at. Damn I hoped he liked what he saw. I was so ready to explode, if he rejected me now, there was a very good chance I may actually shrivel up and die.

Lifting one knee at a time, he got my jeans off like a professional. Even I would struggle with the tight wet material. I tried to flip over. I wanted to see him. I wanted to touch him. Damn did I want to touch him, but he held me in place.

"Zach," I moaned wantonly.

"What's wrong?"

"I need…"

"What do you need? I'll give you anything you want. You just have to tell me." His voice was thick and husky, and I felt an embarrassing gush of wetness coat the inside of my thighs. At least it would've been embarrassing if I wasn't so damn horny.

"I need… I need…"

"Words, Lily. Use your words."

Zach's hands were all over my outer thighs and the globes of my ass. He was touching me everywhere but where I needed him most. When he bent down and bit me, I broke. All sense of right and wrong flew out the window, taking my ladylike manners with them.

"Lily… words… use them."

"You. I need you. I need your mouth. I need your hands. I need your fingers. I need your cock. I need all of it. Now, Zach! Fuck me now!"

A deep chuckle seeped out but instead of turning and shooting death rays at him for laughing at my neediness, I felt Zach's fingers inching ever so much closer to my needy clit. I tried to wiggle to get him where I needed him, but he wasn't having it. It was like he was trying to prove a point. A point that he was calling the shots here and I was just coming along for the ride. And frankly, as long as I was coming fucking soon, I'd go along with whatever he had planned.

Another stinging slap to my ass had me quivering but before the shock and sting could ease, Zach slid one long finger inside me, and I let out an embarrassingly loud, desperate moan.

"Oh, fuck me," I mumbled, fisting his comforter.

"Oh, don't worry, sweetheart. I plan on it."

Just when I was starting to sweat, my nipples straining against my bra, Zach added another finger and pressed his thumb on the rosebud of my ass. I'd never been touched there before. Hell, I'd never even thought about being touched there. But as his thumb circled, not breeching the tight ring of muscle, just applying enough pressure to let me know he was there, my temperature was skyrocketing. Bordering on the precipice of pleasure and ecstasy, I almost cried when suddenly his hands were gone, and I was empty.

Without warning, Zach flipped me over, leaving me flat on my back, staring up at the sexiest man I'd ever met. This man was driving me to the very edge of insanity, and I was loving every second of it. Without warning, his lips latched onto my very sensitive, still-buzzing clit, and I squealed. I'd never been a squealer. Fuck, the last guy I'd gone to bed with complained because I was mute between the sheets but here I was moaning and groaning.

Licking his tongue down the length of my slit, my cries became more frantic. More desperate. "Please, Zach. I need to come."

"Not yet," he growled, sliding a finger inside me while his tongue teased me.

"Please."

"Not yet," he repeated, adding another finger.

"Zach!"

This time he didn't reply. Instead, he nipped at the buzzing bundle of nerves, catapulting me over the edge and sending me soaring straight into nirvana.

21

ZACH

I don't know which sight I liked better. Lily on her knees in front of me in the shower or Lily splayed out on my bed; her whole body taut with pleasure or Lily tangled in my sheets, sleeping soundly looking well and truly fucked. Or Lily sitting on my kitchen bench, sipping her morning coffee, wearing nothing but my station t-shirt and a smile.

"Whoa! Watch it lover boy." Grady chuckled, clapping me on the shoulder.

Looking down at the mess I'd made, I couldn't really blame him. I was still so caught up in reliving every ball-tingling moment of last night, trying to mentally run through my roster wondering when I could schedule a repeat. And would Lily even want a repeat? Shit! Surely, she would. No one in their right mind would turn down sex like that. Sex that had your toes curling and screaming out in pleasure. No. I was sure she'd be up for another round. Or if I was really lucky, maybe two or three.

Grabbing some paper towels, I mopped up the coffee I'd spilled all over the bench before lobbing them towards the bin, missing by a mile.

"Someone's off their game," Samuels smarted as he strolled through the door with a grin on his smug face.

"You look happy. What happened? You hook up last night?"

"Wouldn't you like to know?"

"Not really. What you and Mrs. Palmer do, I don't want to know a damn thing about."

"Who spent the night with Mrs. Palmer?" Collins asked, dumping his bag on the floor at his feet and stealing my coffee. Looks like we were all going to be dragging our asses tonight. Not that I regretted it for a damn second, but still… it was going to be a long night.

"Samuels," I confirmed, making another cup.

"That surprises me."

"It does? Why?"

Without missing a beat, Collins threw back, "I didn't even think she'd want his scrawny ass."

Flipping us the bird, Samuels rose from the couch he was sitting on and started for the door. "You guys are a bunch of dicks, you know that? I'm going to get a workout in, in case you're looking for me."

"No worries, princess. I got more than my share of cardio last night so I'm good. But you have fun with your little weights."

Sipping my coffee, I watched the two of them toss barbs back and forth, slightly worried that one day Collins would push him too far and Samuels would spin around and knock his block off. We may have given Samuels shit and called him scrawny, tiny or princess, but he was bigger than all of us. Born and bred in Texas, the boy was built like the oversized truck he drove around.

Once he was out of sight, Collins turned towards me, and I knew what was about to happen. "So, you and Lily, hey?"

"What about it?"

"You going to share details? Is she as good I imagined?"

"Wait! What? You imagined Lily?" My gut churned. No one should be thinking about Lily, especially like that. And definitely not these horny bastards. I knew what they were like, and their Xrated thoughts and Lily's name should never be in the same sentence.

"Who the hell hasn't? I bet she's a real lady in the street but a freak in the sheets. Am I right? I'm right, aren't I?"

"Collins, stop being a dick before Higgins beats you senseless," Grady warned, strolling back in.

Collins' eyes bounced from me to Grady and back again. He must've read the seriousness in my face because without a word, he was collecting his shit and scurrying out the back to join Samuels in lifting weights.

"Those guys…"

"Are your brothers and they're giving you shit because of it."

"How do you know?"

"Trust me. I've got two brothers who piss me off more times a day than I could imagine."

"Isn't one a cop?" I asked.

I'd heard the rumors, although from what I could gather, it was all pretty accurate.

"Yep. Grant's a cop and my other brother, Grayson he's a medivac pilot."

"Wow! And your dad was chief of police?"

"Yeah. Seems like it's in the Malone blood to serve and protect those in our humble little community."

"Seems so. But Grady, you wouldn't have it any other way."

"Yeah, you're right. And on that note, I'm out. I've got a hot woman at home waiting for me, and if I play my cards right, which let's face it, I always do, tomorrow I'll look as tired and satisfied as you do. Have a good shift. And remember…"

"Two in. Two out. Got it."

"See you in a couple of days."

"Will do."

A quick handshake and Grady was gone. I couldn't imagine what'd been like growing up a Malone. The weight of the expectations would have been stifling. Your dad as the chief of police, your brother following in his footsteps. I was left though with absolutely no doubt in my mind that being a firefighter wasn't just a job for Grady, it was who he was. And he was bloody good at it too.

Pouring the rest of my coffee down the sink, I cleaned up and got to work. There was a mountain of paperwork waiting for me, a mountain I'd been avoiding for days. Now seemed like as good a time as any to make a start.

We'd just finished dinner when the storm rolled in from nowhere. The lightning lit up the night's sky and the thunder boomed. Quickly we cleaned up the mess, knowing what an unexpected storm like this meant. And true to form, within minutes, we were being called out the door. I hadn't even made it to the bathroom.

By the time dawn arrived, I was dead on my feet, but order was restored. Mother nature sure could be a bitch when she wanted to. The winds she'd whipped up were ferocious as trees were ripped from the ground and tossed around as if they were twigs. Powerlines were down, cars were wrecked, roofs were leaking.

When we'd attended the scene of an accident, I'd almost thrown up. Thankfully no one was hurt; the driver had just swerved off the road to avoid hitting debris and ended up in a ditch with his door jammed against the tree. Even though everyone was alright, even though the damage was only cosmetic, seeing the baby seat in the back of his car had me picturing Ava. Something I most certainly did not need to be imagining.

Filing out of the station a couple of hours later, the rumbling in my stomach turned to ferocious growling. Leaving my truck where I was, I walked down the street making a beeline for the bakery and their flaky, buttery croissants. I could devour a couple right now.

Stepping through the door, I was assaulted with the smell of bread. My mouth watered. There was just something about the smell of freshly baked bread that had me salivating.

"Morning, Zach," Phoebe greeted, standing behind the register.

"Morning."

"Just coming off shift?"

"Yeah. Thought I'd grab some food before I head home."

"With that storm it was probably a big night."

"Long night. Very, very long night."

"Well, let's get you fed and off to bed."

Even though I knew what she meant, it just didn't sound right. Or maybe it was the way she was looking at me like I was her breakfast. Sorry, sweetheart. Wasn't going to happen. Not today. Not tomorrow or any other day for that matter.

Ignoring the way her too-small shirt strained the buttons across her chest, I ordered a bunch of stuff and waited for her to box it up. For someone who claimed they were helping me get out of here, she sure did take her time. A couple of minutes later, I handed over my credit card, paid and took the box.

"Get some rest, Zach."

"Will do. Thanks," I said politely, grabbing the box and racing out the door.

I thought I heard her call out behind me, "You're going to need it, big boy," but I couldn't be sure. Maybe I was just hearing things. I was sleep deprived, so it was a possibility.

After some food and sleep I was feeling much more human. The problem was, after two long nights, one of which was much more enjoyable than the other, I'd slept longer than planned and only had an hour before I was due back for another shift.

Stepping into the shower, I let the scalding hot water pound down against my shoulders, hoping it'd relieve some of the aches. Dropping my head, I couldn't shake the image of Lily on her knees, taking me into her mouth, working me over and driving me wild. Squeezing a dollop of body wash into my palm, I reached down and wrapped it around my cock, which was now proudly standing to attention.

"Shit, Lily," I grunted as I stroked harder and faster.

With the picture of her in my head, the memory of her mouth wrapped around me and the way my cum had exploded across her tits had me coming on the tiles embarrassingly quickly. After washing away the evidence, I climbed out of the shower, wrapped a towel around my waist and went to get dressed.

Picking up my phone, I checked the time. If I hurried, I'd have time to stop by and maybe steal a kiss or two before I was due at the station. With that possibility in mind, I moved faster than I think I ever had.

Ten minutes later, I was pulling into Lily's driveway and bouncing out of the car. With every step towards her door, I reminded myself to calm down. I couldn't act like a caveman and just throw her over my shoulder, carry her into the bedroom and keep her there, not that that idea didn't have merit. It was a damn good idea actually, one I was tucking away for another day.

Marching up the steps, I paused when I heard the wood beneath my heel groan. I wasn't exactly a waif of a guy, I wasn't overweight either, but steps shouldn't make that sound. Carefully, I took another step. Again with the creaking and cracking. I wasn't liking this. I wasn't liking it at all.

Knocking on the door, I moved back and waited for Lily to answer. The minutes were ticking by and I was on a time crunch. When she didn't answer, I knocked again. Still nothing. Glancing at my watch, I mentally calculated I had ten minutes, twelve at a stretch, before I had to get my ass moving. As I dug my phone from my pocket, I headed towards the porch swing and dropped down.

Zach: *Hey. At your place. Are you around?*

I wasted two precious minutes trying to come up with the perfect wording and still, that was all I had.

Rocking back and forth, I looked around. Up close you could see the wear and tear aging the house. The paint was flaky in places. The wooden window frames were bulging in areas and the gutters looked like they were in need of some desperate attention.

Minutes ticked down and still no response from Lily. She hadn't appeared either. With the overwhelming weight of disappointment sitting on my chest, I got up and headed to work resolved to try again tomorrow.

22

LILY

THANK GOD FOR LINDA IS ALL I CAN SAY.

Today was a disaster of epic proportions, and I was still trying to get my head around it. Last night the storm had come up, but I was tucked up on the couch with a cup of hot chocolate and a good book while Ava slept like an angel. The thunder rumbled and the lightning lit up the room, but all that was happening on the other side of the windows, and I was too engrossed in what I was reading to pay much attention.

When the lights had started to flicker, I gave up and went to bed. I was still tired, despite my afternoon nana nap in attempt to recover from Friday night's activities. Well, Friday night's activities and the enforced hike I'd made myself go on today. I hadn't realized how unfit I was until I attempted walking up that damn hill.

When Ava had woken me up at three o'clock in the morning, screaming blue murder, I'd tried to turn on the lamp beside my bed, but it seemed the power was out. Hobbling around in the dark, arms outstretched while trying to avoid walking into a wall, I'd stubbed my toe on the corner of the kitchen bench, sending a throbbing pain shooting through my body. Ignoring the desire to reach down and rub it, I pressed on and found a torch and some candles. I never thought I'd see the day when I would be changing a diaper by candlelight, but hey, here we were.

After getting Ava settled – in the bed beside me rather than her crib, because every time I tried to set her down her ear-piecing cries almost deafened me, and tonight, I just didn't have the patience or the energy to fight with her – we fell into a fitful sleep. At least I fell into a fitful sleep. I was so afraid I was going to roll over and squish her while I slept, I doubted I got more than twenty minutes in any one stretch.

By the time morning rolled around, well morning to any normal human being, I was aching and exhausted and not in the pleasant way I had been the night before. After feeding and changing Ava, I rushed to get ready for my own day. We were still without power, and I needed coffee. It wasn't a want. It was a desperate, critical need.

Bundling Ava up, I buckled her into her stroller and headed for the bakery. I deserved a flaky, buttery, full-of-fat pastry and a bucket of coffee. Overhead the skies were dark and the clouds rolling in were menacing but so far not a drop had fallen. Pushing through the bakery doors, I was assaulted with the aroma of strong coffee and moaned loudly.

Settling Ava's stroller in the corner, I went to the counter keeping one eye on her where she laid sleeping quietly. Damn that kid was gorgeous when she was asleep. Her cute little chubby cheeks and her long lashes had cost me hours of just sitting there watching her.

"Lily," Phoebe greeted, stepping behind the register and rubbing her hands against her black apron.

"Good morning, Phoebe," I replied, trying to be extra friendly.

"What can I get you?"

I placed my order and paid before going back over to the table and sitting down. Pulling my phone from my bag, I started scrolling through the picture gallery to kill some time. I hadn't real-ized how many photos of Ava I'd snapped. I had almost every facial expression the kid had, all captured. She did this weird gurgle smile thing when she was in Zach's arms, not that I could blame her, it seemed she wasn't the only one who made weird noises when he had his hands on her. No matter what I did, making silly faces, singing off key, tickling her, I still hadn't managed to coax a real smile out of her. I would, I was determined, I just hadn't got there yet.

Flicking to the next image, my breath caught in my throat. It was one of the first ones I'd taken. Zach was sleeping on my sofa, shirtless with Ava nestled in his arms.

"I heard you went home with him," Phoebe announced, setting my breakfast down on the table, completely ignorant to the coffee splashing over the side of the mug and onto the table.

I didn't answer her. I felt no need to. Who I did and did not spend time with was none of her damn business, nor anybody else's.

"Well from what I hear, Zach's lousy in bed. Doesn't even know how to please a woman and can't even get it up," Phoebe declared loudly, making sure the other people in the bakery heard her snarky comments before stomping off.

Ava whimpered. I reached over and started rolling her stroller back and forth gently, trying to lull her into sleep. "If only she knew, Ava. If only she knew."

As soon as I was done eating, I downed what was left of my coffee and left. The less time I spent near her toxic presence, the happier I was going to be. I'd made it four steps down the footpath when the first fat raindrop hit me. A rumble overhead had me making a beeline for the shop. We could hide out there, and I might even be able to catch up on some work while we waited out the storm.

Four hours later, the storm had passed but I was on a mission and I wasn't ready to stop. I'd eaten all the snacks I could get my hands on, cleaned the windows, rearranged the floor displays and ripped the shelves off the wall in the stock room. They were in the wrong spot, loose and too small. I'd even dug out a clean sheet of paper and redesigned the whole place, carving out a place for Ava.

My phone beeped on the counter where I'd left it, interrupting the music I had pumping through the speakers. Heading out to get it, I didn't see the puddle of water on the floor and slid straight through it. My runners were no match for the slippery tiles.

Everything happened in slow motion. First, I went up, then I went down. And I went down hard.

By the time I'd come to a stop, my ass was planted in the puddle of water, my phone was on the floor beside me, screen shattered, and my elbow was pointing in the wrong direction.

It didn't hurt until I saw it.

Tears filled my eyes and Ava's screams filled the store.

Trying to cradle my arm against my chest, I realized that any movement at all made me want to throw up. Picking up my phone, I looked at the screen. It was bad. It wasn't merely cracked; it was shattered beyond saving. I couldn't even read the screen let alone a message. Taking a chance, I hit the screen, ignoring the glass digging into my finger.

"Lily?"

"Oh, Linda. Thank God you answered."

"What's wrong? Is it Ava?"

"Ah, well… umm… I kinda slipped and fell. Ava's fine, just crying, and I can't pick her up. I've done something to my arm, and I… I… smashed my phone."

I started blubbering like an idiot when I told her about my phone. You'd think I'd be freaking out about the fact my elbow looked completely crazy and was sticking out at a weird angle, or that I couldn't pick up and soothe Ava. But no. I'm the girl who cried over a smashed phone screen.

"Where are you?"

"At the shop."

"Stay there. I won't be long."

With one final snotty sob, I hung up, at least I think I did and tried to stand. At first my feet slipped and tried to slide out from under me, but somehow, I managed to find my feet. My butt was soggy, and I looked like I'd pissed myself. I was a damn mess.

As carefully as I could, I stepped around the water and over to Ava. Poor little chicken. Her cheeks were red and wet from her tears. Reaching in with my good hand, I pushed a sweaty curl from her forehead. Her cries started to fade but her bottom lip still trembled.

"It's okay, sweetie. We're okay. A little banged up, a little bruised, a lot embarrassed but we got this. It's you and me against the world."

While we waited for Linda, I attempted to clean up the mess. Why was it no one ever told you that to clean properly, it meant you first had to make a giant mess. I was down on my hands and knees, a fistful of paper towels mopping up the puddle when Linda came flying through the door, stepping on a pile of rubbish.

"What the hell happened here?"

Looking up, I watched her step carefully through the store, dodging the piles of crap I'd left strewn from one end of the shop to the other.

"Careful," I warned her. I wish someone would've warned me.

I'd made it to my feet when a wave of dizziness hit me, and I wobbled. Without thinking, I reached out to grab onto whatever I could reach. I used the wrong arm. A shot of pain radiated down my arm and I gasped.

Linda's arm wrapped around my waist, and I felt myself leaning into her. Relying on someone wasn't something I was used to and something I was determined not to come to rely on, but right now, it felt so good to have her.

"Honey, what have you done?"

"I don't know."

"Does it hurt?"

"So bad."

"Can you wiggle your fingers?"

Looking down at my hand, slowly I wriggled my fingers, watching with strange fascination as they moved back and forth.

"Okay. That's good. That's really good. Now, we're going to have to get you to the hospital and get that arm put back in place."

"No. It's okay. I can..." I tried to extend my arm to prove everything was fine. Everything was not fine. Nothing was fine. The wave of nausea slammed into me and had me hunching, retching on my own store floor.

Not appearing in the least bit squeamish, Linda sprang into action and took control of the situation, and before I could catch my breath, we were on our way to the hospital and I was being reprimanded for not calling Zach straight away. Even my excuses of a wrecked phone, his night shift and not wanting to worry him with my problems were waved away.

I was lying in the hospital bed, wearing one of those very attractive, flimsy gowns trying not to freeze to death when the doorway was filled by a scowling, hulking presence.

23

ZACH

I WAS FURIOUS.

Like borderline rageaholic right now.

After spending more than an hour on the side of the road helping with a traffic accident, somehow we'd ended up at the hospital waiting for Samuels to get his hand stitched up. Bloody idiot had sliced it open. But I didn't have time to worry about him. As we'd come through the doors, who did I find sitting in the waiting room? Mom and Ava.

Ignoring the reason I was supposed to be there, I stomped over in their direction. "What's wrong? Is Ava okay?"

Straight away my mind started racing that something was wrong with that precious little girl.

Mom smiled at me. She actually smiled. What sort of twisted universe was I in, where she was smiling at me in a hospital waiting room while my mind raced through a million different scenarios? None of them good.

"Calm down there, caveman. Ava's fine." She spun Ava around in her arms so she was facing me and I could see for myself that everything was as it should be. Ava's gummy smile beamed up at me, and for the first time since I'd spotted them, I felt like I could take a breath.

"Then why…"

"Lily had a fall and she's dislocated her elbow."

"What the…"

Seemed forming full sentences wasn't something I was doing right now.

"Zach, she's fine. She's in with the doctors now."

I didn't waste any more time asking questions or trying to piece together answers. I was going straight to the source.

I moved through the emergency department with all the grace of a bull in a china shop. A few of the nurses looked up as I passed their patients, peering through the curtains at each one, searching out the woman whose ass was going to be turned pink from the spanking she was asking for. Why didn't she call me? Did she not think I'd help her?

Running into Sarah, she halted me in my tracks.

"And just where do you think you're going?"

"Ah…"

"I'm pretty sure there's no fire in the emergency department this afternoon."

"Well... um…" I rubbed the knot of muscles in the back of my neck, everything suddenly feeling stiff.

"She's in the last bed on the right. She's going to be fine. Sore for a couple of days and will need help with Ava and everything else," Sarah added, making sure to eyeball me so I didn't miss her message, not that there was any way I could've. She was about as subtle as a slap up the side of the head with a wet fish. "But her ego's taken a pretty decent dent."

"So, she's okay?"

"She'll be fine."

"Thank fuck," I exhaled, letting my shoulders sag.

"Go ahead and check on her. She could probably use the company."

Sarah reached out and squeezed my shoulder in a sign of

support before hurrying away. Shaking my head, I cleared the fog and marched through the ward desperate to get to my girl.

Pushing back the curtain, I saw Lily lying in the bed, her head resting against the pillow and her eyes closed. She looked so tiny and fragile lying there. It was wrong. Everything about this scenario was wrong. She wore a flimsy gown that was sliding off her shoulder and the blanket was pulled up as best as she could manage. Her arm was in a sling, resting against her stomach.

Sighing heavily, I let go of all the fight and frustration I'd been loaded up with ready to confront her for being so silly. It didn't matter. The only thing that mattered was that she was okay, the rest we could deal with later. Together.

Lily's eyes flickered open, and when they fell on me standing at the end of the bed, my hands clenched around the metal bar, her mouth fell open.

"Zach."

"What happened, Lil?" I asked, hearing my voice soften as I said her name.

"Oh, it was nothing, really. I'm fine." She tried to brush it off like it was an everyday occurrence. It wasn't. Or if it was, things were about to change.

"Lily…"

"I just slipped in some water and landed awkwardly." She tried to wiggle in the bed so she was sitting upright. Seeing her wince as she tried to get comfortable had me springing into action. "I'll be fine," she added through gritted teeth, her eyes watery.

"Fine my ass," I grumbled as I rearranged pillows behind her.

"I will be. I just slipped and fell on my ass like a complete klutz. Sure, it hurt, and once these amazing painkillers wear off it probably will again, but it will be fine. And so will I."

"Why didn't you call me?" I asked, pushing the point that was really bugging me.

"Honestly?" I nodded, encouraging her to continue. "I smashed my phone screen so badly I couldn't see a damn thing. I was lucky it was your mom I managed to call and not the pizza delivery guy."

"Where's your phone now?"

Before Lily could answer, my radio crackled to life. Someone was looking for me. I needed to haul ass and get back to work. Technically, I was still on shift. I didn't have time to sit by Lily's hospital bed, but I couldn't leave her like this. Lily must've sensed my hesitation to leave.

"Go, Zach. I'm fine."

"What are you going to do?"

"Honestly, I'm not sure. But I'm a smart girl, I'm sure I can figure it out."

"Lily…"

The radio crackled again.

"Go. I'm fine. I've got this."

Reluctantly I moved towards the bed, reaching out and taking hold of her hand, the one not wrapped in a sling. Giving it a quick squeeze, I bent down and kissed her forehead, accidentally catching a glimpse down her gaping gown. While the gown might've been designed for function and not fashion, making everyone look sick and sad, what Lily was wearing underneath, had my heart rate picking up. A low-cut, lacy black contraption propping up her perky tits. I needed to get out of here and now before I did something stupid, like crawl into the hospital bed with her.

"I've gotta go. Please, take it easy."

"I will."

"And if it's okay, I'll stop by on my way home in the morning." I held my breath, hoping she didn't tell me to stay away. Although, if I was being honest, even if she did, I couldn't promise that I wouldn't show up on her doorstep anyway.

"That'd be great."

"Okay then."

"Okay then," Lily repeated.

With heavy feet, I managed to make it a couple of steps.

"Hey, Zach?"

"Yeah?"

"Be safe."

With a wink, I confirmed, "Always am."

"Good. Oh, and don't forget my coffee in the morning."

"Never."

In a better mood than when I'd barged in, I hurried out of emergency to find Samuels with his hand wrapped up and ready to go. Idiot had tried to block a piece of metal from falling with his hand and sliced it open, even through his gloves.

"All good?"

"Yeah. Just some stitches, a shot and a phone number. I'm good to go."

Shaking my head, I wasn't surprised that Samuels had come in bleeding everywhere and twenty minutes later he was striding out of the hospital with a phone number for probably another notch on his bed post. Guy had the biggest mouth when it came to his conquests. Conquests that we were convinced were actually more talk than actual action.

"Good. I just need two minutes to talk to Mom and we can go."

"Zach, man. Come on. We gotta go."

"Two minutes!"

Not bothering to stand around and wait for him to bitch, I headed over to where Mom was playing with a very cheery Ava.

"See Lily?"

"Yeah. She says she's okay…"

"And she is."

Rolling my eyes, I was sick of hearing how okay she was. She was in the hospital for damn sake. If everything was okay, she wouldn't be. "She's not going to be able to drive or look after Ava while her arm is out of action."

"Probably not."

"She said she'll figure it out."

"And I'm sure she will. Lily's a smart girl. She'll come up with a plan."

Frustration was bubbling. Reaching out for Ava, I stole her from Mom's arms and held her close. She screwed her nose up at me, probably because I stunk like smoke in my turnout gear but when I started talking to her, her chubby little cheeks softened. "Why are all the women in my life determined to drive me crazy? You wouldn't do that to me, would you Ava?"

"Give her a couple of years and I'm sure she will," Mom interrupted, standing up. "Look, Zach, I know you, and I know how big your hero complex is, look at what you do for a living, but Lily's got this. She's smart. Resourceful. If she needs help, I'm sure she'll ask for it. Now, give me back this gorgeous girl and get back to work."

After kissing Ava's cheek and letting her grab at my nose, I handed her back to Mom before kissing Mom's forehead. "Take care of my girls."

"Girls?" Mom questioned, looking smug.

"Yeah, girls. I'll see you in the morning."

"Be careful."

Leaving them, I grabbed Samuels by the scruff of the neck and dragged him away from the nurses' station. I didn't even want to know how many of those women he just hit on. We had work to do and from the way my radio was going ballistic, the sooner we got back out there and gave the rest of our crew a hand, the better.

What a night.

What a fucking ridiculous, exhausting, frustrating night.

I don't think we'd had more than ten minutes in a row to take a breath. Call after call came through. And more than one house fire getting out of control. After the third call, I couldn't for the life of me figure out how people who owned an open fireplace in their home didn't clean their chimneys. It was a proven recipe for disaster. Especially when something had taken residence in said chimney for the summer months.

It was just before dawn when another call came through from Mrs. Davies. Her cat, Fleur, was stuck up a tree. I'd never been called out for this before, but here we were, loading up and heading across town to help the weeping widow.

Fleur was a devil cat. The bloody thing hissed and swatted at us and climbed up to a higher branch. Forty minutes. Forty frigging minutes we spent chasing that damn cat up through the branches before it darted down the trunk and back through the flap in the door.

Thank God it was now over, and I was headed home. Well, after I stopped by and checked on Lily. Mom had text me late last night and explained she was taking them home and would be staying with Lily the night to help out with Ava, and I was so grateful for her being there. I loved that Lily had just opened her life, her business and her home to Mom. I couldn't believe how much her simple actions of inviting her in, wanting her there, had changed Mom in every way. She had purpose again. She was happier, more fulfilled, and the mother I remembered. At some point I had to figure out a more permanent plan, but that was a problem for another day. Today I was delivering coffee and checking in, then going to bed.

Mom was sitting on the porch steps when I pulled into the driveway.

"Morning," I called out as I crossed the grass.

"Ssh. Lily and Ava are still asleep."

"Don't blame them. Why are you up? It's still early," I asked, dropping down on the step beside her.

"I just got Ava back down. She had a rough night. Don't worry, not like that. Just slept on and off. She's fine." My face must've given away my concern. "Zach, you're awfully invested in that little girl," Mom commented, trying to sound casual.

"Can you blame me? She's adorable."

"That she is. But have you thought about what happens next?"

"Next?"

"You know Lily's just looking after her while they find her forever home?"

The bile rose in my throat, making me gag. I didn't like the sound of that. Not one little bit. Even though deep down I knew that was the reality of the situation, pretending it wasn't was a much nicer place to be. Before Ava, I hadn't really thought about having a family, maybe in the distant future, but now she was here, I couldn't imagine a life where she wasn't.

Mom wrapped her arm around my waist and rested her head on my shoulder. Handing her her coffee, together we sat there and watched as morning sunlight erased last night's storm. Lily's front yard had taken a hammering, but it was all cosmetic. A few fallen branches, some of the dirt from the garden bed had washed away and bits of rubbish had blown in, but overall, she'd come through relatively unscathed. God, I hoped I'd been as lucky.

Behind us, the door creaked open and I turned to see the most beautiful woman I'd ever laid eyes on.

24

LILY

"How are you feeling, Lily?" Linda asked.

She'd been a Godsend. I was so glad it was her phone number I'd blindly dialed. Not only had she gotten me to the hospital, but she'd brought me home and taken charge. When I'd gone to change Ava's diaper, I almost howled in agony. Linda had offered to do it, but I was being stubborn and determined to do it myself. While I sat on my bed, sobbing and feeling sorry for myself, Linda took charge getting Ava changed, fed and tucked into bed. Then she turned her bossiness in my direction.

"I'm okay."

"And now the real answer?"

Zach handed me a coffee and quirked his eyebrow.

I yawned loudly and took a sip of my coffee. If I could've found a way to inject it intravenously, I'd be prepping the needle. Sleep had alluded me and I had the headache from hell. Then on top of that my arm was throbbing.

"I need more sleep," I admitted.

"Here here," Zach toasted me with his own coffee.

"Long shift?"

"Yeah. Really long." Zach yawned.

"Well, since I'm the only fully functioning adult here right now, you two need to go to bed and get some sleep, and I'll take Ava out for a walk when she wakes up."

"I can't ask you to do that…"

"You didn't ask. I offered. Now, finish your coffee and go get into bed."

Zach took another sip from his paper cup before tossing what was left on the lawn and standing up and pulling his keys from his pocket.

"Where are you going?" Linda called out.

"Ah, home for a shower and some sleep?"

"Don't be daft. I'm pretty sure Lily has a perfectly good shower you can use."

"Mom! I'm not staying here."

"Why? Because I know about it? Look, Zach, you're not fifteen anymore and trying to sneak Allison what's-her-name in through your bedroom window. We're all adults and you two aren't going to get up to any hanky panky…"

"Hanky panky, Mom? Really?"

"Well let's face it, you both look like absolute shit, and the only thing that's going to happen in there is sleep. Now, I'm going to go check on Ava and move her out of your room, and I don't want to hear another word about it."

Linda strolled past, pinching my cheek before disappearing inside leaving me standing there, clasping my coffee.

"You sure you're okay with this?"

"Honestly, I'm so tired I'd curl up under the tree if it meant I could get comfortable."

"That bad, huh?"

"You have no idea."

"Well then, I need a shower."

"Let's go."

I couldn't believe I was sitting on my bed while Zach was on the other side of the wall – the other side of the very thin wall – naked in my shower. Naked and soapy and wet. Struggling the best I could, I changed into a tank top and a pair of sleep shorts before sliding back in under the covers.

I'd barely laid my head down when Zach strode into my bedroom wearing a pair of boxers and an exhausted grimace. Poor guy looked completely shattered.

Not having a clue what I was supposed to do or say, I blurted out something dumb. "Are you okay on the left?"

Scrubbing his hand across his face, Zach nodded before climbing under the covers. "Oh shit! Do you need anything. Pain killers? Extra pillows? Water?"

Exhausted, sore and feeling more than a little sorry for myself, I answered honestly. "Just you." If I made a fool of myself, I'd just blame the drugs.

With a smile, Zach dragged me gently into his arms, propping a pillow against my side, before snuggling against me.

I woke up starving. It was the best sleep I'd had in weeks and I only had one person to thank for it. The man whose jaw was covered in stubble as he snored beside me. His body was hard and warm. I tried to wriggle out of his grasp, but the arm wrapped around my waist tightened and Zach murmured against my neck. I never would've guessed he was a snuggler, but damn it felt so good being curled up in his arms.

"Where're you going," he mumbled, his eyes not even cracking open.

"Time to get up."

"Five more minutes."

I should've been embarrassed to say that was all the convincing it took to have me conceding defeat and closing my eyes.

When I woke up again, the bed beside me was empty and the sheets cold. I didn't even realize he'd gotten up.

"What's that look for?"

"What look?" I asked, sitting up and rubbing my eyes before slipping my arm from the sling. I needed to straighten it. "Mother-fucker!" I swore as a shooting pain went through my arm, making my eyes water.

"Shit, Lily!" Zach was at my side, taking hold of my hand and helping me settle my arm back in the sling. "That okay?" he asked, adjusting the strap behind my neck and making sure my hair wasn't caught.

"Thanks."

My stomach rumbled loudly. "What time is it?"

"Time I feed you by the sounds of that."

"I'm so hungry. I haven't had anything since... I don't even remember."

"Lily, that's not good."

I was bordering on hangry, something no human should ever be exposed to. Especially Zach. "I didn't do it on purpose. I mean, I was a bit preoccupied..."

"Calm down, sweetheart. I wasn't having a go at you."

"I know. Sorry. I'm just..."

"Well, let's get you fed. What do you feel like?"

"Umm..."

"Anything you want."

"And you won't judge?"

"Of course I'm going to judge. If you make me eat a tofu burger, I'm totally judging you for that. I'm not saying I won't eat it, because I will, but just know, I'll be judging you the whole time."

"That's fair," I agreed. "Well in that case, do you mind calling Carlos and ordering a pepperoni pizza and garlic bread?"

"Seriously?"

"Is that judgement I hear?"

"Hell yeah! Carlos's is the best."

"Good. Start dialing. I'm just going to have a quick shower before food gets here."

"No worries. And don't worry. I've spoken to Mom, her and Ava are currently hanging out at my place. Mom said to let you know she took your car with the seat in it, but they're fine."

"Your mom is an angel."

"She's certainly something. Now get in there so I can order some food."

Taking my time, I did the best with what I had. Trying to shave my most delicate areas with my wrong hand without cutting myself was a challenge and I wasn't even sure I'd done a good job. Guess I was going to have to restrain myself from jumping Zach's bones until I had the situation back under control, although knowing what a complete caveman he was in the bedroom had me giggling to myself. I really doubted a few stray hairs, or a little stubble would scare him off.

Reluctantly I stepped out of the shower, shut off the water and wiped the condensation from the mirror. I wish I hadn't. Turning from side to side I saw the ugly green and yellow bruises on my side from the other night's stupidity. Grabbing a fresh towel from under the sink, I patted myself dry the best I could before wrapping it around my body and darting into my bedroom.

I managed to get some panties on, but my bra was beyond me. Getting it on one shoulder was easy but trying to do the damn clasp up was driving me insane. I tried doing it up in front, behind me, hell, I even tried pulling it off my shoulders doing it up then sliding it back on.

"Lily, pizza's here," Zach's husky voice called out, and goosebumps raced down my spine.

"Just a second."

The door was thrown open and Zach's hulking presence filled the doorway. I panicked. I was standing there in only my panties, my wet towel at my feet and my bra tangled around me holding me hostage.

"I... uh ...shit..." Zach's eyes bounced around the room, looking everywhere but at me. He looked at the ceiling, out the window and at his shoes before lifting his hand to his face, shielding his eyes and turning around. Clearly, he'd been caught off guard with my lack of clothing, but he wasn't the only one.

"Zach, it's fine. It's not like it's nothing you haven't seen before anyway," I said, letting us both off the hook.

"I'm sorry, Lil. I didn't hear what you said and..."

"Nothing to be sorry about. But since you're here maybe you could help me with something."

I must've said the magic word, because Zach was moving towards me, his intense eyes locking with mine. "What do you need?"

"Well, I know you know how to get a bra off, but do you know how to put one on?" I teased, needing to lighten the mood.

"Can't say I've ever needed to, but I consider myself a smart guy, I'm pretty sure I could figure it out."

"Good! Our pizza's getting cold and this damn contraption is trying to strangle me."

"We can't have that now, can we?"

"No, we can't. So, if you could give me a hand…"

With a good-for-nothing smirk on his face, Zach's eyes lit up with mischief, and I was beginning to regret asking for help. "I think I'm up to it."

If he wanted to play, two could play this game. "I have no doubt you're *up* for it," I said as I glanced at his crotch.

His answering groan was all I needed to know I was right on the money.

25

ZACH

Oh boy was I up for it.

I couldn't imagine there was a red-blooded male on the face of the planet who wouldn't be 'up for it' when standing in front of Lily Evans wearing the sexiest pair of black satin panties with a bright red bow front and center and asking for help. Fuck me sideways, did I want to help her. I wanted to help her scratch the itch she didn't even know she had.

As I moved towards her, her raspberry-scented body wash, the one I'd used myself earlier, filled my nostrils, and the semi I'd been sporting went painfully hard. I did not give a toss about the pizza going cold. The lunch I was suddenly salivating for was something deliciously sweeter and much more addictive.

As she handed me the lacy contraption, it took all my restraint to not chuck it over my shoulder and say be damned with it, but the pout on Lily's lips, lips that were dying to be kissed, made me man up and do what she asked.

Rubbing my hands against my thighs – I didn't want my cold fingers to touch her soft skin – I stood in front of her, the feel of her breath on my neck tickling me. Holding the straps out in front of her, Lily wove her arms through the holes, wincing. I watched on, completely mesmerized as she lifted and adjusted her tits, settling the scrap of lace I was wishing were my hands in place.

"Holy fuck…"

"What? What's wrong?" Lily asked, her voice hitching.

"You do that… every day?"

"Do what every day?"

"Play with your tits like that?" I'm pretty sure at this point my eyes were bugging out of my head. I knew chicks wore bras and I knew how to take one off, but I had no idea watching a girl put one on could be so freaking hot.

"I don't play with my tits, I put my bra on. Do you play with your cock when you put your boxers on?" Lily rolled her eyes. I couldn't blame her really. I sounded like a weirdo.

"Ah, yeah. I'm a guy. It's what we do," I shrugged nonchalantly. What was the big deal? I had to adjust my junk so it was comfortable.

"Well that just cements it."

"Cements what?"

"Women are the smarter sex. No doubt about it. Now, are you going to stand there staring at my boobs all day or are you actually going to help me here?"

Grumbling, I watched as Lily spun around showing me her back. "Holy fuck, Lily! What the hell are those?"

"What?"

"Those big-ass bruises all over your back! What happened and who do I need to beat the living shit out of?"

My chest was heaving. I could barely believe what I was seeing. All down one side of Lily's back, her beautiful soft creamy skin was marred with yellow and green bruises. They weren't new ones, so I knew they weren't caused by her fall, but something or someone had definitely left their mark. Clenching my fists at my sides, I tried to calm the storm raging inside me. Even the thought of someone putting their hands on Lily made me want to hit something.

"Oh those." Lily moved away from me, scooping up her dress

from the end of the bed. "They're nothing. Just me being clumsy. If you could just do up the hooks?"

"Uh-uh. No way. I'm going to need a little bit more than clumsy, Lil."

"Fine," she huffed, turning around to face me, her boobs falling out of her still-undone bra, briefly stealing my attention. No one could blame me. They were boobs. Right there in front of my face. The perfect handful with their dusky rose peaks begging to be pinched and licked and suckled until Lily was wriggling around beneath me battling with the line of pleasure and pain.

She snapped her fingers in front of my face, and I dragged my gaze up to find her exhausted expression. "Eyes are up here, buddy."

"I know that."

"Yeah okay. Sure you do."

"Stop stalling, Lil. The bruises? Who am I paying a visit to?"

"Actually, they're your fault," she tossed out carelessly with a shrug.

I think my heart actually stopped.

Stepping backwards, I needed to put distance between me and those ugly bruises I was apparently responsible for. I'd never hurt a woman in my life. I never would. But the evidence staring me in the face said otherwise. Tripping over my own feet and Lily's towel in my haste to put distance between us, I flopped backwards on her bed.

"Lily," I choked out her name.

"Oh god, Zach. Not like that. Hell, we both know you'd be more likely to junk-punch yourself than raise a hand to a woman. You're a lover not a fighter, Zach Higgins."

Reaching out her tiny hand, she cupped my cheek tenderly. Far more delicately than I deserved. Taking hold of her hand, I pulled her carefully towards me before lowering her onto my knee.

"Sweetheart, I'm dying here," I admitted, feeling the sweat bead on my forehead while my heart tried to burst through my rib cage. "What happened?"

With a gentle smile, Lily leaned over and kissed my lips so softly it was barely a whisper. "It was me being clumsy and not thinking. The other night I was determined to get all my boxes of shit put away. Having them filling the lounge room was driving me insane. Taunting me. And I'm a strong, independent woman..."

"Never doubted that for a second, but that doesn't explain these," I confirmed, trailing my finger down her back, Lily shivering at the contact.

"I'm getting to it," she scolded, snuggling against me. Reaching behind us, I grabbed the purple comforter from her bed and wrapped it around us, cocooning us in our very own little bubble. A bubble I never wanted to leave. "Thanks. Now, where was I? You keep distracting me."

"Strong, independent woman."

"Right. I'm a strong, independent woman. I didn't need a guy to do things for me. I was quite capable of doing them myself. Besides, there wasn't anyone to ask, so I started moving them myself."

I could see exactly where this story was going. And although I was relieved, I wasn't the one who physically hurt her, it didn't mean I blamed myself any less.

"I got through the first two fine. Then when I was trying to open the next one, I yanked a little too hard on the tape. It was being a bitch and didn't want to rip, so I yanked harder and fell backwards. I landed on my ass on the floor and hit the coffee table on the way down."

"Ouch!" I winced. That would've hurt like a bitch.

"That's an understatement. I think I laid there on the floor for a good half an hour yoyoing between feeling sorry for myself and berating myself for being so dumb. The damn scissors were sitting on the coffee table, I just thought..."

"That you knew better," I finished for her.

"Something like that."

Relief flooded me. I mean, I wasn't relieved she was hurt or had been in pain, but really, it wasn't my fault. Sure, I was the one who taped the boxes, but no court of law would hold that against me, and from the way Lily was burrowing her head in the crook of my neck, I didn't think she did either. Which was a huge fucking relief.

"Are you okay? And don't bullshit me."

"I'm fine. I think my ego is bruised more than my back."

"I doubt that," I scoffed, leaning her forward and taking another look. Bloody woman. She was a mess, but I wanted her to be my mess. "They're pretty gnarly."

"Gnarly? Is that a word you use down under?"

"You have no idea what we do down under, but I'm more than willing to show you. I mean, what sort of patriotic, kangaroo-loving, beer-guzzling, budgie-smuggler-wearing Aussie bloke would I be if I didn't offer to show you my love for my country? I'm especially fond of the map of Tasmania."

"I don't even think I want to know what that means…"

"I'm sure you'd be mighty impressed with my budgie-smugglers."

"How or why, you'd want to smuggle a bird, I have no idea."

Lifting my hips up, I pressed my cock into her butt as he was coming back to life after that little scare, which quite frankly, I'm surprised didn't scar him for life. Lily looked at me with a smirk. She knew exactly what I was doing, but her growling stomach brought playtime to a screeching halt.

"Come on, let's go feed you."

"I like that plan." Lily slipped off my lap and bent down to pick up her forgotten bra. "Are you going to help me with this?"

"Nope." Snatching it off her, I tossed it across the room, ignoring where it landed. "Go without. Those tits are too pretty to be restrained anyway."

"Has anyone ever told you how annoying you are?" Lily questioned, throwing her dress at me and stepping in front of me, hand on her cocked hip.

"Not recently."

"Hurry up and help me get dressed. I'm hungry and I want to go get our girl."

"Our girl?" Damn I liked the sound of that.

Rising to my feet, I kicked the towel away before helping pull Lily's dress over her head. I may have accidentally on purpose brushed my fingers against the side of her boob causing her to hiss and suck in a breath.

"Yep. Our girl. Ava's as much your girl as mine."

"You have no idea how much I like the sound of that."

"Good! Cause you're stuck with us now."

Fuck me, I hoped so.

26

LILY

I'D EATEN TOO MUCH BUT IT WAS DELICIOUS, NOW I WAS LYING ON THE lounge regretting that last slice of garlic bread.

"So good," I mumbled, rubbing my belly.

"Take these," Zach bossed, handing me a couple of pills and a bottle of water. Damn the guy was good at looking after people. "How you feeling?"

"Not too bad, all things considered."

"Have you given any thought to what you're going to do about work tomorrow?"

"I'm hoping Sage can help out. I can go in, but I'm probably not going to be much use."

"Have you spoken to Sage?"

"Not yet... I need to get a new phone. Mine's stuffed."

"Well, why don't we go get you a new phone and then go see Ava? I can't believe I miss her so much," Zach admitted, unable to wipe the grin from his face.

"What's not to miss? She's adorable."

"Then let's go get her."

"Actually, Zach, before we go, can we talk about something?"

The smile fell from his lips in the same instant that the butterflies in my stomach took flight. "What's up?" His voice was strained and cracked.

"It's about Ava."

"What about her? Is something wrong?"

"No. No. Nothing like that. I just wanted to let you know, I've applied to adopt Ava permanently."

"Okay."

"Are you okay with that?" I thought I was going to vomit. Wringing my hands together, I waited for him to say something. I hoped he didn't hate me. It wouldn't change my decision, I couldn't think of anything that would, but everything Sarah had tried to warn me about had come true.

I couldn't give Ava up. I loved her. The last thing I could ever imagine doing was watching someone else raise my little girl. She owned me. Completely. I loved her. With everything I was, I loved her.

"I think it's a great idea. I've got everything crossed for you."

"You're really okay with it?"

"Absolutely. Ava would be lucky to have you. Have they said what your chances are?"

"They haven't said anything. I've submitted the paperwork but now it's a waiting game." A waiting game that was driving me batty.

"I'm sure it'll all work out. They're crazy if they don't sign on the dotted line."

"Thanks."

"For what?"

"Believing in me. And not hating me for doing it."

Zach scoffed. "I couldn't hate you for that. I admire you. And honestly, thank you. I couldn't imagine someone else giving Ava the life and the love that I know you will."

Wow! Knowing Zach had my back, no matter what happened, felt incredible. I don't know what I would've done if he'd turned his back on me. As much as I wasn't looking for him to walk into my life, now he was here, I couldn't dream of a world where he wasn't a part of it. And my deepest, darkest fear, the one I wasn't ready yet to voice, was that he was only here because of Ava. That I wasn't enough. That I'd never be enough.

"You sure you're okay with this? I mean, you can tell me if you're not."

Squatting in front of me, Zach brushed the hair from my forehead before intertwining his fingers with mine. "Lily Evans. I'm one hundred and ten percent behind you. And Ava will be the luckiest little girl when they make the right decision. And if there's anything, anything at all that I can do to help, I want you to promise me that you'll ask. Don't hesitate; if it means Ava gets to live the life she deserves, growing up with you as her mom, then I'm on board. Just tell me where to sign or what to do."

"You really mean that, don't you?" I confirmed.

There was so much sincerity and so much genuine emotion in what he was saying, it was hard to even consider he didn't mean it. Zach was something else. Maybe they bred them differently in Australia. I'd never met a guy like Zach and I couldn't believe I ever would again. He was emotionally mature and seemingly unafraid of laying it all, heart and soul on the line.

"Every single word."

I couldn't hold back. Leaning forward, I captured his lips with mine and poured every emotion that was swirling around inside me into that kiss. At first, he let me lead but it didn't last. When he took over, our kiss turned feral. His tongue dueled with mine as my body came to life. I didn't know what it was about this guy, but he could turn me into a needy, quivering mess.

Needing more, recklessly I pressed myself against him before yanking back and letting out a pained yelp.

"Shit, Lily. I'm so sorry. I didn't think..." Zach began apologizing as he tried to move away from me.

"This is all on me, Zach. I forgot. You make me forget myself."

A smug smirk crept across his face, and I knew every thought that crossed his mind. He wasn't even trying to hide it. With his hooded eyes alive with mischief and that grin popping his dimple, he was damn sexy, and I was in trouble. Big, big trouble.

Rocking back on his heels, Zach's huge, calloused hands found my calves and began massaging them. It felt like heaven. I don't even remember ever having someone massage my calves before but damn if I didn't want him to ever stop. I went to complain when his hands left my skin, but I didn't get the chance. Grabbing the hem of my dress, he shoved it up over my knees before wedging himself between them.

"What are you..."

"Do you trust me?" he asked, looking up at me from his spot between my thighs.

The lump in my throat stole my voice. Instead, I managed to nod, my eyes locked with his.

Without wasting another second, Zach lifted the skirt of my dress and disappeared underneath, nudging my panties aside and running his finger up my slit.

"Oh, fuck, Zach."

He mumbled something incoherent against my thigh before swiping his tongue where I needed him the most. Without realizing, my hips lifted. When his assault escalated, a powerful combination of tongue and talented fingers, I began fucking his face recklessly.

"Zach, I'm gonna... I'm gonna... Oh my god..." I couldn't form a full sentence. My mind was scrambled. My whole body on fire. The orgasm Zach was coaxing from me was like a tsunami hurtling through me. I was writhing and moaning and screaming, begging for more. All it took was one more crook of his finger in the same moment he sucked my clit, and I exploded loudly.

Throwing my head back, I fisted the cushion, lifting it to my face and smothering myself with it, trying to silence my own screams. As I rode out the aftershocks, I dropped the cushion, sleepily satisfied as Zach emerged from under my dress.

When he rocked back on his heels, our eyes met, and the smug shithead winked at me. "Someone's mighty proud of himself."

"You saying I shouldn't be?"

"Fuck no!"

"Good. I'm pretty sure I didn't hear any complaints."

"Nope. No complaints here. Well, except for one."

"One?"

"I can't feel my legs. Everything's feeling a lot like jelly right now."

Popping up to his feet, Zach reached for my hand. "Come on. Let's get you cleaned up and go get our girl."

Forty-five minutes, an awkward blow job later, and we were walking through the shopping mall trying to replace my shattered phone. Zach's fingers were tangled with mine as he led along, not even batting an eyelid at the curious glances thrown in our direction. We must've looked like an odd couple. I'd forgone my normal heels, choosing flats instead, which made me look tiny when I stood next to him. Or maybe it was just how good he looked in his worn jeans and tight fire department t-shirt that had people taking a second look.

Who knew choosing a new phone would be so painful? Why couldn't I just have the same one I had before? It did all the shit I wanted it to do. I didn't need more fancy gadgets or a better camera. My camera was fine. Eventually we got out of there and Zach ushered me through the food court, stopping to buy me a pretzel.

"Anything else you want?"

"I'm good," I mumbled through a mouthful of salty goodness.

"Then let's go get Ava. I can't wait to give her a hug."

After helping me into his truck, making sure his hand slipped and settled on my ass as he went, we headed towards his place. Staring out the window, we passed the shop, and I started to worry that I was getting in over my head. Did I really think I could pull this off? I mean, running a business, being a full-time mom, not to mention trying to fix up Grandma's house and turning it into a home. Then there was Zach. Where'd he fit? Did he want a role in my life? And if he did, how big of a role? I'd never cut him out of

Ava's life and, when the time came, when she was old enough to understand, she'd know that he was the man responsible for giving her her amazing life and bringing her into my world. But what did he want to be to her? A father figure? The doting uncle who spoils her with toys and candy? Or an old friend who we said hi to on the street from time to time?

"Mom! We're home," Zach announced, guiding me through his back door.

Linda appeared, her blouse covered in something white which she was dusting off. "Good to see you two awake again. Have a nice nap?"

I got the distinct feeling there was more to her question, but thankfully she left it at that.

"It was great," I offered.

Zach turned towards me. "Great? Just great? I was going to go with incredible, but I guess I'll just have to try harder next time."

I felt my cheeks burn. I couldn't believe he was putting me on the spot like that in front of his own damn mother. Well, two could play at that game. "I'll take your incredible and raise you to mind-blowing."

"Mind-blowing, huh?"

"Absolutely."

"Wow! I don't think I've ever had a mind-blowing nap. Maybe I should go find some of what you're getting, Lily. You're positively glowing."

Zach groaned and scrubbed his hand down his face. "Geez, Mom. I don't need to hear about that."

"Well you started it. Besides, I'm not dead. I deserve a good nap now and again."

"Stop! Please for the love of all that's holy, stop talking about... about that."

"You're never going to be able to think of it the same way again, are you?" I asked Zach who looked like he was about to throw up all over the floor.

"Never! Where's Ava?"

"Asleep in your bed."

"I'm going to check on her," Zach declared before fleeing like someone had lit his ass on fire.

As I sat down at the kitchen table, Linda handed me a glass of water before sinking into the chair opposite me.

"You really like him, don't you?"

I couldn't lie. I didn't even want to. "He's a great guy."

"I know. I raised him. But that's not what I mean, Lily, and you know it." Nodding my agreeance, I let her continue as she looked towards the door where he'd vanished through a moment earlier. "And he's fallen for that little girl."

"I don't blame him. It's impossible not to."

"You're right about that. But she's not the only one he's in love with."

27

ZACH

AFTER I'D BUNDLED THE GIRLS INTO THE CAR, NOT BEING ABLE TO think of any other way to string out their visit, I threw a load of laundry into the machine. I had three-day shifts starting tomorrow and then three days off, and I couldn't wait. I loved working. I loved the guys I got to work with each and every day, but right now I had a huge list of shit I wanted to get done.

"Dinner's ready," Mom called.

As I sat down at the table, she slid a plate piled high with steak and vegetables towards me. After pouring drinks, she set her own plate down which was half empty.

"Is that all you're eating?" I wasn't really happy by her tiny portion.

"I'm not very hungry."

Something wasn't right. I watched as she pushed her carrots around her plate before sipping at her water. When I tried to engage her in conversation, it was like talking to a brick wall. She wasn't giving me anything. Even mentioning Ava's name only got me a strained smile.

When she set her knife and fork down, I swallowed my steak

and picked up my drink taking a long gulp. I had a feeling I was going to need it.

"Zach, I want to talk to you about something," Mom began.

I could see how nervous she was. She was fidgeting and refusing to meet my eye. I hated this bullshit. She was my mother. My only mother. The mother I'd moved halfway around the world to be close to. Whatever she wanted to talk about, I was going to listen.

"What's up?" I asked cheerily, wiping my mouth with my napkin.

"The lease on my place is coming to an end…"

"Already? I didn't think it was so soon."

"End of next month."

"Okay."

"I want to move."

"Where to?"

"Here."

"My house?"

"Not necessarily. I want to move to Sunnyville. I'm over here all the time anyway. With you living here. And Lily. And the shop. I like it here. It's less…"

"Less what, Mom?"

"Less lonely."

Fuck that hurt my heart. I knew she wasn't doing well over in Kellyville and I'd done my best to get over there as much as I could, but obviously I hadn't tried hard enough. I'd let her down and left her alone and I hated myself for it. I'd do better. I wouldn't let her down again. I refused to.

"I'm so sorry, Mom. I didn't…"

"Zach, you have nothing to be sorry about. I'm your mother, not someone you need to save."

"See, that's where you're wrong. *Because* you're my mother, *I* should be looking after you."

Reaching over, I took hold of her hand, feeling how cold her fingers were.

"Sweetheart, you're a good man. You've got a huge heart and I'm so proud of you. But you've got your own family now. They need to be your priority. I just want to, if it's okay with you, be close enough to be a part of that life."

"Mom, you're always going to be part of my life. And I'd love to have you closer. These last few weeks have been great. I mean, I come home to cooked meals and a clean house. I haven't eaten frozen pizza once." My smartass response made her smile before she pulled her hand out from under mine and slapped my shoulder.

"I'm not going to be your housekeeper, Zachary."

"So, are you moving in here?" I asked, mentally adding more renovations to the never-ending list. If Mom was moving in, I needed to get her bathroom finished off and her room. The rest could wait. I wanted her to be comfortable and feel at home.

"Not sure yet. Haven't really gotten that far. I wanted to make sure you were okay with it before I started making any firm plans."

"Well, I just need to know when you want me to help you pack the rest of your stuff and where I'm delivering it."

Rising out of my seat, I stepped behind her, wrapped my arm around her shoulders, and kissed her head. She smelt like home. It was always the same smell. The scent of my safe place.

"I'll let you know."

"Okay then."

She picked up her fork and started eating, this time normally. Obviously, the weight of the conversation hadn't been sitting well with her, but now it was out there, she could relax.

"So, Lily said she talked to you about her wanting to adopt Ava."

"Yeah."

"What do you think? Really think?"

"I think it's the right thing to do. I think it'd break her heart to have to give her up," I admitted.

"Not only her heart," Mom added.

"What's that supposed to mean?"

"Zach, that little girl lights up your world. She might not be yours by blood, but you love her just the same."

"I do," I confirmed. There was no point in denying it.

Mom rose from the table and started clearing the dishes. "Leave them. You cooked; I'll clean up."

"That'd be great. Thanks."

I'd just finished stacking the dishwasher when Mom reappeared with her overnight bag slung over her shoulder. "Should I be worried where you're going at this time of night?" I teased. "Do I need to give you a curfew?"

As far as I knew, Mom hadn't dated since Dad. She'd never even mentioned the idea. I'd like to think I was old enough and mature enough to be okay with it if and when the time came, but I wasn't sure. I'd be better than Maddy, that was for sure. Maddy had been Daddy's girl, and when we lost him, for a period, we lost Maddy too. She went off the rails, and I know Mom spent many, many nights pacing up and down the porch worrying. It would've devastated her if Maddy had been lost to us forever. We'd already lost Dad, losing her too would've been more than we could survive.

"Ha ha. You think you're so funny. If you must know, I told Lily I'd stay at her place for a few days and give her a hand with Ava. She didn't tell you?"

"Not a damn word," I muttered, rubbing that spot on my chest that was suddenly aching.

"It's just to help her out while she's down an arm."

"Oh, makes sense."

"Then why do you look like you did when I told you Norbert died?"

"Did you have to bring Norbert up?"

"Zach, you loved that dog, and you were eight when he died. It's okay that you spent a week sleeping in his kennel, crying yourself to sleep."

"Still can't believe you tell people about that," I grumbled, my eyes watering as I remembered the damn dog who'd followed me everywhere. He was the world's best dog and my best friend, even if he did sleep on the end of my bed, snoring and farting.

"It was adorable, Zachary. And so were you. Now, if you could stop pouting, I've gotta get going."

"I'm not pouting."

Mom walked over to where I was leaning against the sink, drying my hands on some paper towels. She hugged me before grabbing her purse and heading out the door. "Stay safe, Zach."

"Always," I confirmed, and Mom disappeared, leaving me standing in my all too quiet house.

Wandering around, I catalogued everything I wanted to get done and began wondering where I was going to find the time to do it all. Feeling restless, I grabbed a beer and went and sat outside on the step. Staring up at the night's sky, I dug my phone from my pocket and shot off a text to Maddy. I don't know why I wanted to talk to her; even though we'd once been close, those days were long gone. Maddy was my sister and I loved her, and God forgive anyone who crossed her because I had no hesitations of going into battle for her, but with time and distance we'd grown apart.

Zach: *How's life in Sydney?*

My message was pathetic, but I didn't know what else to say. When she didn't reply, I stuffed around with my phone, losing time playing some stupid game. I should've done something productive like gone for a run or headed to the gym, but that seemed like a lot of effort. When the rain started falling, I headed back inside, plugged my phone into my charger and climbed into bed.

The next three days were monotonous. My alarm woke me with the sun, and I fell out of bed, changed into my running shorts and was out the door five minutes later. Running the same five-mile loop I'd been doing for weeks, right by Lily's front door. Then I was home eating breakfast and showering before heading to work. At lunch time each day, I'd head down to the florist to check how things were going, only to get reamed out from Lily for checking in.

Damn woman was stubborn as a mule, much to Mom's amusement. I'd tried lying, saying I was there to talk to Mom or see Ava,
but she wasn't buying it. Apparently, Lily didn't like the fussing.
Wasn't going to stop me from dropping in, if anything I was highly
entertained by her attempts at a tantrum. I'd grown up with a
drama queen; hell Maddy had gone on to be an actress, so Lily was
going to have to up her game if she wanted me to buy the annoyance she was trying to sell.

After my last shift for the week, I'd headed to Hooligans for a
beer with the boys, which turned into two. Then three. Then before
I knew it, Samuels was helping me into the back of an Uber, sliding
in beside me and taking me home.

After drinking my body weight in beer, Samuels had been
tasked with getting me home safely, I was in no state to do it
myself. So, he bundled me into an Uber and got me inside before
passing out on my couch. When I woke late the next morning, I had
to move. The walls felt like they were closing in on me. But it was
more than that. If the dodgy renovations were responsible, something we'd find out in the coming days once the investigators
worked their magic, then like hell was I letting a tradie get
anywhere near Lily's place. I'd do it myself. At least then I'd know
it was done right and she was safe.

Leaving Samuel's ass in the air and snoring on my couch, I
threw my tools in my truck, grabbed a coke from the fridge and
headed over to Lily's. I had work to do.

28

LILY

Four days with my arm in a sling was four days too many. The knot kept digging into my neck, I barely got any sleep, tossing and turning most of the night, and getting dressed was another nightmare altogether. And if that wasn't bad enough, this week Ava, my sweet, beautiful little girl, had morphed into the devil. She screamed. She was awake all freaking night and slept like an angel all day. On top of that, she wasn't eating, and I was beyond stressed.

Linda kept assuring me that it was nothing, that she was just feeding off my frustrations, but it didn't seem to matter how many times she repeated it, I just couldn't accept it. After I dropped my barely eaten burrito on the floor at lunch when Ava screeched, the only thing stopping me from getting up and taking her to the doctor was Linda's calm head. The woman was a Godsend. She wasn't my mother or even my family, but she'd stepped up and was saving my ass. She was everywhere I needed her to be even before I needed her. She'd taken over bathing Ava, changing her, and rocking her to sleep. I hadn't realized it was even possible but I both loved and hated her for it. There was no doubt she was saving my ass, but I hated that I couldn't be the one to look after her.

After she'd buckled Ava into her car seat, she'd promised me tomorrow would be better before jumping into her own car and heading in the opposite direction. With Ava finally settled, I stood in the street outside the shop and just took a breath.

Forty minutes later I pulled into my driveway, surprised to not only find Zach's truck parked on the street, but stuff all over my front lawn. Putting the car into park, I climbed out and rounded the side to get Ava, but Zach was already there.

"Hey," he greeted with a lopsided grin.

Holy fucking hotness, Batman. The guy was standing in front of me wearing deliciously low-slung shorts with a tool belt buckled around his waist, a pair of heavy work boots and a baseball cap. That's it. No shirt. No tank. His bare chest was glistening in the sun, streaked with sweat and dirt and what looked like sawdust.

When he reached through the door and lifted Ava out of her seat, a toothless smile covering her face followed by some gurgling and drooling, my heart melted.

"Thanks," I forced out, my throat as dry as the Sahara.

"I thought you could use a hand." Zach nodded, indicating the arm that was still restricted by a sling.

Turning away, I forced myself to take a breath and grabbed my shit from the front seat. Including the mountain of Chinese food I'd picked up on my way home that I was embarrassed to be hauling inside.

"How was your day, beautiful?" Zach crooned.

I went to answer but thankfully hadn't managed to splutter a response, because when I turned around, I saw he was one hundred and ten percent focused on Ava, who looked more than comfortable snuggled in his arms. Shaking my head, I squashed the disappointment and headed towards the house.

I was just about to put my foot on the bottom step when Zach's hand wrapped around my bicep. "Careful. Some of the boards are a bit loose."

That was an understatement and a half. Half my damn porch

was missing. Turning back to face Zach, I asked the obvious. "Ah, Zach...what happened to my porch?"

"Lil, your porch was a disaster waiting to happen. I knew it squeaked but damn! When I started ripping up the loose boards, the beams underneath were completely rotted through."

"Oh."

"I've still got to replace the steps but figured you'd need to be able to get in the front door, so I'll do them tomorrow."

"Good call. But you know you don't have to do this. It's your day off. Shouldn't you be sleeping or washing your truck or doing whatever it is guys do on their time off?"

He shrugged off my question like it was nothing. It wasn't nothing. It was everything. The man was building me a damn porch. "I'm going to need your input on what new railing you want. And I think you should put one down the steps."

"I can do that. But first, I need to eat. Come on inside and help me eat all this food before I make myself sick."

"You don't have to feed me, Lily."

"And you don't have to build me a porch, but here you are. So, get your cute butt inside."

"I'm filthy!"

"I'm counting on it."

Trying to look sexy with a run in your stockings and arm in a sling wasn't easy, but I put as much sway into my hips as I could muster. I could hear Zach chuckling behind me which made me feel a bit better. The first time in a couple of days if I was being honest.

"Have I got time to give Ava a bath and clean up first?"

How could I say no? He was a complete mess and watching him give Ava a bath could make this bad day a whole lot better. Besides, Chinese food reheated. "Absolutely."

"Come on then, pretty girl. Let's go get you cleaned up."

Unsnapping his tool belt, Zach carried Ava towards the bathroom, and I heard the water running. After dumping the food in the kitchen, I ducked into my bedroom to change. Standing there in my underwear, staring at the cupboard, I had no idea what to put on. I needed to look cute but not like I was trying to look cute. Flipping through the rack of clothes, I hadn't found anything when I heard Zach bellowing.

"Lil! Need some help in here!"

"Coming," I replied, racing through the house.

Rounding the corner, I stepped into the bathroom and burst into a fit of hysterical laughter. There was no way I couldn't. The look on Zach's face was priceless.

"What happened?" I spluttered, covering my mouth to stop the giggles.

"She exploded. Everywhere! I'm covered in shit!"

Zach was flustered. I'd never seen him like this. It was so damn adorable. The guy ran into burning buildings for a living, had muscles on top of muscles but had been bought to his knees by Ava's poo explosion. Ava was smiling and babbling away to herself, looking completely unaffected by the whole situation.

"Can you please stop laughing and help me?"

"What do you want me to do?"

"Get this shit off me!"

"Oh, calm down. It's just a bit of poo," I snickered, opening the drawer and pulling out a couple of wash cloths – there was no way one was going to cut it.

"Just a bit of poo? It's running down my leg and into my sock!"

"Oh, poor baby. Now move over so I can get to the tap."

Holding the cloth under the warm water, I started cleaning Ava up while she squirmed in Zach's arms. He was holding her out in front of him, elbows locked and deep-set scowl on his face. If he was trying to express his disappointment to her, then she completely missed the point.

It wasn't until I looked up in the mirror and caught Zach shooting me an evil glare that I realized I was standing there in my underwear. Only my underwear. Could this day get any worse? I didn't think it could.

Once Ava was clean, Zach looked at me like he was waiting for instructions. "Let me grab a diaper and then we can set her down in her crib."

"What about me?"

"What about you?"

"Don't I get a sponge bath too?"

"You're not a little kid," I confirmed.

"Nothing little about me," Zach replied confidently with a wink. "But I do need to get cleaned up."

"Well, big boy, I'm sure you can handle it."

It took us almost half an hour for the three of us to get cleaned up, dressed and sitting down to eat. Ava was lying on her mat gnawing on her own fist. I drained the last drop from my wine glass and got up to get a refill.

"Want another beer?"

"Nah. I'm fine, thanks though."

"Well, I need one," I explained, refilling my glass almost to the top. I don't know why people even bothered to have gigantic wine glasses if they only half filled them. Seemed like a waste to me.

"Rough day?" Zach asked as I flopped back onto the couch.

"You have no idea."

"Wanna talk about it?"

"Maybe after. I need food first," I deflected, trying to buy myself some time. The last thing I wanted to do was dump my problems on him.

Although he didn't look convinced, Zach accepted my decision and heaped a spoonful of rice onto my plate. "Well then, eat up."

I ate until I almost burst. I didn't know why I did this to myself. I knew I needed to stop. But it was always one more mouthful or one more egg roll. The problem was, when it came to Chinese food and chocolate, my will power was zilch. Leaning back against the cushions on the couch, I rubbed my very full belly. I closed my eyes just for a second, and when I opened them up again, all the dirty dishes had been put away, there was a blanket pulled over me, and there was no sign of Zach. He was gone. Without even saying goodbye, he'd left. And I felt like complete shit.

29

ZACH

LILY WAS A STRANGE CREATURE. SHE'D BARELY SET HER FORK DOWN before she started snoring on the couch. Creeping around her as quietly as I could, I cleaned up, checked on Ava before heading back outside to tidy up the mess that had been her front porch, and pack away my tools for the night. While I wasn't completely happy with the progress I'd made this afternoon, I'd worked some of the frustration out of my now-aching muscles and had something to actually show for it, not just sore knuckles from taking it out on the boxing bag hanging in my garage.

As beautiful as Lily was, she looked shattered. Haunted even. Something was stressing her out and sapping all her energy, and every bone in my body was telling me to find whatever was making her miserable and fix it.

In my pocket my phone buzzed again. It'd been going off all day and I'd ignored it. At first it was because of the bloody hang-over I was suffering through. Now, it was because the last thing I wanted to do was talk about it. I knew I'd have to at some point, but not right now. I had three days off and I wasn't going to waste them talking about my feelings.

I was just stacking the last of my tools into the back of my truck when Lily appeared at the top of the steps looking sleepy and stunning.

"You're leaving?"

"Just heading home for the night. I'll be back in the morning to keep going. I can't leave your porch like that."

"No, I guess not."

Walking back up the path to where Lily was standing, I watched as she folded her arms across her chest, propping her boobs up. Most of the time I was pretty sure she wasn't even aware what she was doing. It was no wonder so many guys at the station were giving me shit about her. They were just jealous bastards, and I was well aware I was a lucky son of a bitch.

"Does seven work for you?"

"Seven?" Lily looked confused as she shivered. As night had fallen so had the temperature, and the breeze was making it quite cool. She needed to be tucked up back inside where she wouldn't catch a chill.

"In the morning? If I can get an early start, I'm thinking I can rip out the steps and put them back in before you get home."

"All in one day?"

"Yeah. It's not too big of a job. And I've got all the stuff, so should be fine."

"How much is this going to cost me?" Lily asked, her voice wavering slightly.

"Cost you? Nothing. There's no way I'd charge you. I'm doing a friend a favor." Even as I said it, I realized how much I hated it. The last thing I wanted to be was Lily's friend, but if that's all that was on offer, then I was taking it. Not having her as part of my life wasn't an option now.

Lily must've picked up on my word choice too. Like the seductive siren she is, Lily carefully stepped down off the porch, cradling her arm as she moved towards me, her hooded eyes locked with mine.

"And what if I don't want to be your friend?"

"You don't want to be my friend?"

"No, Zach. I don't want to be your friend. Actually, the last thing I want to be is your friend."

"Okay then." I gulped, waiting for the kicker.

"I want to be yours. I want to be able to hold your hand in the street without second guessing it. I want to order Chinese takeout for two…"

"I thought you already did that?" I teased, earning me a very much deserved slap to the stomach.

Reaching out, I grabbed the hand she'd hit me with and yanked her forward until her chest was crushed against mine, mindful of her arm. "Are you saying, Lily Evans, that you want to be my girlfriend?"

"I don't know. Do you want to be my boyfriend, Zach Higgins?"

Lily looked up at me, her eyes twinkling with mischief. "Fuck yeah I do," she confirmed no louder than a whisper before she jumped up, throwing her good arm around my neck and twining her legs around my hips before capturing my lips in the most intense kiss of my life. One that nearly had my knees buckling as I palmed her ass.

Eventually we pulled apart puffing and panting. "So, you're my girlfriend."

"I guess I am."

"And is there a policy about sleepovers with your girlfriend?" I asked, rocking my hips, nudging my growing erection against her pussy. Even through the thin material of her clothes, I could still feel her heat.

Leaning down, Lily nibbled on my earlobe, earning her a squeeze of her ass cheeks. "It's compulsory," she confirmed.

"Thank fuck for that," I growled, carrying her inside and throwing her down on the bed.

The first round was hard, hot and needy and over way too quickly for a grown man. But after a short intermission, I was up and raring to go for round two and, this time, I was going to make it count. Using my tongue, fingers and cock, I wanted to prove to Lily how much she meant to me and how much I treasured her. But soft and steady weren't Lily's strong points. Even though it started out that way, the closer she got to her crescendo, the more feral she became. And when she clamped down on my cock as I drove inside her, she milked everything I had from me, leaving me sated, satisfied and sleepy.

It was almost midnight and we'd just climbed back into bed after a shower. Lily had dropped to her knees and got very dirty before letting me clean her up. Seeing cum marking her tits made me almost beat my chest and go all Tarzan on her. Now she was lying in my arms, her head resting against my chest while her fingers traced small circles on my stomach.

"Are you sure about this?" she asked timidly. Gone was all the confidence and all the bravado. Lying there in the dark, stark naked, Lily wasn't so sure anymore.

"Absolutely."

"Good."

"You?"

"Mmmm." It wasn't exactly the heart-stopping, life-affirming declaration I'd been hoping for, but I was taking her sleepy agreement as enough.

"Wanna tell me about your bad day?"

It was late and I should've let her sleep, but if something was bugging her, I didn't want her fretting. And if she told me now, tomorrow would be better. I was going to make sure of it.

"It doesn't matter," she deflected.

"Of course it does, Lil. If something or someone's upsetting you, then you share it with your boyfriend. It's a rule."

"I didn't realize there were so many rules to this girlfriend boyfriend thing. Maybe you should write them down for me, you know. So I don't forget."

"You won't forget," I assured her. "Besides, if you do, I'll spank your ass, so you remember next time." Feeling her shiver in my arms was all the assurance I needed to know she wasn't completely turned off by the idea. She liked it, a lot. "Now, spill. What happened today that made your day so shitty?"

"It was nothing really. I was just being silly."

"No, you weren't. You're not silly, Lily. Nothing you do is."

"I just got a call from Child Services about my adoption application for Ava."

"And?" Now I was well and truly wide awake. No wonder she'd been off balance. I hadn't even taken the call and already I was sitting up a little straighter.

"They want to do a home visit," she continued.

"That's good, isn't it?"

"Yes and no. I don't know."

"What's got you worried about it?" I probed, needing to get to the bottom of the actual problem.

"What if... what if..."

"If what?"

"What if they don't like me? What if I'm not enough? What if they take her away?"

Lily pulled out of my arms and climbed out of bed. I watched as she moved around the room, only illuminated by the moonlight spilling through the gap in the blinds. When she pulled a shirt over her head, she sat down on the end of the bed and turned back to face me. I hated the distance between us. This wasn't how this conversation was supposed to go. She was supposed to stay in my arms and together we'd figure it out. I'd assure her that she was everything Ava could ever need or want in this world and then Lily would feel better. Instead, she was moving away and getting dressed.

Sitting up, I arranged the blanket in my lap not needing my cock to pop out as a distraction right now. "Firstly, Lil, no one that's ever met you has ever not liked you. It's just not possible. You're the most amazing woman I've ever met. And I'm not just saying that because I'm sleeping in your bed. You're kind and compassionate. You care about people. And not just in that fake pretend-to-care way either, you really do care."

"You believe that, don't you?"

"One hundred percent. As for not being enough, how could you not be? Ava is happy, safe and loved. She has everything she needs, including the most important thing in the world…"

"What's that?"

"Someone who wants her. Someone who wants to see her succeed. Someone who'd move heaven and earth to help her achieve her dreams. Someone who will stand by her no matter what. Someone who will stand in front of her and defend her until her dying breath. And someone who loves her. Unconditionally."

"You really think I'm all that?" Lily raised her hand to her face and wiped away what I imagined were tears.

I was over the distance. It was bullshit and it wasn't working for me. Snagging her ankle, I dragged her over the covers until she was back where she belonged. Wrapped in my arms. "No, Lil. I don't think you're all that."

"You don't?" She tried to pull away again, but this time, I wasn't letting her go.

"You're more. And you're going to give that little girl the world. I know you will."

"How do I convince them of that?"

I wished I had the answer to that one, I really did. "You just be you. They'll see it. I'm sure of it." God, I hoped I was right. I couldn't imagine what would happen if they didn't.

"Thank you, Zach. You know, you're pretty amazing yourself."

Shrugging my shoulder, I grabbed the hem of her shirt and dragged it up over her head, exposing her to the cool night air before rearranging the covers back over her.

"Yeah, I know. But right now, as awesome as I am, I need to get some sleep. My new boss, she worked me pretty hard today. First with construction on her front porch and then she turned demanding between the sheets too. I don't know if I can keep up with her."

Lily's hand snaked down my chest and wrapped around my cock. "I'm pretty sure you can keep up with her anytime."

If Lily was going to throw down a challenge like that, then I was definitely going to rise to the occasion. And just like the good little soldier he was, he did just that.

30

LILY

ZACH AND I QUICKLY FELL INTO A ROUTINE. HE'D CLIMB OUT OF BED IN the morning and make breakfast while I got Ava organized, and then we'd sit down and eat together, family style. Over coffee and waffles, he'd pepper me with questions he insisted I make the final decisions on, so he could keep going on the porch. True to his word, yesterday he'd carried us down the steps and then ripped them out. By the time I got home, new, non-squeaky and sturdy steps replaced the old rickety ones. Then we'd argue over dinner about Zach going home, and each night I'd win the argument and he'd crawl into bed beside me.

Today was going to be different though and I wasn't sure I was ready. He was going back to work today so there'd be no hot tradie out the front of my place and no reason for me to hurry home just to see him covered in sweat and dust, those tattoos glistening in the dying afternoon sunlight.

Over coffee this morning, something had been up with him, but he was being tight lipped. He kept changing the subject back to me and Ava. She hadn't had a good night. Actually, that was an under-statement, she'd had a perfectly shitty night. After throwing up all over herself and all through her crib, she'd turned into a clinging koala, at least that's what Zach kept calling her. But sadly, only to him. Every time he went to set her down or hand her over to me, she screamed even louder. In the end, somewhere around four, we'd given up and Zach had spent the rest of the night on the couch with Ava sleeping soundly on his chest. Lucky girl. But even though they'd passed out, I hadn't managed to turn my brain off so I could get some sleep. It went into overdrive. With the home visit from Child Services only days away, this was what I was afraid of. Not being what Ava needed. Tonight was yet another example. She didn't want me. She wanted Zach. What happened when he wasn't here? Was she just going to scream and screech until she went hoarse?

Now I was at work, Sage and Linda were babbling incessantly about I don't even know what, and Ava was passed out in her portable crib in the back room which had become her second bedroom.

"Have you got the flowers for Mrs. Margaret?" Linda asked, leaning on my workbench which was buried under a pile of crap.

Usually I was organized, tidy and everything had its place, but today, like everything else, it'd gone to shit. There were flowers falling on the floor, a puddle of water on the bench and the pink ribbon I'd thrown in my tantrum was balled up in the corner. I was so fucking over this sling. It was driving me batty. Pulling it off, slowly I stretched my arm out waiting for the pain to shoot up my arm. It ached but nothing I couldn't manage. Besides, the pain was the lesser of the two evils.

"Mrs. Margaret?" I asked, having absolutely no idea what Linda was on about.

"Yes. The bunch of colorful flowers ordered by her daughter Sarah to be delivered to the hospital. Apparently, she's taken a tumble and broken her hip."

Ah yes. Those flowers. "Can you give me twenty minutes?" I asked, embarrassed.

I was better than this. I was. I knew I was. I just had to get my shit together and get back on track and I'd be fine.

"Sure. I'll go..."

"Actually, Linda?"

"Yes?"

"Would you mind doing me a favor?" I was embarrassed to ask, but one thing I was learning, even though it was possibly the hardest lesson ever, was asking for help didn't make you weak. It didn't make you a failure. If anything, asking for help made you strong and, I was hoping, could make my life just a little easier.

"Absolutely, Lily. What do you need?"

A month off? A hug? A bottle of vodka? A week of really good sex? Eight hours of uninterrupted sleep? A maid? No. Even though the ideas went through my head, I wasn't going to voice any of them. Especially not to Linda.

"Would you mind having a look at the order book and getting together a list of what else we need for today? I need to get this place sorted out. Having stuff everywhere isn't working for me and I want to see if we can smash out what we need to and close early so I can tidy up a bit."

"Tidy up a bit? Did you just say tidy up a bit?" Sage asked, butting into the conversation as she stashed her phone in her back pocket.

"Yes. Since I decided to, rearrange... yeah, rearrange, let's go with that, I can't find anything. It takes me forever to get stuff done and I need that stock room put back together," I admitted, grabbing a handful of white roses from the bucket, pricking my finger on the thorns "Bitch!" I muttered to myself, popping my now-bleeding finger into my mouth.

Sage and Linda exchanged glances before giving each other a high five. "Hallelujah!" Sage exclaimed dramatically.

"What?" I asked, not really liking the fact they had inside jokes I wasn't a part of. I knew I was the boss and I wasn't going to always be included, but I didn't think this place was like that. At least I hoped it wasn't. I wanted us to be a family or, at the very least, friends.

"We've been dying to do this for a couple of days but didn't know when you were going to let us," Linda offered.

"So, you hate it too?" I asked, shocked. Neither of them had said a word about my purging binge, other than the constant nagging about taking it easy and not overdoing it.

"So much!" Sage's bluntness was reassuring.

"Okay then. That's the plan. First, we get the orders done, then we put this place back together," I declared, feeling a little lighter now I knew a solution was in sight.

"Don't forget to schedule lunch in there somewhere. I'm starving."

"You're always starving, Sage," Linda scolded. I wondered if Linda had seen Sage's idea of a well-balanced meal yet. Unless it was smothered in cheese or deep fried, Sage didn't want to know about it. It was disgusting and I was jealous as hell. If I ate even a quarter of the shit she did, my butt would be the size of a bus, but somehow Sage never put on a pound.

We did it. Well almost. After getting all the orders sorted, Sage and Linda both took off to do deliveries and organize lunch. As soon as they were out the door, I flicked the lock and closed for the afternoon. Even though I told them repeatedly I was fine, my arm was aching. Digging a couple of pain killers out of my bag, I downed them quickly before dragging a stool into the back room where Ava was chewing quietly on the pink stuffed rabbit Linda had bought her.

Taking advantage of the quiet, I dug my phone from my bag and checked my social media accounts. I hadn't posted in a while, but when I clicked on my profile, I saw the word 'single' staring back at me and realized how much I hated it. I wasn't single. Not anymore. I had a real boyfriend. He was a hot-as-hell, tattooed firefighter who I couldn't get enough of. Feeling slightly drunk on the knowledge that Zach was mine, I updated my status to being in a relationship. Then the option came up to add who I was in that relationship with. Not sure I had the balls to go that far, I set it down on the bench and leaned into Ava's crib.

After changing her diaper, something I was mastering with one hand, I went back out the front and looked around. I had absolutely no idea where the hell to start. How I'd made such a mess of everything, I wasn't sure.

Picking up the bin, I set it down next to my bench and started throwing shit out. If it was broken, busted or ugly, in it went. Next, I started emptying buckets and washing them out, but it was way too quiet in here. I didn't want to annoy Ava, not when she was likely to drop back off to sleep any minute now, but the quiet wasn't inspiring me. Instead, I started singing to myself.

"Wow! And here I was thinking a cat was being murdered in the back lane."

Spinning around, I saw Sage standing there smirking. I would've killed her but when I spotted the paper bag in her hands with the Hooligans logo on it, I changed my mind. Hooligans takeout was possibly the best thing to happen to me today. Well, the best after the incredible orgasm Zach had coaxed from my body just before dawn.

"Burgers?" I asked excitedly.

"And fries and milkshakes."

"Do you know how much I love you right now?" I declared, heading over to the sink and washing my hands, my stomach growling loudly.

"Yeah, yeah. And if Phoebe walked in here right now with a hunk of chocolate cake, I'm sure you'd say the same thing to her."

"Not likely," I grumbled.

It was no secret Phoebe and I weren't best friends. It wasn't that we hated each other or there was really a reason for us not to be, it just was what it was. We were civil and polite, but we weren't planning on having a slumber party anytime soon.

"What's not likely?" Linda asked as she breezed through the back door, dumping her purse on my now-clear work bench.

"Phoebe and Lily being besties."

"Ah, yeah. I can't imagine that would happen. Especially not now."

"What do you mean especially not now?" I asked, reaching for a handful of fries and stuffing them in my mouth.

"Ah..."

"What have you heard, Linda?" Sage prompted, jumping up and sitting on the edge of the bench before taking a massive bite of her burger.

"Oh, I'm sure it's just gossip."

"Even so, I need to know any and all town gossip," Sage insisted.

"It's nothing. It's just from what I heard, Phoebe's had a thing for Zach for a while." Linda looked over at me, her apologetic eyes making me feel sorry for her.

"Oh that. Don't worry about that. That's old news." Sage dismissed it like it was nothing. "Everyone in town knows about her crush."

"They do?" I asked, my voice catching.

"Ah, yeah."

"Well, I didn't," I snapped, feeling like shit. How did I not know this? Did I live under a rock?

"Well, that's because, Lily, you're too nice of a person to get caught up in gossip. Well, that and the fact you pretty much have your head up your..."

Sage didn't need to finish her sentence. We all knew what she was getting at.

"Do not!"

"Do too. When was the last time you went out?" Sage challenged. I opened my mouth to reply, but she lifted her hand, cutting off my answer. "And the speed dating thing that I dragged you kicking and screaming to doesn't even count."

I pouted.

I know I did. Because she was right. I did live under a rock. Under there was a nice place to be sometimes. There was no drama. No backstabbing bitches. No problems. I'd dealt with enough of them already in life. I was so ready for a calm and easy couple of years. If there was such a thing.

"Anyway, it doesn't matter. Lily and Zach are together now, so it doesn't really matter what Phoebe thinks or wants," Linda stated, sounding just like a mom.

"You know?"

"Know what, dear?"

"That Zach and I are together?"

Linda smiled around her straw as she sipped her milkshake. "Sweetheart, I knew you were together before you two did."

"Lily, hate to break it to you, but we all did."

"Oh."

"Yeah, oh. Now, why don't you strut your sexy ass down the road and see that delicious hunk of man meat of yours and ask him if he can bring his tool here after work and help you screw something?"

"Sage!" I can't believe she'd say something like that, especially in front of Zach's mother. Oh wait. It was Sage. It's exactly something she'd say in front of his mother.

"What? Someone needs to put those shelves back up, preferably straight this time. And from what I hear, Zach's good with his hands."

"Oh my god! If you stop talking, I'll go."

"Good. You might want to wipe the ketchup off your face before you get there though."

Grabbing a wad of napkins, I wiped at my face like a mad woman only to have Sage snickering. "That was mean," Linda told her before turning her attention back to the counter.

"You two suck."

"So do you. Now, go talk to lover boy and see if he can help you."

"What about…"

"What about what? What excuse are you trying to use this time?" Geez the sass in Sage was strong today.

"Ava," I replied, like duh.

"Ava's fine… I've got her. You go see Zach. Tell him I said hi,"

Linda assured me, nudging me towards the door and handing me my purse.

Knowing I had pretty much no chance of winning this argument, I threw my hands up in the air, defeated. "Fine! Fine! I'm going."

"Good. See you in a bit." Sage skipped around.

Standing out on the street in front of my store, I stared down the road. Digging my sunglasses out of my bag, I started walking. It wasn't far and it was a beautiful day, I was going to enjoy the ten minutes of peace and quiet while I could.

Rounding the corner, Station 13 came into sight and my heart took off. I was excited to see Zach. It'd been less than six hours and forty-five minutes since he'd kissed me goodbye, but I missed him already. I couldn't wait for him to come over tonight so we could snuggle on the lounge. For someone so hard and lean, Zach was the best snuggler.

The rig was parked out the front and the crew were crawling all over it. Everything was open and someone, I think it was Samuels, was holding the hose, but I couldn't see Zach and, trust me, there's no way I'd miss him. I'd spent hours studying the ink on his arms, wondering why he got certain symbols and the meaning behind them. There was no way I wasn't going to see them.

Then, like the heavens had opened for me, God's gift sauntered around the back of the rig, looking all sorts of hot. Zach Higgins was every woman's fantasy. Well, he was definitely mine. In his turnout pants and tight navy station t-shirt with his aviators covering his eyes, my mouth watered and I almost tripped over my own feet. Coming to a stop, I forced myself to take a breath before I ended up face first on the pavement.

"Bout time, kangaroo boy," I heard someone tease before tossing something at him. Something Zach caught easily and set down beside his feet.

"Yeah, yeah. What'd I miss?" Zach's deep baritone made my steps hasten. It was like I couldn't get to him quick enough.

Turns out, I wasn't the only one.

As I went to cross the road, a cab pulled in front of me, coming to a halt at the station. When it moved on, I had enough time to hear the shriek before a tiny blonde bombshell wearing black leather pants and a blush-pink sweater, one tight enough even I could see from here how perfect it fit her, threw herself into Zach's arms.

Hugging her tight, Zach growled. "What are you doing here?"

"Didn't you miss me?"

"Like you'd never believe."

I felt sick. Like someone had kicked me in the stomach. I had to get out of there. Turning back the way I came, I jogged along the road, avoiding as many people and dodging as many conversations as I could. Right now, I had no words. I felt like the rug had just been pulled out from under me. No. it was worse than that, I felt like a loser the world was laughing at. At least, my world was laughing at me.

I made it back to the store in record time and fell through the door, leaning my back against it and sliding down. My dramatic entrance and the ringing of the bells caught Sage and Linda's attention. I didn't think I could handle one of their interrogations right now. I just wasn't up for it. And Linda, what the hell was I supposed to say to her? Zach was her son. Her only son. A wave of dizziness washed over me, and I dropped my head between my knees and focused on my breathing. I didn't need to fall apart right now. I couldn't. I had people counting on me to hold my shit together. Ava was counting on me. And unlike Zach Higgins, I didn't let people down.

"Oh sweet! You're back. Although have to admit, that was a much quicker quicky than I thought, but yay! You're here. What time's Zach stopping by to fix these shelves. We've come up with an awesome idea," Sage babbled.

"He's not."

"He's not, what?"

"Zach's not coming. I'll call a carpenter tomorrow."

"Why isn't Zach coming? You're his girlfriend. Installing

shelves is definitely a boyfriend's job. If he's slacking already, Lil, then maybe..."

"Well maybe you should go explain to him the rules of being a boyfriend, Sage. Don't forget to include the 'you don't make out with blondes who aren't your girlfriend on the street' too."

"He didn't?" Sage asked, dropping the bucket full of soapy water she'd been carrying and splashing it all over the floor. "He wouldn't. No. Zach's not like that."

"Not like what?" Linda asked, appearing from the back, Ava in her arms.

I reached for my girl, and Linda handed her over without question. I needed her right now. I needed Ava to ground me.

"Apparently Zach's a cheating scumbag."

31

ZACH

From the moment I left Lily's place, today had been an absolute shit show.

I'd gotten to the station right on time, which was my first mistake. On any normal day, showing up on time I would've considered being late. I was always, every single shift, at least twenty minutes early, but today, I just didn't want to. For the last couple of days, I busted my ass trying to get Lily's porch finished and I still hadn't, which just pissed me off. But that wasn't the cause of the thorn in my side. No, that was this morning's meeting.

I'd barely gotten through the door when Collins and Malone were in my face, both pissed because I'd ignored their messages for the last few days.

"Your phone broken, Higgins?"

"No. Just needed a few days."

"Well Chief wants to see you before you head out today."

"I'm sure he does."

"Stop being a dick, Higgins. People around here were worried about you after what happened, and then you went off the grid."

"I'm fine," I spat out through gritted teeth.

I wasn't fine, but I wasn't about to tell them that. Frankly, it was none of their business. All they needed to know was when the time came, I had their back and I hoped they had mine. Apparently, that wasn't enough.

"Sure you are," Collins tossed out before Malone shot him a look that silenced him and had him excusing himself.

"Look, Higgins, I know we don't know each other that well and you're still new around here, but I wasn't always this awesome. A few years back, two of us went into a building, but only one came out. I was pretty badly injured and for a long time I let my scars rule my life. Dylan was actually the one who basically told me to pull my head out of my ass."

"Shit, man. I had no idea."

"Why would you? Anyway, the point of my story isn't to get your sympathy."

"I wasn't—"

"Yes, you were. It's written all over your face."

"Sorry."

"Don't be. But the point is, eventually I talked. And you need to as well."

"I'm…"

"Fine. Yeah, I know you are. But, Zach, you didn't move. Standing outside that building you didn't suit up. You didn't follow procedure. And that's not like you."

I hung my head in shame. Everything he said was true. In the moment it mattered, I was useless. I didn't grab my equipment and I didn't follow them towards the house. Instead, I stood there, unblinking unable to look away. My legs were like cement. I couldn't move even if I'd wanted to. The call had come through, and like all those calls that'd come before it, we suited up and headed out. The difference was this time when we arrived on scene everything was wrong.

The guy who'd called it in was out the front screaming. His wife and daughter were still inside and there were flames billowing from every window. Samuels and I had grabbed the guy, holding him back. He was determined to go in and save his family. His pained cries ripped my heart in two. He was a strong bastard, fighting to get free and run in. While I stood there holding him back, keeping him from helping the people he loved the most in the world, I couldn't help but think of Ava and Lily. If it'd been me in that guy's shoes, it would've taken the whole fucking national guard to stop me barreling in there, my own life be damned.

As the minutes ticked by, my hope and the fight within the guy faded. It was taking too long. They should've been out already. They should've been safe. Behind me the ambulance waited. Samuels and I started steering the guy, who was like a dead weight in our arms, towards the stretcher. He needed to be checked over for smoke inhalation but also, I had this disgusting feeling in the pit of my stomach that he was going to need help.

The guys started to get the fire under control but there was still no sign of his daughter or wife.

"How old is your daughter?" I asked nervously.

"Amber is six months old. She's the most beautiful little girl you've ever seen. She's always happy..." His voice broke as tears streamed down his face.

Six months. Shit. I'd been hoping he said six years. At least then she could run and would've had a fighting chance.

When they were found amongst the smoldering ashes, I didn't have the strength in my arms to hold him up any longer as he crumpled to the ground. He let out the most painful howl I could ever recall hearing, one that I was positive would haunt me for all my days.

"No one's judging you for not being okay, Zach. We just want to help you. So go, talk to Chief and do whatever he suggests. You did everything you could to save them. We did everything we could to save them. It was an accident. An electrical fault with the renovations is responsible for this tragedy, not you."

"I should've done something..."

"What? What more could you have done?"

"I...I...I don't know."

And that was the problem. For the last few days, whenever I

stopped, whenever silence engulfed me, that's what I was trying to figure out. What more could I've done? What more I should've done? But I still had nothing. Not one damn idea.

Grady clamped his hand down on my shoulder and squeezed. "You're a good guy, Higgins, and I know how much this is hurting you, but you have to move past it. If you don't... you'll destroy your future, and that would be a god damn shame."

Malone left me standing there, staring at my scuffed boots and replaying everything he'd said and everything that had happened. Even though in my head I knew he was right, my heart couldn't catch up.

Half my shift was wasted talking to the chief then the department psych they had on call. It didn't seem to matter how many times I told them I was fine; they weren't buying it. They wanted to know about my childhood and how I'd handled my father's death. Nosy bastards. At one point I wanted to pick up the computer screen and hurl it through the wall, but that would probably just prove their point that I was unhinged. The last thing I wanted to do right now was give them more ammunition.

At least it was a slow day and I didn't miss much. There was only one call out; a kid had got their fingers caught in the drain down at the local elementary school, so we'd gone to help. As soon as we'd pulled to a stop out the front, the rig was swamped by kids asking us to flash the lights or turn on the sirens.

Thankfully, by the time we made it back our shift was almost over. We were just doing final checks, making sure everything was stocked and ready for the next team when someone called my name.

Walking around the other side of the rig, I was stopped by the sight of a blonde I wasn't expecting to see any time soon.

Without waiting for even a hello, she threw herself towards me, catching me off guard, and although I stumbled back slightly, I managed to catch her and stay standing.

Hugging her tight, I growled. "What are you doing here?"

"Didn't you miss me?"

"Like you'd never believe."

To the whistles and cat calls of the guys who'd stopped what they were doing and were watching the show, I set her back on her feet. Damn she looked good. Happy almost. "Zach, I'm so glad to see you."

"Missed you too, Maddy. I can't believe you're really here."

"I know."

"Why didn't you tell me you were coming?" I asked.

Maddy looked vulnerable. Not something I was used to, and I didn't like it. Not one little bit. "I didn't want you to tell me not to."

"I'd never do that. You're my little sister. You're always welcome."

"Well, I'm glad you said that, big brother. Any chance you've got a spare bed at Casa Higgins? I need somewhere to crash."

"There's room in my bed for a pretty girl like you," Samuels smarmed as he stuck his hand out for Maddy to take.

I growled at him, but the asshole didn't even flinch. And Maddy, well she hadn't changed a bit either. She just smiled even wider at Samuels' shameless flirting.

"I might just take you up on that," Maddy replied, equally as flirty and offering him a wink.

Oh shit. Someone save me. If these two are already making eyes at each other I was going to need a drink.

"Maddy's staying at my place. Now, why don't you go put your bags in my truck, then we'll head over to Hooligans and grab a drink."

"Sounds great."

"I'll give Lily a call and see if she wants to join us."

"Who's Lily?"

"Lily's my—"

"Lily's his girlfriend and baby mama."

"WHAT!" Maddy's overly dramatic screech woke every dog in the surrounding neighborhood. "You're a dad? You didn't even tell me!"

"It's a long story," I offered, trying to calm her down.

"Well, it sounds like a long story that's going to need tequila. So, hurry up, big brother. I'm thirsty and you've got a story to tell."

"Let me help you with your bags," Samuels offered, picking up Maddy's bright pink suitcase.

I rolled my eyes. Could this day possibly get any freaking longer?

32

LILY

I WAS ON A MISSION; SORE ARM BE DAMNED. OKAY, MAYBE NOT BUT I wasn't letting it slow me down. Not today. While Ava lay on the floor on a patchwork quilt I'd found in the cupboard, one I remembered from my own childhood, I started purging. It was long overdue and strangely cathartic, but I wasn't slowing.

After I'd seen Zach fawning over the blonde with the perfect ass, I'd tried to get back to work at the store but Linda and Sage practically chased me out the door after I knocked over the third bucket of flowers, flooding the floor.

Annoyed at the world, I'd stopped by the grocery store and stocked up on supplies; chocolate, chips, cookie dough and ice cream, before coming home and attempting to eat my weight in sugar. It wasn't until I went to dig through the pantry looking for the chocolate icing I remembered buying that I started my cleaning binge. When I couldn't find it, I pulled everything out of the pantry, checking the use by dates and rearranging. After the pantry, feeling pretty good about myself, I moved on to the drawers filled with baking trays. Grandma could bake. She made the best shortbread cookies I'd ever had and even though we'd spent hours in the kitchen together, I'd never got the hang of it. Mine always turned out too dry and crumbly, or worse, too wet and flat. Knowing my skill set didn't including baking, I started throwing away pans that had seen their best years.

Grabbing another chocolate cookie, I popped it into my mouth as my phone chirped on the counter.

Zach: *Hey, pretty girl. Feel like dinner tonight at Hooligans?*

What was I supposed to say to that? Was the message even meant for me or some other 'pretty girl' in his life? Up until today, I thought I knew, but now, now I wasn't so sure.

Even though part of me wondered who the real Zach Higgins was, I knew he was determined. If I didn't reply, there was a very real possibility he'd just show up on my doorstep, looking as sexy as ever, and I'd instantly forget the reason I was angry with him. He had this magic power over me. One that made me forget myself and my own name with only a smile.

Lily: *Not tonight. Got a headache so having an early night. Have fun.*

"Hopefully that should keep him away," I told the room, setting my phone on silent and turning my attention onto to the linen cupboard.

I was trying to fold a fitted sheet when a knock at the door interrupted me. Groaning, I hoped it wasn't Zach, a thought that annoyed me because until I'd seen him with that woman wrapped in his arms, there was no one else I'd rather have standing on my porch.

"Just a minute," I called out, stepping over the mountain of old towels and threadbare sheets that were destined for the bin, making my way to the door.

Glancing around the room, I caught sight of my reflection and hesitated. I looked like shit. My hair was sticking out in every direction. I was sweaty, smelly and looking my absolute worst. Oh well, as Grandma would always say, 'if you can't love me at my worst, you don't deserve me at my best.'

Opening the door, I was relieved to see Linda standing there in her sweats.

"Linda, what are you doing here?"

"Checking on you, sweetheart. Can I come in?" Her voice was filled with that warm motherly tone and I realized that if I lost Zach from my life, that meant I lost Linda too, something I was sure I wasn't ready for. Somehow, she'd been the person I needed in my life when I didn't even know I needed her.

"Of course, please. And excuse the mess, I was…"

"You were?"

"Cleaning."

"Cleaning or avoiding?" Linda challenged.

"Both?"

"Thought so." Linda picked up the sheet I'd tossed on the sofa and folded it quickly.

"How did you do that?"

"Do what?"

"Fold a fitted sheet? Are you a witch or something? Those things are ridiculous."

"They're not so bad. Now, where's your sling, young lady?"

"Ah…"

"And why isn't it on your arm?"

"It was in the way and slowing me down, so I took it off. I think it's in the kitchen."

Linda marched past me before returning with the torture device and holding it out for me. Not wanting to piss her off, I slid it into place, adjusting the knot at my neck that kept getting caught in my hair.

"That's better. Now, sit down and tell me what's got you cleaning like a mad woman."

Dropping down into the couch, I wished I'd thought to pour myself a glass of wine. "Happy now?" I asked, hearing how horrible I sounded. Linda was the last person who deserved to be on the end of my snotty attitude. "I'm sorry," I apologized quickly.

"Don't even worry about it," she dismissed with a wave of her hand. "Now, what's wrong? And don't even bother to tell me it's nothing or you're fine, because I won't believe you."

She wouldn't either. And I wouldn't lie to her. I just wondered how much I could tell her without trashing her son.

"I just feel like a fool, that's all. Nothing a night of binge eating chocolate and keeping busy can't fix."

"Is that what you had for dinner?" Linda asked, pointing at the pile of chocolate wrappers and cookie crumbs on the coffee table.

"Ah…"

"Lily! That's no example to set for your daughter," Linda scolded, and I felt my cheeks burn with embarrassment. She was right. Eating your feelings wasn't healthy and not something I wanted Ava growing up to do.

"Sorry. It won't happen again."

"It will, but that's okay, Lily. You're not perfect. I know that might be hard to hear, especially when everyone in this town seems to think you're a saint, but you're not perfect. And no one expects you to be. You're human. You have faults and flaws just like the rest of us. It's what you do, who you are despite them that makes you someone to be proud of. And you, Lily Evans, are an incredible woman. You're kind, compassionate, caring and your Grandma would be so proud of you."

"You really think so?" I snorted through the runny nose.

"I know so."

Linda hugged me, squashing my arm between us and, despite the shooting pain, I didn't want her to let go. I needed her to hold me. To reassure me. To tell me that everything was going to be okay.

"Thank you."

"Anytime, sweetheart. Now, what did my idiot son do to upset you?"

"What makes you think I'm upset?" Linda gave me that 'you're kidding, right?' look which had me caving instantly. "It's nothing. Zach is…"

"Not here. So how about you tell me the real reason. And don't tell me you're still upset about what you saw this afternoon with the blonde. I'm sure once you spoke to Zach that was all sorted out very quickly… Wait! Lily, you did speak to Zach, didn't you?"

"Ah, well… not really."

"Not really? What does that even mean?"

"We exchanged messages but…"

"But you didn't ask him about it, did you?"

Shaking my head, I felt like a fool. I wasn't sure why I was insisting on playing these games. This wasn't high school. This was real life. My life. I should be better than this. I *was* better than this. Most of the time anyway.

"Oh, Lily. You need to talk to him. I'm sure there's a perfectly good explanation for whatever it is you think you saw."

"And what if there's not?" And that right there was the reason I hadn't gone and asked him in the first place. I wasn't sure if I wanted to know. I was terrified the truth was going to hurt more than what I already was.

"Let me ask you, why did you fall in love with my son in the first place?"

Wow! Talk about being put on the spot. "I don't… I didn't say…"

"Yeah, yeah. You two haven't exchanged I love yous yet, but it's obvious you do. So, what is it about Zach that made you love him?"

As much as it pained me to admit it, Linda was right. I did love Zach, and maybe that's why this hurt so bad. Why I was acting like such a brat. Why I was hiding from my problems. "Because he's kind. And he's real. And he's got a good heart. And he's… he's a good man."

"And do you think he's any less of those things after what you saw today? Keep in mind, you don't really know what you saw."

"No."

Linda was right. I didn't know the real story behind the woman at the fire station and until I did, I was going to keep dreaming up scenarios in my mind and torturing myself.

"Then you need to talk to him."

"You're right. I do. But maybe tomorrow. I'm a mess."

"Sounds like a good plan to me."

"Thank you, Linda. And not just for tonight either. Thank you for everything. Without you helping me for the past couple of weeks, everything would've..."

"Worked out anyway," she finished for me.

"Not what I was going to say. What I was going to say though, was everything would've been so much harder without you. I wish there was a way I could repay your kindness."

"There is." Linda smiled softly, not missing a beat.

"What's that? Name it and it's yours."

"I need a cuddle from my granddaughter before she goes to bed." Linda smiled, looking over at Ava who was chewing on her teddy bear's ear.

"Granddaughter?" I choked, bending down and scooping her up; something I was getting rather good at with only one arm.

"Yes. Granddaughter."

I placed her in Linda's arms and watched her dote over the precious little girl. It was amazing. A month ago, I didn't have Ava in my life and now I couldn't imagine a world that didn't revolve around her. So much of my calm, orderly world had been upended, including a move across town, but I wouldn't change a thing. Ava was everything I ever wanted and never thought I'd have the chance to have. Giving her up wasn't an option.

Sarah had warned me this would happen. That I'd fall in love with her and when the time came for her to go to her forever home, I wouldn't be able to say goodbye. She'd even questioned me when I'd signed the paperwork to be a foster carer. But I'd known better. I'd sworn I'd be able to do whatever was best for the child. I truly believed I would. And to some extent, I still did. The difference was, I truly believed I was what was best for Ava. No one would ever love her like I did. Now I just had to prove it.

"Are you okay with her?" I asked, looking at Linda.

"Absolutely."

"Great. I'm just going to go unpack a few more boxes, if that's okay?" I confirmed, eyeing the towering pile of boxes still filling my living room. If Child Services were going to come and do a home inspection, then they were going to look at my home, not the storage shed we were living in.

"Should you be moving them with your arm?"

Probably not. "I'm fine," I lied, focusing on carefully opening the first box before shoving it along the carpet into the spare bedroom.

Two hours later and Ava was tucked up in bed, while Linda and I hauled the last of the unwanted blankets out to the living room so I could put them in the car and take down to goodwill tomorrow.

"Coffee?" I asked as I moved into the kitchen.

"No thanks. It's late. If I have a coffee now, I won't sleep tonight."

"Good thinking." I hadn't even thought about that. My brain was in a fog and I wasn't thinking more than one step at a time.

"Actually, Lily, I had an idea I was wondering if I could run by you," Linda asked, sliding onto the bar stool at the kitchen bench. She was a sweaty, disheveled mess. I probably was too, but she looked nervous. Like she was afraid to ask me whatever it was that was playing on her mind.

Handing her a bottle of water, I took a long chug from mine before jumping up onto the bench. "What's up?"

"Your apartment. The one above the store. Were you thinking of keeping that?"

"Are you interested?"

"If you're looking to rent it out. My lease is up next month and since I spend all my time in Sunnyville anyway, I'd talked to Zach about moving over here. He was surprisingly fine with it."

"Of course he was fine with it. You're his mother. He moved halfway around the world to be closer to you. He's not going to baulk about living in the same town."

"Yeah, you're probably right. But while I'm sure he's okay with us living in the same town, I'm not sure us living under the same roof is the best idea."

"Then the apartment is yours," I confirmed.

Having Linda living there was a relief. While I hadn't been in a hurry to do anything with it, having it resolved was one less thing I had to worry about, and I was a big fan of that. She'd be the ideal tenant too. No loud parties. She knew the shop hours and what it was like downstairs, so she wasn't likely to complain. She was meticulously clean, almost to the point of hospital-grade cleanliness. And most importantly, I trusted her.

"We still need to sort out rent and utilities…"

"We can do that. But for now, here," I handed her a chocolate bar. "Instead of champagne. Welcome to the neighborhood."

"You're sure about this? I mean, really sure? I don't want you just saying yes because I'm Zach's mom. You need to be certain this is what you want."

"Linda, the place is yours. For as long as you want it. We'll work out the finances, but I'm not worried. You can move in whenever you want. I'd offer to help you, but I don't know I'd be much use until I get this damn thing off my arm."

Linda set her half-eaten chocolate bar on the bench and moved towards me. Feeling this was a moment, I slid down the bench and reluctantly set my own chocolate aside. She wrapped me in a hug so tight it brought tears to my eyes. Not from the pain, but from the comfort that overwhelmed me. There was no doubt in my mind, I'd made the right call. No matter what happened between Zach and I in the future, I was setting up my life, Ava's life to be the brightest I could make it.

33

ZACH

Now I remember why I don't party with Maddy. Chick is wild. And not in a good way. I'd tried to get some food into her between shots, and I think she ate maybe a handful of fries, but then the dancing started. Maddy was as outgoing as you could imagine. At least she was when she was full of booze and let loose. I still had no idea why she'd shown up out of the blue like this, but I knew she'd been going through a rough time for the last couple of months.

I don't remember everything that happened last night, probably a good thing, but I do remember warning Samuels that if he so much as looked at Maddy like that, I was going to cut off his hand and slap him in the face with it.

"Morning," Maddy grumbled as she strode into the kitchen wearing only a t-shirt and a pair of sunglasses. If only the magazines could see her now. The soapie star wasn't so glamourous after a night out.

"You're trouble," I told her, blaming her for the pounding migraine I was rocking. The idea of climbing back into bed and sleeping the day away sounded so good, but I was on shift in... "Shit!"

"What?"

"I'm going to be late. I start work in ten minutes."

"Sucks to be you."

"You know what, Maddy? Sometimes you can be a real bitch."

She shrugged like it was water off a duck's back. I guess she'd been called worse. Hell, I'd called her worse, not that I was proud of it, but Maddy had this unique way of pushing every single one of my buttons at the same time just to see what happened.

"Takes one to know one," she sing-songed, cradling her mug like it held the cure to her hangover.

After a quick cold shower, I got dressed and was standing back in the kitchen in record time. While I tugged on my boots, Maddy poured coffee into my to-go cup. "Thanks. What are you going to do today?"

"I don't know. Maybe crash for another couple of hours then unpack. I don't know. What time do you finish?"

"Unpack? So, does that mean you're staying?"

"Well, ah. Maybe just for a couple of days. If that's okay?" she asked, her voice trembling.

"Mads, stay as long as you want. There's plenty of room here. But you should know…"

My phone rang and I waved her a goodbye as I jogged out to the truck. I was late, hungover and tired. Not to mention not looking forward to the ribbing the guys were going to give me about Maddy. I had a feeling it was going to be a very long day.

I was halfway through the most boring shift from hell when Mom appeared carrying a tray of snacks. The guys raced up, thanking her and ushering her through to the break room, but as I came out of the office I'd been doing paperwork in, I saw her smack away Collins' hand when he went to grab the jelly donut. That sucker was mine and Mom knew it.

"Hey, Mom. What's all this about?" I asked, snagging the donut and taking a huge bite.

"I actually came to see if you had a second?"

My heart sank and panic took over. No conversation that ever started with, 'have you got a second' or 'we need to talk' ended well. I glanced around, and the guys got my unspoken message and made themselves scarce.

"Sure, what's up? Is everything okay?" I looked her over from head to toe. She looked okay, but I guess looks could be deceiving.

"Everything's fine. No, it's nothing like that. I've been talking to Lily…"

"Is she okay? She wasn't answering my calls or messages last night. Is it Ava? Shit! It's Ava, isn't it? Something's wrong, I know it. You can tell me, Mom; you need to tell me."

"Zach! Calm down and take a breath. Ava and Lily are both fine."

Phew! I don't know what the hell I would've done if something was wrong with them. I still didn't know why Lily was dodging my calls but I'd figure that out after work. I was not going out drinking tonight, no matter what Maddy suggested. I was picking up takeout and, with a little luck, spending a nice quiet night curled up on the couch with my girls.

"Oh. Okay."

"You seem relieved."

"That's an understatement," I admitted easily. I'd given up trying to fight the truth. Pretending to be tough and macho wasn't me, not when it came to them anyway.

"You really love them, don't you, Zach?"

"Yeah, I do."

"Have you told Lily?"

Rubbing that spot on my chest that was suddenly aching, I shook my head. I'd shown her, in every way I knew how, but I hadn't actually said the words. I didn't think I needed to.

"Well then, you need to go and talk to her. Sort out this… this silly misunderstanding so you can be happy. Be a family."

"Misunderstanding?" Now I was confused. What misunderstanding? Last time I'd seen Lily everything was good. Better than good. Everything was perfect. I couldn't have asked for anything more. Now Mom was telling me there was a misunderstanding that needed sorting out.

"Just talk to her, Zach."

"I will," I promised easily. There was no way I was going to rest until this was sorted. "Is that what you came to talk to me about?"

"Actually, no."

"Then what's up?" I popped the last bite of the donut into my mouth and licked the sugar from my fingers.

"I'm going to move into Lily's old apartment. The one above the florist."

"You're what?" I coughed. That wasn't what I was expecting.

"Lily's going to rent me the apartment. I can live here in Sunnyville but we can both still have our own space. I won't be under your feet all the time."

"Mom, you're never under my feet," I lied. It was just an itsy bitsy little white lie. It wouldn't hurt anyone. Sure, having Mom pretty much living in my house for the past few weeks had its downside, but it also had quite a few upsides. I was going to miss the clean piles of laundry on the end of my bed and the home cooked meals waiting for me when I came through the door after a long shift, but I understood. I was too old to live with my mother, and it really wasn't what I wanted, but I would've done it without complaint if it made her happy and kept her safe.

"We both know that's not true. But anyway…"

Before she could continue, the alarm sounded, and I had to get to work. "I'm sorry, Mom. Can we finish this later?"

I was already moving towards where my turnout gear was sitting, ready and waiting for me to pull on.

"Go! Do what you need. We'll talk later."

"Thanks, Mom," I leaned over and placed a quick kiss on her cheek.

"Be safe."

"Always," I assured her.

"It's all good, Mrs. Higgins. I got your boy's back. Two in. Two out. Always," Grady promised her before jumping into the front seat, me following hot on his heels. It was time to get to work.

As we flew through the streets towards the primary school, the sirens blaring and the lights flashing, I realized I hadn't told Mom Maddy was in town. "Fuck!" I was going to be in so much trouble for this one.

Kids, matches and dry grass were never a good combination. A group of ten-year-old misfits had stolen their fathers' cigarettes and tried smoking on the edge of the football field after practice. They'd tried and succeeded. What they hadn't been counting on was the wind igniting their forgotten smoke further than they'd intended. It only took us twenty minutes to put it out and less time than that for the culprits to be dobbed in and parents called. The way one of the mothers was storming across the field, hands on hips, nostrils flaring, I was glad as hell I wasn't one of the ones who was about to have his ass handed to him.

Grady, being the goodie two shoes he was, talked to the principal, smoothing things over and assuring him that no real damage was done. Then, for some unknown reason, the asshat decided to drop me in it, telling Principal Ward that I'd be more than happy to come and talk to the kids about fire safety.

"Why can't you do it?" I grumbled as I tossed my helmet on the back seat before climbing in after it. "It was your brilliant idea. You do it."

"Not a chance. Besides, Higgins, the kids will love that weird-ass accent of yours."

Flipping him the bird, I sunk into the seat and sulked. Now I had to figure out what to say to a room full of kids that didn't make me sound like an old condescending jerk. Fantastic. Like I didn't have enough problems.

"So Maddy…" Samuels started as we stripped out of our gear and set it up for the next call.

"Don't even go there. Not today," I grumbled.

"What's wrong, Skippy? Woman troubles?"

"I've got so many women causing my head to spin without Maddy's arrival. I'm not sure I can handle whatever shit she's here to stir up."

"Maddy seems like a great girl. A little wild, but she's young," Collins commented.

"She is. And I love her. I do. But damn is she a handful when she wants to be."

With a cocky smirk I wanted to wipe off his face, Samuels couldn't help himself. "I could take her off your hands for you. I mean, if you want."

The look I shot in his direction had him backing out of the room quickly.

Collins slapped me on the back. "Fuck, Skip. You're a scary bastard when you want to be. You know that?"

They had no idea.

The women in my life might drive me to the very edge of sanity and sometimes over the edge, but I'd protect them, I'd defend them, and I'd love them until my dying breath. I only had to survive the inevitable fireworks when they all ended up in the same room. God help me.

34

LILY

I'D BEEN DODGING ZACH FOR A WEEK. WELL, ALMOST A WEEK. FIVE days, three hours and twenty-seven minutes, but who was counting? He still sent messages and I replied, I wasn't rude, but I didn't encourage him either. When he called, I let them go to voicemail. I hadn't listened to them yet. Instead, I let him fill my message bank. I knew I was weak and the moment I spoke to him or heard his voice, I'd probably crumble and, right now, I didn't have time to do that.

Tomorrow was the day.

Child services were coming to do their home visit to determine whether or not I was fit to be Ava's full-time legal guardian.

Avoiding Zach hadn't really been hard. I'd been so busy preparing for what was coming I hadn't had time to worry about it. Not if you didn't count those lonely hours I'd spent lying in bed staring at the ceiling wishing I had someone here to tell me it was all going to be okay. That no matter what happened, I was strong enough to survive it. But there wasn't. I was alone and that was just how it had to be. I wasn't going to be one of those women who stood by and allowed cheating. I deserved more than that.

Everything was ready. Yesterday I'd managed to convince the

doctor that my arm had healed enough to get rid of the awful sling. Reluctantly, he agreed but only after I promised not to overdo it. Sage and Linda were going to cover the store, all the orders had been prepped ahead of time and the mountain of boxes that'd been stacked in my lounge room were gone. How I'd accumulated so much shit, I had no idea. I didn't even know what to do with some of the random crap I owned so I used the opportunity to purge. Anything I didn't recognize, hadn't used or never would use went straight in the trash. It felt awesome.

I still had a lot of work to do but I had a plan. Slowly but surely, I'd fix up Grandma's house, starting with a visit to the nursery on the weekend. This place needed to be brought back to life and the best way I knew how was with flowers. I wanted the garden full of color so when I got home each day, it was a happy place.

Stacking the last of the groceries in the cupboard, including the store-bought cookies I planned on offering the representative tomorrow, I heard my phone chirp.

Zach: *Are you home? Mind if I stop by?*

Why did he have to make it so hard? He was being so… so… Zach. Just because I hadn't seen him, didn't mean he'd been any less attentive. When I'd stopped by the store earlier, I realized how lucky I'd been. The girls had been run off their feet and the guilt was weighing on me. Needing to be helpful, even if only in some little way, I'd ducked up to the bank, leaving Linda to man the counter, and when I returned there was a box sitting beside the register waiting for me containing a chicken, mayonnaise and lettuce sandwich and a brownie.

"Shame he forgot the drink," I muttered to myself, feeling guilty for accepting his gifts even though I was keeping my distance.

"You mean this drink?" Linda asked, pulling a glass bottle of my favorite old-fashioned lemonade from behind her back. "When he dropped it off, I put it in the fridge for you so it stayed cold."

"Oh. Thanks." I swallowed down the dry hunk of sandwich that was lodged in my throat.

"I don't mean to pry…"

"But let me guess, you're going to."

"Something like that. I'm guessing from the disappointed look on Zach's face when he realized you weren't here, and the guilt written all over your face right now that you two still haven't straightened out whatever mess you're in."

"I was at the bank!" I protested weakly.

"Today you were at the bank. But last night when he called?"

"Fine. We haven't talked but honestly, there's no point. I saw what I saw. I really don't have the energy to listen to any of his excuses. I have to focus on tomorrow."

"I know you do and that's why I haven't pushed."

"Why do I feel like there's a but coming?"

"Because there is."

Picking up the brownie and taking a huge bite, I figured I was going to need the chocolate to hear whatever was coming next.

"Lily, you're an incredible woman. Kind, honest, generous."

"Thank you."

"I'm not finished."

"Oh."

"While you're all of those wonderful things, you're also stubborn as a mule."

"I have to be."

"Why? Why do you think you have to be stubborn?"

"Because I'm the only one I have to rely on. I'm all I have. I have to be strong and brave and, on occasion, stubborn."

"And you don't think Zach could be someone you could come to rely on?"

"I did. But now… now I'm not so sure."

Linda shook her head sadly. "I'll leave it alone. It's not my place, and I don't want to get in the middle, but I have to say one last thing. Talk to him. If it turns out what you think you saw was exactly that, then tell him that's the end. And if it was something different, aren't you better off knowing?"

"Mmmm." I didn't really have words. What was I supposed to say to that?

"Now, is there anything else you need done before tomorrow?"

Relieved by the change of topic, I looked over Linda's head to where the shelves still sat on the floor. Last night after everyone had left, I'd tried to install the new shelving myself, but my stupid arm was still too sore to actually be useful.

"Nope. I think everything is good. Thank you for everything this week, Linda. I couldn't have survived it without you," I told her honestly.

"Yes, you could've. You can survive anything you set your mind to, Lily. Just keep that in mind."

I watched as she grabbed her purse and headed for the door, leaving me pondering her words. Once I was alone, Sarah having taken Ava for the afternoon to give me time to panic and freak out, I got to work. Everything was clean and tidy, but I found myself going over it again. I was fidgety. I couldn't sit still. Even though it was my home being judged, I was tired of trying to work in a pigsty. The sooner this place was back to normal, the less stressed I'd be. At least that's what I was telling myself. When an older gentleman stumbled through the door to buy his new girlfriend a bunch of flowers, I almost pounced on him, grateful for the distraction.

I was just flicking off the lights and locking the door when my phone chirped again.

Zach: *Have I done something to piss you off?*

It was on the tip of my tongue to reply, 'why don't you go ask your blonde', but I wasn't going to be that callous. I decided to take the high road. I just needed to get through the next twenty-four hours and then I could face everything else.

Lily: *Sorry. It's been a crazy week.*

He replied almost instantly.

Zach: *Wanna talk about it?*

Yes. No. I don't know. It would be good to share what I was feeling with someone but right now I wasn't sure I trusted Zach. And I had to hold my shit together. Once I got through the Child Services visit tomorrow, then my world could fall apart, but until then, I had to keep going.

Lily: *Tomorrow? Sorry I'm wiped and headed home to bed*

When his reply didn't come, I tossed my phone into the bottom of my bag and climbed into the car. The sooner I picked up Ava the sooner I could get my fill of baby snuggles and all would be right in my world again.

Zach's reply didn't come until I was changed into my pajamas and sliding between the sheets absolutely exhausted. I hadn't lied that I was wiped out; I was beyond stuffed, but my floors were clean enough to eat off. Closing my eyes, I waited for sleep to swallow me, praying I hadn't missed anything.

Crawling out of bed, I was like a zombie. I didn't think I'd actually slept a wink. After a quick hot shower, I pulled on my favorite pink polka dot dress with a wide white belt and sweetheart neckline. After fastening Grandma's pearls around my neck, I felt ready to take on the world. Getting Ava up and dressed seemed effortless this morning and she was surprisingly happy. Maybe it was just because she was completely oblivious to the chaos surrounding her.

She was late.

I was sweating and pacing, and she was late. The fresh

lemonade I'd made this morning was getting warm and I was beginning to panic. Who am I kidding? I was in full-blown melt-down mode, minutes away from losing it, when there was a knock at the door.

"Oh my god!" Grabbing a tissue, I dabbed at my face, trying to clean myself up without wiping off the face full of makeup I'd spent way too long applying. Twice.

Scooping up Ava from where she was kicking her legs and trying to get her tiny toes in her mouth on the blanket on the floor, I went to answer the door.

"Good morning," I greeted the stern-looking woman holding a clipboard as cheerily as I could muster.

"Miss Evans?"

Pushing open the screen door, I stepped out into the morning sunshine. The scent of freshly cut timber surrounded me, bringing flashes of a shirtless Zach back to the front of my mind. Now was definitely not the time to be having these dirty thoughts.

"That's me. Lily Evans. Thank you for coming."

She looked me up and down, and I wanted to run back inside and hide under my blanket and wait until the scary lady went away. Hugging Ava closer, I pressed a kiss to her forehead.

"I'm Emery Jones from Child Services. I'm here to discuss your application and review some information."

I gulped.

I had the distinct feeling I was about to be fucked, and not in the way that ended in orgasms.

Emery was peering over the top of her glasses which were attached to one of those fancy chains around her neck. She wore a perfectly pressed navy skirt that finished just below her knee and sensible black leather shoes with a low heel. Her navy blazer covered her silk cream blouse that was buttoned to her neck. But it was the tightly wound bun on her head that made me think Emery Jones belonged in a library behind the counter scolding kids for talking louder than a whisper.

"Of course, Mrs. Jones. Please come in," I invited with a wave while Ava cooed. Adjusting her in my arms, I tried to keep her weight from my sore arm. It was fine and I was using it again, I still wasn't going to push my luck though. I'd spent enough days in the stupid sling.

"It's *Ms.* Jones. And thank you," she corrected before stepping over the threshold and coming inside.

This wasn't going well.

Forty minutes later, we were sitting on the couch sipping tea. She'd walked through the house, not saying a whole lot but murmuring and making notes on her clipboard. A clipboard I would've paid money to sneak a peek at.

"There's just a few final details I need to confirm," Emery stated as Ava started to wail.

Picking her up, I realized very quickly what the issue was. Her diaper had leaked all over the back of her pretty pink dress. "Do you mind if I clean her up quickly?"

I didn't have a choice. Ava would always come first. Always. Even if it wasn't on Emery's carefully scripted plot.

"Please go ahead. I'll wait here," she replied, and I hurried out of the room, holding Ava at arm's distance.

While I got Ava cleaned up, something that required a quick change of everything, I talked to her like she could understand me. "You had to do that this morning, didn't you, pretty girl." Ava just smiled at me like I was the funniest thing in her world. Once she was dressed into a yellow dress with a white cardigan we headed back out to where Emery was waiting.

"Sorry about that."

"No worries. We can't schedule that sort of thing."

"No, we can't," I confirmed, taking my seat on the sofa and holding Ava on my knee like a shield from whatever was coming.

"If you're right to recommence…"

"Absolutely."

"Okay. There're just some things I need to confirm. I understand you own this home?"

"Yes. It was my Grandma's home. She left it to me a few years ago when she passed."

"I'm sorry to hear that," Emery replied automatically, without emotion.

"Thank you."

"It says here that you own your own business too?"

"Yes. I own the florist shop on Main Street."

"And it does well?"

"Yes. We're the only florist in Sunnyville, so we have the monopoly on weddings, funerals and school dances." I smiled, desperate to lighten the mood.

"It says here you're single."

I winced. Even though it was true, hearing it being said so bluntly stung. "That's correct," I confirmed, swallowing down the lump in my throat.

"Hmm," she murmured, scribbling something on her damn clipboard, rubbing salt into the wound. "Do you have a support network?"

"I have an incredible support network. My best friend Sarah, she works at the hospital and has been amazing. She's a mother to two young children and been a wealth of information."

"Anyone else?"

"Sage and Linda are both incredibly supportive and have made it abundantly clear that they're only a phone call away."

Flipping through her notes, the silence that hung in the air was suffocating me. "It says here Sage is your employee. Is that correct?"

"Well... ah... yes."

"And Linda? There's no mention of Linda in your application. Where does she fit?"

"Linda Higgins is an amazing woman. She's my friend Zach's mother. She's a retired bank teller who's recently moved from Kellyville. Linda has been helping as Ava's nanny when I'm working. She adores Ava and treats her like her own grandchild."

"And Zach? Who's he?"

I'd been hoping to avoid this. "Zach is actually the fire fighter who..." I looked down at Ava. She couldn't hear this. Even if she was too young to understand, I never wanted her to hear this. "... Who found her. He stayed with her in the hospital until I was called. He's deeply fond of her."

"Just her?" Emery's eyebrow quirked, and I knew exactly what she was insinuating, and the last thing I needed was for my relationship with Zach to be a deciding factor here.

"Zach and I are friends, obviously. He's amazing with Ava and I truly believe he loves her. I'd never stand in his way from getting to know her."

Behind me, my phone rang on the counter.

"Do you need to get that?"

"No, no. It's fine. Voicemail will get it."

I don't know if she was satisfied with my answers about the people in my life, but she moved along.

My phone fell silent but only for a breath before ringing again. After the fourth ring, I apologized and got up to answer it. Whoever it was, was obviously desperate to get a hold of me.

Picking it up, I answered, trying to keep the frustrations out of my voice. "Hello?"

"Lily! Where have you been? I've been calling."

"I am in the middle of something, Sarah. What do you need?"

"You need to get to the shop straight away. There's been an accident."

35

ZACH

"Incoming!" I heard yelled out before the bathroom door was pushed open and I dropped my hands to cover my junk, shampoo dribbling down my forehead into my eyes.

"What the fuck, Maddy? Get out! I'm fucking naked!"

"Well obviously, dumbass! I didn't think you showered in your clothes."

"Then get out!"

Why the hell was my sister standing in the bathroom door when I was in the shower? We hadn't shared a bathroom since I was six, and I wasn't interested in starting now. I was all for saving the environment, but communal showering to save water was a few steps too far for me.

"Calm your tits. It's not like I want to see that cocktail wiener you're so fond of," Maddy replied, still staring at her phone while I tried to snake an arm out of the shower and grab a towel to cover myself.

"Maddy! What do you want?"

"Oh yeah. So, Jake just called…"

"Don't care. I just woke up from back-to-back night shifts. Someone else's problem. I've got plans," I cut her off quickly. I didn't want to know. Today I was sorting shit out with Lily. The world might fall down around me, but that was someone else's problem. Today getting my girls back was all that mattered.

"If you'd let me finish..."

I knotted the towel around my waist and stepped out onto the mat. Running a hand through my hair, I wasn't surprised that it was still full of suds. The sooner I could kick Maddy out of the bathroom, the sooner I could finish showering.

"Hurry up then," I grumbled, folding my arms across my chest.

"There's been an accident." I went to reply, but Maddy's next words stole my breath. "At Lily's store."

"What?"

"He's been blowing up your phone for ten minutes. When he couldn't get you, he called me."

"Is Lily..." I couldn't even get the words out. If I didn't say them then they wouldn't be true.

"I don't know. Jake just asked me to let you know. He thought you'd want to know." I was already pushing past her out of the bathroom, all thoughts of hot water forgotten. I walked into my bedroom dropped my towel and pulled on the first thing I found. A pair of khaki shorts and navy t-shirt. I didn't know if they were dirty or clean and frankly, I didn't give a fuck.

I grabbed my keys and was out the door within a minute.

"Wait up! I'm coming too," Maddy called out as she jogged toward the truck still doing up her too-short shorts.

As soon as Maddy was in the front seat, I told her to call Samuels. "See if he can tell you what's going on."

Backing out of the drive, she pulled her phone away from her ear. "He's not answering."

"Fuck!"

"It'll be fine, Zach," Maddy offered weakly. We both knew she didn't know that. She couldn't know that. I appreciated her saying it all the same.

"Why's Samuels got your number anyway?" I asked, turning the corner.

"We're friends. We talk." Maddy shrugged like it was nothing. It wasn't nothing. If Maddy was crushing on someone, this is how she acted. It was when she wasn't serious, she bounced around, throwing it in my face.

"Hmm. We'll talk about that later. We're here."

I drove too fast but I didn't care. Turning the corner into Main street, I couldn't see the florist or any sign of Lily. The rig was there and a couple of cop cars blocking the street, not to mention the busy-body onlookers filling the sidewalks.

Parking illegally out the front of the butcher, I jumped out of the truck and ran towards the florist. I didn't know what I was expecting but it certainly wasn't what I found. And from the look of the people standing around, no one else was either. Besides, it's not something you see every day.

"What the hell?" I pushed past the people gathered on the street and walked straight into Grady who was standing back talking to the paramedics.

"Whoa! You can't go in there, Higgins," he told me, nudging me backwards a step or two.

"Fuck off, Malone. Lily's in there."

"We don't know how stable it is. We can't just run in there. You know the drill."

"Fuck the drill. There's a bloody car hanging out the front window of the shop. If Lily's in there, I'm going in to get her. So, get the hell out of my way."

Someone tapped me on the shoulder, and I spun around to see Chief standing there. I couldn't remember the last time I'd seen him on scene, so I knew this one was important.

"Higgins."

"Chief."

"I hear you think you're going in?"

"Lily's—"

He pointed over my shoulder. "Right over there."

I spun around so fast I almost tripped over my own feet. I had to wait until Samuels' big boof head moved out of my way but then there she was. Clinging to Ava, wrapped in her arms, her mouth gaping open and her eyes wide.

Ignoring the directions of the crew, I took long strides towards her, not letting go of the breath I was holding until I was standing right in front of her.

"You're okay," I exhaled, feeling my shoulders sag under the weight of relief.

"My store…"

"Can be fixed," I finished for her. "Are you hurt? Ava?"

"We-we're fine."

Lily's glance flicked from Maddy to me and back again, but she didn't say a word. Instead, she burrowed her head against my shoulder but only for a second.

"Lily… I've got to…"

"Go! Go! I'll be fine. We're fine."

"I'll be back… and then we'll—"

"Zach, go!"

I didn't want to leave them. Technically I wasn't on shift and I wasn't even supposed to be here, but there was no way I was going anywhere. Not until everyone was accounted for. Safe and sound. Bending down, I quickly dropped a kiss on Ava's head before taking Lily's lips. She tasted like her favorite cherry Chapstick. I couldn't wait until I could have more. It'd been too long.

"Zach, go! I'll stay with them," Maddy offered, moving towards Lily and Ava.

"Higgins!" Someone yelled my name, and I spun around to see Samuels waving at me.

"Thanks, Maddy. Stay here. I'll be back."

Jumping over an upended trashcan, I headed over to where Samuels was. A moment later Chief, Grady and a few of the others on scene joined us.

The bright red beetle with its front half buried through the shop window wasn't as bad as it looked. There was a lot of glass and a fair bit of damage, the door was blocked, and the brick work was keeping the driver in the car, but overall, the building wasn't going to fall down so that was a plus.

"Mom and Sage?" I asked, pulling my phone from my pocket to see if I'd missed a call from her. Annoyed there was nothing, I dialed her number and somehow, over all the noise I heard her unmistakable ringtone. She was the only person I knew who actually liked the sound of the old-school telephone.

"We haven't heard."

"She's in there."

"If she is, we'll get her out. Safely, Zach."

"I'm helping."

"No, you're not," Chief stated.

"Unless you plan on having me arrested, I'm helping." I issued the ultimatum defiantly.

Chief huffed, unimpressed. I'm sure I hadn't heard the end of this but for now, he was going to let me get on with it. "At least put a decent pair of shoes on. There's glass everywhere."

Taking that as his approval to get to work, I asked about the plan. Twenty minutes later and we were helping the driver from the car. A driver I recognized despite the smell of booze on her breath and the cut on her forehead.

Helping Phoebe down from the wreckage, she was lifted onto a stretcher and wheeled over to the awaiting ambulance, police escorting her with every step. I knew she was drunk; it wasn't going to take a test to prove that; the fact she could barely slur her own name was a dead giveaway, but I had this sinking feeling there was more to the story. Phoebe could've crashed her car into any tree or store front or anything else on Main street, yet it was Lily's florist where she'd jumped the gutter and ended up going through the front window.

Now, onto more pressing and more important matters.

"Mom?" I called out over the hood of the car into the darkened shop.

36

LILY

I watched Zach spring into action, and it was sexy as hell. Seeing him stand up to his boss, take control, consumed by the need to help. If anyone ever questioned why people went into these sorts of jobs, it is because they never for a second saw it as a job. It was a lifestyle. It was who they were. They weren't the sort of people who could sit on the sidelines watching someone struggle or in pain, they needed to be in there, on the front line helping. And Zach was one of them.

"He's amazing, isn't he?" I whispered to Ava while she fidgeted in my arms. I was probably holding her a little too tight but after everything that had happened already today, there was no way I was loosening my grip.

"I've never seen him in action before," said the blonde I'd seen in his arms the other day, the one who'd caused the white-hot jealousy to consume me as she watched on with awe.

"He's pretty awesome," I confirmed.

"I wouldn't say awesome," she smiled, "but he's good at what he does. I'm Maddy by the way. Zach's little sister and his favorite pain in his ass."

Shifting Ava in my arms, I reached out and shook her hand. His sister? How had I managed to get it so wrong? I was an idiot. An idiot who'd wasted too much time. Before I had a chance to fall too deep into my own pity party, a murmur went through the crowd behind us.

"Is that?"

"It can't be."

"It is."

Turning back to face the disaster that was the front of Daisy's Flora, I saw Zach helping Phoebe clamber out of the wreckage. She was the one who'd done this. She was the one who'd driven her car straight through my front window.

"Phoebe?" Maddy gasped under her breath.

"You know her?" I asked, unable to keep the surprise from my voice.

"Kinda. Not really. I mean, I ran into her a couple of times at the bar. But I wouldn't say I know her."

"She works at the bakery down the street. She's had a crush on Zach for years. I think it's pretty much fizzled now…"

"It hasn't."

"Excuse me?"

"It hasn't. When she found out I was Zach's sister, it was almost like she wanted to be my best friend. She asked so many questions about him and our family."

My stomach lurched. My throat went dry. Looking over at the drama unfolding, I watched as Phoebe was helped onto a stretcher by the awaiting paramedics. From where I was standing, I could see the trickle of blood across her forehead and hoped she was okay. I mean, I was pissed as all hell at her for destroying my store, but it didn't mean I wanted to see her hurt. I wasn't that heartless. "What'd you tell her?"

"That I didn't know. Honestly, Zach and I haven't really been close. I mean, I've talked to him more in the last week than I have in the last two years, so I'm not really in a position to know what his hopes and dreams are."

"Oh."

I hated that disappointment fluttered through me. Stupidly, I'd been hoping that I was part of what he wanted. Me and Ava. At least, that's what he'd led me to believe. But I guess the blame wasn't all on him. I'd ghosted him since I'd seen him with Maddy and gotten the story completely wrong. It was probably my fault.

"I might not have lied to Phoebe, but that didn't mean I told her the full truth either."

"You didn't?"

"Hell no! I don't know that chick from a bar of soap. I wasn't about to give her all my brother's secrets."

"Makes sense."

"But I will tell you something…"

"You don't know me either."

"You're right. I don't. But honestly… I'm sick of hearing your name come out of my whiny brother's mouth. You and that adorable little munchkin."

"He mentions us?" My heart swelled and I found myself standing a little taller.

"Nah."

"Oh."

"He doesn't mention you. More like he doesn't shut up about you two."

"Wow."

"Not expecting that, huh?"

"Honestly, no."

"I believe that. But from that look on your face, I'd say you're not completely opposed to the idea either."

"I wouldn't say opposed exactly. More like relieved."

"You're good for him."

"You don't know me."

"Don't need to. You make him happy. That's all I need to know."

Standing there with Maddy, I looked at her and realized I'd judged her way too harshly. When Zach had said his sister was an actress, I was expecting some vapid, attention-seeking diva, but

Maddy seemed surprisingly grounded. Almost normal. Well until we heard Zach call out "Mom?"

"Wait! What the hell? My Mom's in there?" Maddy screeched looking at me.

"We don't know. She could be," I answered honestly.

"Why?"

As quickly as I could, I explained how I'd come to know and depend on her mom and how much Linda meant to me. Like she was a second mother. As I spoke, Maddy transformed from the easy-going woman I'd been chatting with, to one wringing her hands and on edge.

"So, my mom could be inside and she could be hurt?"

"I'm sure she's fine. Besides, Zach's working on it. I'm sure he'll get her out and we'll see for ourselves."

"Hope so," she replied, her answer barely a whisper.

Maddy had gone pale. Like pass-out pale. Seeing Jake heading in my direction, I called out for him to bring some water. With Ava in my arms, I couldn't catch Maddy if she went down and I didn't like my chances of getting her to look after herself right now.

"Lily," Jake said, stepping in front of me and blocking my view of what was happening, which in all honesty, didn't appear to be much. Everything was going in slow motion, and while I understood it, it was frustrating as hell.

"Just give it to me straight," I told him.

"It's not good. There's a lot of damage…"

"Obviously, Jake. There's a car hanging out of my front window."

"Ah, yeah. Are you okay?"

"You came over here to ask if I was okay?" I confirmed.

"Yeah."

"Were you sent over here, Jake?" Maddy interrupted.

"Maybe."

"By my bossy big brother?"

"I'm not answering that," Jake deflected.

"Then that's a yes."

"Madeline…"

"I told you not to call me that," she growled, poking him in the ribs and making him flinch.

Wow! Maddy mightn't have been in town long but it was obvious to anyone near these two that their chemistry was off the charts.

"Jake, can you go tell Zach I'm fine. We're fine. Just get Linda and Sage out of there and then we can all go have a much-needed drink."

"Sounds good," Jake agreed as he scampered back towards the rig where there was a group of firefighters pointing and arguing.

"He's a good guy. Bit of a flirt, but I'd say you already knew that," I said off the cuff, aiming my comment directly at Maddy.

She mightn't have wanted to hear it, but from the way her cheeks turned pink, I'd say I hit the nail on the head. "We're just friends," she confirmed.

"For now."

Action amongst the rubble caught my attention. Zach was moving towards the front door, an axe over his shoulder.

"Oh shit."

The words were out before I had the chance to stop them. I didn't know what he was about to do, but an axe was never a good sign. Holding my breath, I watched as he lifted it up over his head before bringing it down with a crash.

The thinning crowd behind me gasped.

Three more swings, the muscles in his arms bulging, and he was forcing his way inside. I didn't give a shit about the damage. I knew he wasn't taking an axe to the front display without good reason. Besides, at this point, did it even matter if there was a bit more mess to clean up?

I took a step forward.

"Would you like me to hold Ava for you, Lily?"

Spinning around, I saw Emery standing there. She looked so out of place it was almost comical. There was dust and broken bricks and glass everywhere, and she was standing there in her suit and glasses.

"I...I..."

Fuck me! I was so screwed. Part of me wanted to hand Ava over and sort this out, while the other part of me didn't want to look like I was abandoning her. I'd promised her Ava was my priority and that wasn't a promise I'd made lightly. It was one hundred percent true.

"Please. You need to go and find out what's going on."

She was right. Reluctantly, I placed Ava in her waiting arms, running my hand down the soft skin on Ava's arm as I stepped back. "I'll just be a minute," I said, not sure who I was telling.

I was terrified.

My feet were frozen on the spot.

What if I'd just handed over Ava to Emery and she didn't give her back. What if this was the end? My heart was thumping so hard in my chest it hurt.

"Lily!" Zach's voice called out across the debris.

"Go. I've got her. And we'll be right here when you get back. Won't we, Ava?" Emery confirmed.

I wanted to believe her. I really did. My heart wouldn't let me. I was so scared. Emery must've read the fear written all over my face. "Lily, go. You're a great mom. And Ava's going to be lucky to have you. But part of being a mom is doing what's right. It might be the hard thing to do, but it's the right thing to do. You're leaving Ava with someone. She's not alone. And I can see that it's the absolute last thing you want to do."

"It is," I confirmed.

"Lily." She reached out and touched my arm, and for the first time I realized that while on the surface Emery may come across cold and hard, beyond that she was soft, caring and sweet. "I know you're waiting for me to tell you you're going to be a mom, but what you can't see, is you're already a mom. A wonderful mom. And that's the recommendation I'm going to be making."

"You are?"

Seriously, right now you could knock me down with a feather.

"Lily!" Zach called again. Looking over my shoulder, I saw him beckoning me.

"I am. Now go and see what that gorgeous man wants."

With one final look at Ava, I carefully made my way over to where Zach was standing in the doorway, the abandoned axe leaning up against the wall, or what was left of it.

"Are they in there?"

"They are."

"Are they okay?"

"Yes, Lily. We're fine. Can you tell that son of mine to stop following the rule book so damn closely and get us out of here?" Linda called out, and I let go of the breath I'd been holding. Hearing her complaining about Zach was music to my ears.

"I can try, Linda. But you know how he is." I winked at Zach, and he slapped my ass in front of everyone. He didn't care and, after the initial shock wore off, I realized I didn't either.

"Well then, Lily, flash him your boobs or something. Just get me the hell out of here!"

Ah, there was my girl Sage.

Zach turned to me, his eyes alive with mischief. "Well?" he murmured, leaning down. I felt the warmth of his breath against my neck, and I realized how much I'd missed him. And it was all because I was a dumbass who refused to ask questions. That wasn't going to happen again. Here and now, I made a pact with myself to not let things fester. Front up and ask the question. The worst that could've happened was Zach confirmed what I was seeing and broke my heart, which happened anyway because I refused to pull up my big-girl pants and ask him about it.

"Maybe later," I suggested. "But how about we get your mom and Sage out first?"

"Do we have to?"

"Yeah. We do."

"Grr. Fine. You okay if I make a mess?" Zach asked.

"You mean, now you're asking. After you let yourself in with an axe?"

Zach reached up and rubbed the back of his neck, his arm muscles bulging and frying my brain. "Do what you need to. Get them out and then we can go home."

"Yes, ma'am."

Now it was my turn. I reached out and slapped his ass, repaying the favor.

"Guess we know who wears the pants in this relationship," I heard behind me, turning to see Jake headed my way.

"Piss off, Samuels," Zach groaned before bending down and kissing my cheek softly.

"Get them out. And, Zach…"

"Yeah?"

"Hurry."

"On it."

37

ZACH

"WELL, IT'S GOOD TO KNOW WHERE YOUR BALLS ARE," SAMUELS started as he stepped up beside me. Quirking an eyebrow at him, I had no idea what the hell he was on about, but then again, I rarely did. "Safely tucked away in Lily's purse."

Ah, so that's where he was headed with this one. Guess he thought he was funny. Little shit.

"At least I have some."

"Your sister didn't seem to mind having mine in her—"

"Samuels! If you even finish that sentence, we'll need to call for another ambulance to come and cart you away after I've put my boot so far up your pretty-boy ass your teeth rattle."

"Someone's touchy."

"Boys! A little less bitching and a little help would be nice."

"Sorry, Mom," I replied.

Samuels and I got to work, slowly but steadily removing the crap in the way so we could get through the front door to where Sage and Mom were. From what I could figure, they were both fine. Sage had a cut on her leg which Mom said wasn't too bad but other than that, no real damage. A bit of a scare and some spilt coffee, but in the scheme of things, everything was okay.

It felt like it took forever, but eventually we'd cleared a path wide enough we could get inside.

Before I stepped through the gap, I couldn't help but look over to where Maddy and Lily were standing. The women in my life were going to send me gray before my time, but I wouldn't have it any other way. Now I just needed to get Mom sorted and we could all go home. Together.

Lily nodded and I stepped inside. Looking around, I saw the place was totaled. It was going to break Lily's heart when she saw this. Right now, she was putting on a brave face, worried more about Sage and Mom than anything, but once she knew everyone was safe and sound, her heart was going to break. There were flowers and buckets scattered everywhere. The table where she spent hours bundling together her arrangements was upended and one of the legs bent so badly, I knew it couldn't be saved.

Moving past the counter, which was covered in mess, I saw Mom and Sage standing in the doorway of the stock room, arms folded.

"Took you long enough," Sage smarted.

I could see why Lily loved that girl. Sage had spirit and fire. Way too much for me, but I admired the hell out of her for it.

Mom moved towards me first and hugged me like she was going to lose me. I wasn't the one who'd been trapped inside a florist shop when a car decided to come through the window. But instead of making fun of her, I just hugged her back, just as tightly.

"Well, I know how you like to make a dramatic entrance," I replied.

"That I do, Zach. That I do."

"Well, how about we get you ladies out of here?" Samuels offered.

"I like that idea," Mom confirmed, loosening her grip only slightly. I had a feeling she wasn't going to let go anytime soon.

"You got your mom?" Samuels asked.

"Think you can handle Sage?"

"If I can handle your—"

I couldn't help it. He'd been bugging me for days. I slapped Samuels up the side of the head, messing up pretty boy's hair.

"No one can handle all this awesomeness," Sage commented, moving towards Jake.

Bending my knees, I lifted Mom into my arms and carried her back out the way we came, Samuels and Sage hot on my heels. As we stepped outside into the sunlight, a round of applause broke out. We headed straight for the awaiting ambulances. Even though they kept telling us they were fine, and to me they looked it, there was no way either of them were going anywhere without at least being checked. I'd tie Sage to the bed if I had to, although I was slightly concerned she might like that.

As I set Mom down on the stretcher, she went to stand, but I kept my hand on her shoulder, holding her in place. "Humor me, Mom, please?"

She looked less than impressed with the idea but thankfully, she stopped fighting me.

Taking a step back, I waved Lily and Maddy over. I knew they were just as worried as I was.

"Oh, Mom?"

"Yes?"

"There's someone here who wants to say g'day."

"G'day? I haven't heard that word in a long time."

"Well, this Aussie girl travelled a long way just to say it to you," I told her before stepping back and making room for Maddy to take my place.

"Madeline?" Mom spluttered, sitting up, much to the annoyance of the paramedic who was trying to wrap the blood pressure cuff around her arm.

"Mom. I'm so sorry," Maddy apologized quickly before bursting into tears.

I felt Lily's presence beside me before I saw her. Her thin arm snaked around my waist, and I immediately dropped mine over her shoulder. She didn't seem to even notice that I was covered in sweat and dirt, messing up her pretty dress.

"Where's Ava?"

"She's with Emery."

"And Emery is?"

"Come meet her. She's from Child Services. The meeting was this morning."

"Oh shit. I'm so sorry, Lily."

I knew how much she'd been fretting about this, and even though I wasn't going to tell her, I'd been freaking myself.

"What are you sorry for?"

"Everything. Not being there. Not helping you get organized. And now this," I gestured at the shitstorm behind us.

"Zach, there's absolutely nothing to be sorry for."

"There's not?"

"Not at all. Emery's going to recommend that Ava stay."

"She is?"

Lily nodded, and without thinking I picked her up and spun her in a circle. When I stood her back down on her feet, she laced her fingers with mine before leading me over to where Ava was babbling in a very severe, very serious-looking woman's arms.

As soon as Ava spotted me, she stretched out her chubby arm making a grabbing fist with her hand. I let go of Lily and reached for her, not missing the way Emery's eyes widened. I didn't give a shit what she thought of me. As long as Ava was on my side, I was good.

"Hey there, pretty girl. Did you miss me?" I cooed softly, all my attention directed at Ava.

Lily must've been feeling left out, because she nudged my arm before reaching for Ava's hand, letting her wrap her fist around Lily's finger. Tucking Lily under my arm, we stood there completely unaware of the world around us, safe and happy in our little bubble.

"Damn you guys make a cute family," Sage called out.

"They really do, don't they?" Emery asked, stealing my attention from my girls.

"I'm sorry. I'm Zach Higgins," I introduced myself.

"I guessed as much. I'm Emery Jones. I'm with Child Services."

"Well, it's nice to meet you. Although, I can promise you, this wasn't planned."

"I'm sure it wasn't. Now, if you'll excuse me, I have a report to file. It seems like everything here is just as it should be. Ava's happy and cared for and loved."

"She really is," I confirmed, kissing her head. Even I hadn't been aware how much I could fall in love with the little girl, but it was undeniable. Ava owned me. She'd completely stolen my heart and I'd fallen.

"Anyone who looks at the pair of you could see that. And that's what I'll be putting in my report. Keep doing what you're doing. You two are going to make great parents. Ava's a very, very lucky little girl."

"No. We're the lucky ones," Lily confirmed, her arm that was banded around my waist tightening as we watched Emery walk away.

Once we'd had a moment to ourselves, I had to ask. "Hey, Lil?"

"Yeah?"

"How are you doing with all this?" I pointed at the store front.

"I have no idea. For now, everyone's okay and that's what matters. I guess I'll deal with the rest tomorrow. I'm insured so I guess it will just take some sorting out. But Phoebe... I can't believe it."

"She was definitely drunk. Or very close to it. I could smell the booze on her when we helped her out of the car."

"Well, at least she's not too badly injured."

"Damn girl! You're too nice for your own good. If it was me, I'd want to beat her ass!" Maddy big noted.

"Maddy, you wouldn't know how to beat anyone's ass," Mom confirmed, her arm wrapped around Maddy tightly.

"Are you sure you should be up and walking around?" I asked worriedly, sounding more like the parent than her son.

"Zach, I'm fine. The lovely paramedic over there, Josh, he gave me the all clear. I'm perfectly fine. Just a bit of shock. Nothing a good cup of coffee won't fix."

Looking over Mom's head, I caught Josh's eye. He was a good guy. We'd met a few times at various call outs, and I knew he was thorough. When he gave me the thumbs up, I decided I'd take Mom's word for it.

"Well, let's go get you a coffee then."

"Zach?"

"Yeah, Maddy?"

"Give me the keys. I'll drive Mom home and make sure she gets her coffee and a slice of that cake I found. Why don't you take Lily and Ava home?"

While I liked her thinking, handing the keys to my precious truck to Maddy wasn't so easy. "Do you even know how to drive?"

"Of course."

"You know in America they drive on the other side of the road?"

"Pft! I'll be fine. It can't be that hard."

"Children!" Mom raised her voice, causing Maddy and I to both smile widely. "I'll drive."

"Then I want you all at my place for dinner. No arguing," Lily instructed. Damn! Seeing the bossy side of Lily come out did things to me it probably shouldn't. Especially not in front of my mother.

"Sounds good. Text me and tell me what to bring."

"Yourselves."

"A family dinner sounds perfect," I confirmed.

Lily ducked over to check on Sage who was still sitting on the stretcher getting the cut on her leg cleaned up, I watched on silently as Mom and Maddy reunited. I'd been arguing with Maddy since she arrived to stop hiding and just talk to Mom, but she kept coming up with excuses. It wasn't until she'd fallen through the door the other morning, drunk as a skunk ranting and raving about how Mom hated her for not following her to America and choosing her career that all the pieces of the puzzle dropped into place. A career that Maddy insisted Mom never approved of in the first place.

Bloody women.

Now look at them. All it took was a hug, a couple of spilled tears and they were as thick as thieves. Why they couldn't just listen to me, I had no idea. I guess in the scheme of things, it didn't really matter. They'd sorted it out now and were laughing and crying together. God help me.

"You ready?" Lily asked, returning to my side.

"Everything okay with Sage?"

"Yeah. She's going to swing by later. I invited her to join us for dinner. I hope that's okay."

"Of course it is. Sage is your family."

"Yeah. You're right. She is."

"And speaking of family, I think it's time you took yours home. It's been a rollercoaster of a day. And I can't speak for Ava, but I could use a nap."

"Then that's what you're going to get."

"And you're joining me, aren't you?"

"If that's what you want?" Because Lily had rocks in her head if she thought even for a second, I was letting either of them out of my sight in a hurry.

"It's exactly what I want… for starters." Lily winked up at me, and I found myself lengthening my strides. I'd never gotten a better offer.

38

LILY

"Get your sexy ass moving, Lily. Mom and Maddy just pulled up," Zach called out to me.

I was running around the bedroom like a chicken with my head cut off wearing only my underwear. I was running late. Like seriously late. But it wasn't my fault. Nope. I was taking none of the blame. This was all on Zach. Zachary Higgins and his wicked ways.

As soon as we'd bundled Ava into the car, she was out like a light so by the time we got home, there was no waking her. She was lucky like that. The world could implode around her, and she'd sleep through the lot. But that meant Zach and I had time to ourselves. Time Zach insisted we make up for.

After the third orgasm he'd wrung from my body, I laid in his arms and we talked. And talked. And talked. I apologized for judging him about Maddy and then pulling away, and he apologized for being so easy to push away, promising that from now on, he was going to be like a leech on my ass.

He was worried about what I was going to do about the store, but I wasn't. I knew it'd all work out. The last couple of weeks had been hard, but I'd been through harder. And maybe the reason it didn't seem so overwhelming facing it head on this time, was I knew the family I had around me wouldn't let me fall. And if for some reason I did stumble along the way, I had no doubt they'd be right there to pick me up, dust me off and help me on my way.

"I want to rebuild the store," I told him.

"Then that's what we'll do."

"I want to preserve what Grandma originally built, but I want to make some changes too. It was her place, Daisy's Flora, but now I want it to be Daisy and Lily's."

"It get it You want to put your own mark but keep your Grandma's memory alive. I think it's a great idea. Would you change the name too?"

"I'm not sure." And that was the truth. While I had a few ideas on improvements I wanted to make, I hadn't really given it much thought. I guess now was the time to.

The house smelt like garlic and tomatoes and cheese, and my stomach rumbled. I'd skimped on breakfast, been too nervous to eat and then we'd been too busy making up for lost time to eat lunch, and now I was ravenous.

Grabbing a dress from the cupboard, I tugged it over my head before pulling my hair up in a ponytail. Taking a quick look in the mirror, I was swiping on some lip gloss when I noticed the bite mark on my neck.

"Zachary!" I boomed, and he appeared instantly in the doorway looking very much the housewife. He was wearing my pink apron with white lace trim tied in a bow at his side. It had a huge tomato splatter on the front, so it was probably a good thing he was wearing the apron. But it was the wooden spoon in one hand and the baby in the other that had me forgetting all about the branding he'd left on me.

"Why are you smiling?" I asked, moving towards him.

"Because you look beautiful. The freshly fucked look suits you."

"You're such a sweet talker."

"I know."

"Keep it up and you might even get lucky later."

"Oh, I'm getting lucky. You can bet your ass on that."

"Honey, we're home. Put your clothes on and come feed me!" a voice echoed through the house which had us laughing.

"Maddy," we said in unison.

"Welcome to my life," Zach grumbled as Ava tried to grab for the spoon. He let her take it easily only to have her bop him in the center of the head with it.

"Admit it. You wouldn't change a thing."

With a wickedness in his eye, one I was starting to understand and appreciate more than I could say, Zach bent forward and kissed me like we were alone. Like he wasn't holding Ava and his mother and sister weren't waiting in the other room. It was a kiss that buckled my knees, flooded my panties and sent my heart into overdrive.

"Not a chance."

My stomach growled embarrassingly loudly. "Come on. I need to feed you. You're going to need your strength."

I took Ava from his arms. "Promises, promises," I teased, slipping past him and out to greet our guests, leaving him to adjust the very prominent bulge in his pants I hadn't missed.

I found Linda and Maddy in the lounge room, and they both raced towards me, fighting over whose turn it was to hold Ava. There was no doubt about this little girl being loved. They were calling dibs on who got to nurse her, and Ava was basking in the attention.

"I picked up a bottle of red," Maddy said, handing me a bottle of wine that was well out of my budget. It was one of those fancy Australian Barossa Valley blends I'd tried at restaurants once or twice but couldn't bring myself to cough up that much for a bottle just to drink at home by myself. "Hope it goes with whatever you're cooking."

"It smells delicious," Linda added as Ava grabbed hold of her nose, making her words squeak.

"It really does. And I wish I could take the credit for it, but I was actually asleep so Zach…"

"Zach turned into a master chef and whipped up dinner," he

finished for me before retreating into the kitchen and stirring the huge saucepan on the hotplate.

"Well thank you, chef. But what are we eating?"

"Why don't you sit down, and you'll find out."

"Wait for me!" Sage called out, blasting through the front door like the whirlwind she was.

"You're just in time," I told her, taking my seat, while Zach opened the wine and started pouring before grabbing himself a beer from the fridge, setting it in front of his plate and a huge salad in the center of the table.

"Want some help?" Linda offered as Ava was stolen from her arms by Sage, much to Maddy's annoyance.

"I've got it," Zach replied confidently with a wink.

There were only some minor swear words exchanged before he carried a few overflowing bowls in and set them down. From the size of the servings he was dishing out, I had a feeling Zach had forgotten he was feeding four women and not the guys at the station.

"Is this…"

"Your grandma's spaghetti recipe. Yes, Lil, it is."

"I haven't had it…"

"I know. But tonight, at family dinner, we're having it. I know how much you wish she was here, and she'd be so proud of you for everything, and this is as close as I could get to having…"

I leaped out of my chair, spilling my wine on the tablecloth and knocking my chair to the floor as I threw myself in Zach's arms. At first, he had the look of pure panic on his face, like he thought he'd fucked up and I was about to burst into tears; actually there was a very good chance the waterworks weren't far away, but they weren't sad tears. They were happy tears. Very, very happy tears. Grandma couldn't be here, but he'd done everything he could to make her a part of our first official family dinner. She might be gone, but she most certainly wasn't forgotten.

"Fuck I love you," I told him as I smashed my mouth down

over his, only slightly aware of the clapping and cheering behind me.

"Love you too, Lil. You're it for me. You and Ava. You're my family now. Today. Tomorrow. And forever. I've completely fallen for you."

"Excuse me, lover boy?"

"What, Maddy?" Zach growled, not taking his eyes from me.

"There're kids and parents in the room. Keep little Zach in your pants."

Zach rolled his eyes so hard as he let out an exasperated sigh.

"Maddy?"

"Yes, Lily?"

"Let me assure you, there's nothing little about Zach." I winked at her, and Zach burst out laughing.

"Ew! Too much information."

"Isn't that what families do?"

"It's what this one does," Linda confirmed. "Welcome to ours, Lily. You and Ava will fit right in to all our craziness."

"What about me?" Sage's outburst caught us off guard.

EPILOGUE

ZACH

"Lily Higgins! If you're attempting to move that bed…"

"You're going to what?"

I'd just finished my shift and I was tired and aching. Winter sucked. People thought fire pits were a great idea, but they had no idea how to light one and, possibly more importantly, how to keep one under control.

Walking into the back bedroom, the room that was going to be Ava's new princess bedroom, I found my very pregnant wife down on her hands and knees, the bed pulled out from the wall, with a guilty look written all over her face. Lily was carrying our miracle baby, the one she never dreamed she'd get to have, but even knowing how lucky we were didn't slow Lily down at all. My wife was a solider.

Stretching my hand out, I helped her to her feet and watched as she attempted to brush the dirt off her knees.

"I told you I'd do that when I got home."

"I know, but I thought I could—"

"Yeah, yeah. I know what you thought. Now, what do you want me to do?"

Twenty minutes and four changes of her mind later and Lily was happy. And you know what mattered most in my life? Keeping Lily happy. Happy wife, happy life.

"She's going to love it," I assured her, wrapping my arm around her shoulder.

"Do you think? Maybe we should've gone with…"

"This is perfect."

"Well, she deserves the best birthday ever."

"Birthday and adoption day."

"I'm so excited she's legally ours. I mean, not that it mattered… I just want to know that…"

"I know, Lil. I'm the same. I love that little cockblocker more than anything, but knowing she's ours forever, that means everything."

"To me too."

Lily smiled up at me as I lifted my finger to her hair and pulled something pink out of it before setting it on my palm showing her.

"Oops! Frosting."

"How did frosting get in your… you know what, I don't even want to know."

"Probably best. Ah!"

Lily grabbed at her belly and I moved even closer to her. "What? What is it? What's wrong?"

I wasn't even embarrassed that I was that father. Ava already had me dressing up as Elsa from *Frozen* and dancing around the living room belting out 'Let It Go' at the top of my lungs, if anyone thought for a second that I'd be any less attentive to my son who was only a few weeks from making his grand entrance, then they didn't know me at all.

"Your son's been kicking up a storm all day."

"That's good," I replied, earning me the stink eye from Lily. "I mean, it's not good that he's kicking, but it's good that he's healthy and strong."

"Yeah, yeah. Keep trying to pull your foot out of it. Just for that, you're giving me a foot rub tonight," Lily instructed, making it sound like a threat.

The thing was, every night for the past couple of months, Lily and I had sat on the sofa after Ava was in bed, with her feet propped up in my lap and I'd rub her them while she read to me from one of her many pregnancy books. It'd taken many, many months of practice for me to knock Lily up, something that wasn't exactly torture, but our son was our miracle. One Lily had been convinced wasn't an option. And now here we were. Each night, we'd sit there in the quiet, just the two of us talking or arguing over names. Our son was still nameless and probably would be until he popped his head out and his mother named him. I knew it wouldn't matter what she named him, I was going to love him as much as I loved his mother and sister.

"I'll give you more than a foot rub," I suggested, wriggling my eyebrows in Lily's direction.

"What time is your mom dropping Ava off?" Suddenly Lily didn't look so tired.

"She's not."

"What?"

"Apparently it's girls' night. Maddy's in town, so Mom, Maddy and Sage have invited Ava to stay for girls' night."

"And I didn't get invited?"

"Well… You did."

"But?"

"But I may have declined your invite, telling them you were busy preparing for the party tomorrow."

"Zachary Higgins!" Lily pouted and, for a second, I wondered if I shouldn't have spoken for her. Pregnancy hormones were a bitch. Just when you thought you knew someone, wham! They're knocked up and morphing into someone you barely recognized. In Lily's case, she could go from playful and flirty to pissed off at the drop of a hat. Something I should've learned around the fourth month mark, but here I was, closing in on her due date still completely bloody clueless.

"Lily, you and I have the whole night to ourselves. Do you know what that means?"

"You're ordering me Chinese while I have a bath and then we get to go to sleep in our bed without Ava squirming between us?" Lily's eyes lit up.

"Something like that." Lily might have thought we were having a quiet night in, but trust me, once my wife got going, there was nothing quiet about her. And I planned on making our last night before we became a family of four one to disrupt the neighbors.

THE END

Want to keep up with all of the other books in K. Bromberg's Everyday Heroes World? You can visit us anytime at http://www.kbworlds.com/ and the best way to stay up to date on all of our latest releases and sales, is to sign up for our official KB Worlds newsletter HERE.

Are you interested in reading the bestselling books that inspired the Everyday Heroes World? You can find them HERE.

BOOKS BY REBECCA

Picturing Perfect

Fighting Back

Breaking Free

Finding Forever

A Merry McIntyre Christmas

Meet the McIntyres Boxset

ACKNOWLEDGMENTS

Firstly, this book was really for Marnie. She requested/demanded a tattooed book boyfriend who Margaret didn't steal, so I introduced her to Zach Higgins.

But on more serious note, thank you to the amazing team who helped me get there. Kathryn – your pretty images are incredible, and I love how you can see straight into my brain and what I'm thinking, even if I can't explain it.

Margaret and Mum – your proofing skills are unparalleled, and I appreciate you more than you know.

Leesa and Dana – you ladies, my Aussie K Bromberg World support group, helped me when I was struggling and debating whether to persist or walk away.

And possibly most importantly, Kristy. Thank you for letting me part of your amazing Everyday Heroes world. Your stories drew me in when I read them, and I found myself never wanting to leave. Then you opened up the option allowing me to join and I'm forever grateful.

I hope you loved Zach and Lily's story, but if you want to know more about what happens to Zach's annoying little sister Maddy – stay tuned :P

Rebecca
xoxo

ABOUT THE AUTHOR

Rebecca is a clumsy, introverted, bubble bath loving, chocoholic who'd rather read a book than go shopping. And don't even mention shoe shopping!

Rebecca is a lucky girl - one of four kids to schoolteacher parents. Wife to a football obsessed husband. Aunt to the most crazy/adorable little girls. And sister to two very determined sisters and one easy going brother.

Rebecca lives in Canberra Australia and spends way too many hours a day working the day job.

She is a book whore who can easily (and happily) read a book from start to finish in on sitting and spends her spare time writing.

ALSO WRITTEN BY K. BROMBERG

Driven
Fueled
Crashed
Raced
Aced

Slow Burn
Sweet Ache
Hard Beat
Down Shift

UnRaveled

Sweet Cheeks
Sweet Rivalry

The Player
The Catch

Cuffed

Combust
Cockpit
Control
Faking It

Resist
Reveal

Then You Happened

Hard to Handle

Flirting with 40

Hard to Hold
Hard to Score
Hard to Lose

Printed in Great Britain
by Amazon